DANCE OF FIRE

YELENA BLACK

BLOOMSBURY
LONDON NEW DELHI NEW YORK SYDNEY

Bloomsbury Publishing, London, New Delhi, New York and Sydney

First published in Great Britain in March 2015 by Bloomsbury Publishing Plc
50 Bedford Square, London WC1B 3DP

www.bloomsbury.com

Bloomsbury is a registered trademark of Bloomsbury Publishing Plc

A CIP catalogue record for this book is available from the British Library

ISBN 978 1 4088 2998 1

Typeset by Deanta Global Publishing Services, Chennai, India
Printed and bound in Great Britain by CPI Group (UK) Ltd, Croydon CR0 4YY

1 3 5 7 9 10 8 6 4 2

DANCE OF FIRE

For my readers, and for all those who love the dance

PROLOGUE

For the first time since Margaret's disappearance, Vanessa slipped on her older sister's pointe shoes.

Carefully she raised one toe and then the next, steadying herself until she was *en pointe*. She raised her chin to the light as a flash of colour seared her mind. Thin red lips, trembling. A nude leotard clinging to a girl's ribcage, and a slender, delicate foot.

'Margaret,' Vanessa whispered. She shut her eyes, holding on to the image.

Her sister extended her leg, pointing her foot as if positioning herself for the start of a dance. But it wasn't a dance at all. With some difficulty, she dragged her toe along the floor, slowly, carefully, forming letters.

I'm still here.

It was a message from her sister, Vanessa realised. She was out there, somewhere. Margaret Adler was alive.

Two And A Half
Years Earlier

From the Diary of Margaret Adler
February 27

Margaret Adler is dead.

That's what Hal told me when he gave me my new identity papers.

'The only way we can hide you is if you become somebody else,' he said, blinking. 'So that means Margaret is gone.'

'Gone,' I repeated. The freighter's steel decking thrummed beneath my feet, putting watery miles between me and my old life, my family. Hal and Erik chose this means of escaping New York because it is so low-tech, so unglamorous.

Kind of like this cheap notebook I'm writing in. At least I know it can't be hacked.

'Erased,' Hal said, as though gone *hadn't* been clear enough. '*You can't contact anyone.*' I barely know Hal, though Erik swears he can get anything done. He looks like a comic-book nerd – or a cybercriminal. '*It's too risky.* He might find you.'

By *he*, Hal means Josef, my old choreographer at the New York Ballet Academy. The one who almost destroyed me.

I nodded. 'OK,' I told Hal. *The floor rocked as the boat shifted, and the light over our heads swayed gently.*

'Instead, you are …' Hal opened the passport, and I read my new name under my photograph: Margot Adams.

'Who's this?' I asked.

'Now? It's you. But before …' He shrugged. 'A girl who died in a tragic car wreck a few years ago. Her body was never found.'

Which is creepy enough that the hair on my arms stands at attention. 'I'm pretending to be a dead girl?'

Another shrug. 'Not *pretending. You* are *this dead girl.*'

The door to the hall banged shut as Erik sauntered in. *He is lean, with a dancer's body, young and handsome. And I* think *he likes me; I can see it in his eyes when he smiles. I find myself stealing glances at him when he's not looking. He isn't like other boys I've met. The way he carries himself, so confident, so serious.*

I owe Erik so much. It is only thanks to him that I escaped Josef at all. Erik was visiting NYBA, and unlike everyone else, he had heard of dancers like Josef – who used the art of dance for evil. He believed me when I told him what was going on. And that I thought my life and soul were at risk.

He smuggled me out of NYBA, introduced me to his childhood friend Hal, and came up with the plan that got us on to this *freighter bound for England. If it wasn't for Erik, I would be dead. Or worse. I can almost still feel his hand on the small of my back as we waited by the dock that day, his body shielding me from the incoming fog.*

Which is why I'm here. No more Josef. No more being forced to dance, to try to summon something deadly, dangerous ...

I shake my head and close my eyes. Now it is time to get some sleep.

Next stop: London!

CHAPTER ONE

Hazy white light made the wooden floor of the studio glow with warmth. Vanessa stood *en pointe*, arms arched in *allongé*, muscles tense, straining to maintain position. Waiting. Until, with a whisper of breath at her neck . . .

His touch.

He moved behind her, his fingers spread, his right hand cupping her waist. His left hand hovered, barely grazing her shoulder. She shuddered as something within her awakened, his warmth coaxing her limbs to life.

Together they danced across the worn yellow floorboards to the wall of mirrors, where she could see herself all in white, like a phantom – leotard and tutu and even a light dusting of ghostly make-up. Her stark-white pointe shoes drew an ashen line across the wood.

Her partner wore black. He pulled her closer until she felt his chest rise and fall against hers. Her fingers ran along the cut of his shoulders, his muscles damp with sweat.

He spun her away before she saw his face, his own steps echoing behind her with a quick scraping patter, their shadows entwined, dancing together and breaking apart in the gauzy light. His cheek pressed warmly against hers, and she could smell his cologne – like ocean and summer and sand. A fine film of sweat glued her leotard to her chest, and she could practically taste salt on her lips. He gently turned her towards him.

Justin.

He smiled.

She spun, again and again, glimpsing his face with each turn. His messy, sandy hair, his blue eyes. All the light in the room seemed to gather in his smile. With each spin, his lips grew brighter, taking on hints of yellow, then a searing orange.

A warm breath rose within her, propelling her faster, faster. Justin's face began to change, becoming ashen, his eyes sharpening to a metallic grey. She felt her heartbeat, echoing his name. *Zep. Zep. Zep.* Something was wrong. She turned, unable to stop, as the colour continued to drain from his cheeks, and his eyes brightened with inhuman fire. He looked upwards, his motions strangely mechanical, as though possessed by something otherworldly.

She faltered and lost her balance, falling out of her turn and into his arms as he rasped, *Your kiss will bring me home again, my love*. And then he opened his jaws wide, revealing the flames that filled him and reached out to swallow them both.

Vanessa awoke to find someone attacking her face.

'Sweetie, you drooled!' Her mother was dabbing at her chin with a handkerchief.

'Mom, stop.' Vanessa swatted her mother's hand away. 'Seriously.' She glanced around – no one else on the plane seemed to be paying attention, not even the businessman with the handlebar moustache on her other side. Like Vanessa, he'd fallen asleep on the long flight from New York to London. Only she was sure *he* hadn't been dreaming of a cute boy filled with flames . . .

Vanessa craned her neck forward, pushing strands of red hair out of her eyes. Justin sat a few rows ahead, on the other side of the aisle, reading. He looked entirely normal, not like there was a demon inside him. They hadn't been able to get three seats together, and Vanessa's mother wasn't about to sit by herself.

'What are you looking for, dear?' her mother asked, a little too loudly.

'Mom, please,' Vanessa said, leaning back in her seat and unzipping her hoodie.

'Please *what*?' Vanessa's mother said.

'Please be quiet.' Vanessa placed the sweatshirt on her lap. 'You're giving me a headache.'

For a moment her mother's expression softened, and Vanessa was reminded of when her mother had been full of love and laughter, a former ballerina who'd stepped out of the spotlight to raise a family. Then her mother blinked and was herself again – worried, tense, ready to snap at any moment – the way she'd been ever since Vanessa's sister Margaret had disappeared three years ago.

'You know, some daughters would be nice to their mothers,' her mom said, 'because their mothers put their own lives on hold to travel halfway around the world so their daughters could take part in a ballet competition.' She paused, staring at the small television screen embedded in the seat in front of her. 'I wonder what it would be like to have a daughter like that.'

'I'm sorry, Mom.' As usual, even after a seven-hour flight, her mother was impeccably dressed, not a hair out of place, her make-up perfect and her clothes unwrinkled. She had the sort of flawless beauty that a ballerina was supposed to have. That Margaret had. And Vanessa did not.

Her mother placed a hand over Vanessa's. 'That's all right, dear. You're just nervous about the competition.'

'Um, sure,' Vanessa said, even though she wasn't thinking about the competition at all.

'They invited you at the last minute, without having passed any of the preliminaries,' her mother said. 'That means a lot. The Royal Court is one of the most prestigious European dance companies, and they don't make mistakes.'

'If you say so,' Vanessa mumbled.

'I'm just glad you have an opportunity to dance,' her mother continued. 'Dad and I were so looking forward to seeing you in

The Firebird. I despise how your choreographer ran off with his assistant like that. What a scandal!'

Vanessa winced. The *truth* was that Josef, head choreographer at the New York Ballet Academy, and Hilda, his mentor, were both dead, casualties of the demon they had raised – with Vanessa's unwitting help. Now the demon was still out there in some form, and Vanessa could hardly begin to guess what havoc it might wreak. She and Justin were on their way to London in an attempt to track down the evil entity and stop it. And she also hoped to find Margaret along the way.

'It's a shame your father is going to miss the competition,' her mother said with a sigh, 'but he'll be there in time for the holiday.' She forced a smile. 'Christmas in London. It will be so nice to be away.'

Since Margaret's disappearance, it had been impossible to enjoy the holidays without bittersweet memories: building snowmen, watching *A Christmas Story* and drinking hot cocoa, opening presents, Margaret flitting around in new pointe shoes and tights.

'Tell me more about that boy,' her mother said, changing the subject.

For a second, Vanessa's heart raced. *Zep*, she thought. He'd been her first boyfriend and a fellow New York Ballet Academy student – and he'd turned out to be a monster. But her mother didn't know about Zep.

'That Justin. He's tall and handsome,' Vanessa's mother said, 'but who *is* he? What is his family like? Why he is travelling alone?'

'He's *not* alone,' Vanessa said. 'He's with us.'

When it came down to it though, Vanessa didn't know all that much about Justin. He was older than she was, a senior. He had tried to help her back at school, warning her away from Zep. But she hadn't listened. She'd loved Zep, and he had betrayed her. It was only after the truth came out that she realised Justin was actually a good guy. Not just good, great. He and Vanessa had kissed once in the snow in front of Lincoln Center, but then Justin had got all stiff and strange. It was as if the kiss had transformed Vanessa into a different person, one with the capacity to hurt him.

And now Vanessa felt the same way about him. She thought of her dream, of the demon's words. *Your kiss will bring me home again, my love.* Even though she was no longer its host, were she and the demon somehow linked? Could it inhabit someone else, or use that person to get close to her? Was her dream just a dream or was it something more – a vision?

'Is he a good dancer?' her mother asked.

'I guess so,' Vanessa said. Truth be told, she had never thought Justin was particularly talented. He'd even dropped her once in a rehearsal, though he claimed he did it only to keep her safe. But now they were going to partner in the *pas de deux* on the second day of the competition, and Vanessa would see what he was really made of.

'You *guess*?' Her mother shook her head. 'Not just anyone can compete at London's Royal Court. Your other friends weren't asked to compete, Vanessa – just you and Justin. That must mean something.

'Are you two . . . ?' her mother went on, looking uncomfortable. 'You know.'

Vanessa raised an eyebrow. 'Are we *what*?'

'Don't make me say it,' her mother said. 'An . . . item.'

Vanessa laughed. 'No. We're not.' *At least, I don't think so . . .* she thought.

'Good. What is he, eighteen? You're only fifteen, Vanessa. You don't need a boyfriend. Focus on dance.'

'Right.' This was safer ground, and her mother seemed to relax.

She took out the invitation Vanessa had received, which was folded crisply and tucked inside her purse.

The Royal Court Ballet Company
1 Theatre Square
London, England

Dear Ms Adler,

Congratulations!

You have been selected to audition for the Royal Court Ballet Company. All expenses will be paid for you to attend the Eighty-Sixth Annual Scholarship Competition.

A world-renowned dance troupe based in London, the Royal Court is one of the most prestigious dance companies in a country famed for its contribution to ballet. The scholarship allows dancers of exceptional

promise to train with the company for two years,
launching them on a career the upper bounds of which
can only be imagined.

The letter went on to describe how the competition worked: one intense week in which ninety-six students from all over the world vied against one another in a series of three auditions, two days apart. At the end of the week, only two dancers would remain – the winners.

'Just imagine,' Vanessa's mother said with wide eyes. 'You could win!'

'Maybe,' Vanessa said. 'I doubt it though.'

'Don't think like that, dear.' Her mother clicked her tongue. 'If the other competitors see you as weak, they will dance right over you. If you *think* you're a winner, then you'll *be* a winner.'

'Easy for you to say.' Vanessa was a good dancer, maybe even a great one, but she hadn't inherited her mother's passion for dance.

Margaret had.

Margaret. All Vanessa knew was that her sister was alive – probably – and on the run. No doubt she'd fled NYBA because Josef had been using her to attempt to summon a demon – Margaret must have been terrified. Now Josef was dead, but his trail led back to other dancers in London. Vanessa's hope was that once she found them, they would somehow lead her to her sister.

A few months ago, Vanessa would have laughed. A demon? Raised through dance? But she had seen it, felt it; it had inhabited her, tried to consume her from within. Almost destroyed her.

There was a *ding!* followed by an announcement that they were beginning the descent into Heathrow Airport. Up ahead, Justin turned and locked eyes with Vanessa. His sandy-coloured hair was sticking up at the back, and he looked tired – like he'd woken up not long ago. But something about his expression made Vanessa's stomach flutter, and she thought again about the dream she'd just had.

Your kiss will bring me home again.

What did that mean? Could kissing Justin endanger him?

'Seat belts, please,' the flight attendant said as she moved down the aisle, blocking Vanessa's view.

Vanessa leaned back and slipped her earbuds in, though she kept the volume on mute. Beside her, moustache man awoke from his nap. He rubbed his eyes and took out a copy of *The Times*.

Vanessa skimmed the headlines over his shoulder. *Man United Loses in Late Rally* seemed to be about soccer, and *Cameron Coalition Falls Apart* was clearly about politics.

'Dear, it's rude to read someone else's newspaper.'

Vanessa sighed. 'Fine, Mom.'

Never mind the demon. She wondered if having her mother by her side all week might be the most challenging part of the competition.

'There he is!' Vanessa's mother said as passengers rushed past them towards customs. 'Oh, Justin!'

Justin was standing in front of the boarding gate, his backpack slung casually over one shoulder. He was wearing a grey sweater that was loose around the neck, a snug pair of jeans and crisp-looking white sneakers.

Vanessa had to admit he looked good.

Her mother drifted ahead, pulling out her phone to call Vanessa's dad, as Vanessa and Justin fell in behind her. 'How was your flight?' she asked.

'Fine,' Justin said. 'Yours?'

'Oh, fine.' Vanessa wasn't sure what else to say. Was Justin nervous about the competition? Had he been in touch with Enzo? They hadn't exactly spoken since the end of the semester. Even though they'd been in touch to make arrangements for the trip and choose their *pas de deux*, it had all been by text, short and sweet and businesslike. There'd been nothing personal, nothing about their kiss in the snow.

'Being in England already makes me want tea,' Justin said, eyeing a restaurant in the terminal. 'And, like, a crumpet.' He smiled at her suddenly, his blue eyes warm and friendly.

'Crumpet,' Vanessa repeated. She'd never actually had a crumpet. She didn't even know what one was. Why had she just repeated the word *crumpet*? Oh, God.

'Watch where you're going!' an older woman yelled as she cut across the walkway, nearly knocking Vanessa to the ground.

'Careful,' Justin said, catching Vanessa's shoulder. 'You OK?'

'I'm fine, thanks.' Glued to her phone, her mother hadn't even turned round.

Justin gave her shoulder a gentle squeeze, and Vanessa felt her stomach flutter. 'Good,' he said. 'Let's go.'

Forty-five minutes and one stamp on her passport later, Vanessa was through customs. Her ears were full of English accents – everyone sounded like Russell Brand or the old dowager on *Downton Abbey*, which was weirdly comforting.

'You may not know this about me, Justin, but I abhor being late,' Vanessa's mother said. 'That and Chinese food. Neither are good for you, you know.'

Justin stifled a laugh, but Vanessa just shook her head. She already knew her mother was crazy.

Their overnight flight was supposed to have arrived just before 8 a.m., but now it was nearly ten. Vanessa could see the weak morning sun hiding behind grey clouds, and she shivered as the three of them stepped outside into the cold December air.

Vanessa turned on her cellphone while they waited. A few text messages came in at once. The first was from her friend TJ: *Be safe. Don't do anything I wouldn't do.*

There was one from Steffie that said, *Say hi to Justin for me*, and one from Blaine: *Kiss Justin for me*. Blaine was spending the holiday at Steffie's house in Cincinnati, while TJ was in Manhattan, trying to convince her parents to let her fly to London and spend Christmas with Vanessa and her family. All of them were hurting – missing their friend Elly, who'd gone missing in September and was probably dead, murdered by Josef or Zep. Vanessa shivered, remembering dancing with

Zep, kissing him, how crazy she'd been about him, while all the time he was working with Josef to raise a demon. What a creep.

'Anything interesting?' Justin said.

Vanessa stuffed her phone into the pocket of her jeans. 'Not really.' She could feel the blood rushing to her cheeks, and she turned away.

'Come on, let's hail a cab,' Vanessa's mother said, but then Vanessa spotted their last name – ADLER – on a cardboard sign.

She immediately recognised the man holding the sign: Enzo. He was a member of the Lyric Elite, an organisation of dancers who fought those who would use the power of their art for evil. An organisation that she hoped would help her find her sister. Enzo had shown up at NYBA too late to help with the demon, but he had got her and Justin invited to the competition as a first step towards working with the Lyric Elite.

Vanessa guessed he was twenty-one at the very most, with black hair that parted in the middle and tumbled down on either side of his forehead, framing his angular face. Enzo had dark eyes, olive-coloured skin and an ultrawhite smile. On first glance he didn't look like much, but when he walked towards them she saw he had the posture of a dancer, precise yet graceful, his muscular frame suddenly appearing weightless.

'Oh!' Vanessa's mother said, stopping short when she recognised her last name. 'Why, Justin – did you hire us a taxi?'

But Enzo cut off Justin's response. 'Mrs Adler,' he said, stepping forward.

'Yes?' her mother said.

'I'm from the Royal Court Ballet Company.'

Vanessa's mother's eyes flashed with understanding. Instinctively she brushed her fingers over her hair. 'Why, yes, of course you are.'

Enzo grabbed her mother's silver Tumi bag and began to roll it towards the street. 'Please come with me. If we're lucky, we'll make it just in time for orientation.'

He strolled over to a white BMW parked behind a row of taxis. He clicked open the trunk and heaved all their bags inside. As her mother slid into the backseat, he looked at Vanessa and Justin and said, 'I'll bring you up to speed later. But we have to *hurry*. If you don't turn up on time, you're in danger of being disqualified before you've even started.'

CHAPTER TWO

Through the back windows, Vanessa watched the staggered rooftops roll past as they sped along the M4 towards the city centre. London looked so different from New York. The buildings here were shorter, the sky bigger, the clouds lower and greyer – as if they'd been hanging over the city for so long that they drooped with exhaustion. A thin, cold rain had begun to fall.

'You're lucky – your schedule has already been laid out for you,' her mother said, flipping the pages of a small guidebook. 'But I'll have to find some way to occupy myself. There are almost too many things to do.'

Lucky? Vanessa didn't feel lucky. She closed her eyes and saw again her dream of Justin, his mouth a pit of flame. She felt a tickle of heat in her chest. 'You could always go shopping.'

'Of course, dear – that's what I'm talking about. Harrods will take *at least* a day, but then there's Harvey Nichols, and Liberty, and – oh, it's too much for just one week.'

'Yeah, it's way more tiring than winning an international dance competition,' Vanessa mumbled. Though her mother shopped so much it almost seemed competitive.

Nearly half an hour later, the city skyline was replaced by a vast patch of countryside, a huge city park so quiet and idyllic that it looked like a painting. RICHMOND PARK, a sign read. Vanessa pressed her face to the window as a flock of blackbirds swooped over the landscape towards a distant steely lake.

The white peaked roof of a building was just visible past the trees. 'Welcome to the White Lodge,' Enzo said, steering the car down a dirt carriage path. 'Once upon a time, royalty stayed here at weekends, but these days it's the home of the Royal Court Ballet.'

The lodge *looked* like something fit for a king or queen. The front was taken up by four immense white pillars framing tall glass windows, and two staircases swept down from either side of a marble balcony to meet in a flight of broad stone steps. It was like an ivory mansion carved out of ice – in the middle of a city park.

Vanessa opened the car door and stepped out into the drizzly air.

Justin came up behind her, his arm brushing hers. 'What do you think?' he whispered, handing Vanessa her suitcase. 'Pretty impressive, eh?'

At the wintry sight, Vanessa couldn't help but think of the white figures that had been frozen into the wall in the basement dance studio in New York – the silhouettes of dancers who had died while in thrall to Josef and his attempts to raise a demon. Now Josef was dead, and the demon was – where? What did it want? Dread rose in her.

'You need to hurry,' Enzo said, looking at his watch. 'I drove fast, but you're still quite late.'

'Listen to the man,' her mother said, shooing them away. 'You don't want to make a bad impression.'

Justin reached back and took Vanessa's hand, and she felt a jolt of electricity at his touch. Together, they took the stairs two at a time, and were breathless by the time they reached the entrance. Behind them, she could hear her mother following at a more leisurely pace. The doors creaked as Vanessa pushed them open.

Inside, the yellow glow of a chandelier welcomed them. The grand foyer was polished and clean, with the sweet aroma of a museum. The walls were decorated with portraits of ballerinas and dancers frozen in time, their arms extended, their legs spread in *jetés* or tangled beneath tutus in a breathtaking array of colours – violet, sage, salmon pink and blueberry as well as white. Some of the pictures were from productions Vanessa knew – *Swan Lake*, *A Midsummer Night's Dream*, or *Don Quixote* – but others left only an impression of unbearable grace.

'Wow,' she breathed, her voice quiet, as though this really *were* a museum.

They made their way through the foyer, which was lined with head shots – more distinguished alumni probably. But then Vanessa noticed a familiar face among the photographs. *Margaret?* No, she realised, it was Pauline something, a promising young French dancer she'd heard about.

'These are the competitors,' Justin said from behind her. The portraits filled the entire hallway, their eyes staring back at the empty corridor, eerie, lifeless.

Vanessa realised she didn't see her own portrait or Justin's among them. Was it because they'd registered at the last minute?

A woman in her mid-twenties came down the hall towards them, her heels clicking against the tiles. 'You must be Ms Adler,' she said, surveying Vanessa's sneakers and jeans with the slightest hint of distaste. 'And Mr Cooke. We've been expecting you. I'm Jennifer, the dorm manager.'

Vanessa nodded. 'Sorry we're –'

'Late?' The woman pointed them down the hallway towards a theatre. 'Orientation has already begun. Leave your bags with me, and I'll make sure they get to your rooms.'

Vanessa and Justin gently pulled open the heavy doors of the theatre, and together they slipped into the darkness.

The auditorium was dim, the only light from spots focused on the stage. A man stood in front of a velvet curtain, his face pale in the white light. He was tall, lean and bald, with sharp black eyes. Vanessa and Justin tiptoed down the aisle and took two plush red seats in the rear.

'– and I am Palmer Carmichael, master choreographer of the Royal Court Ballet Company.' The man paused, and the room filled with thunderous applause.

'Never heard of him,' Justin whispered. 'Have you?'

Vanessa shook her head. Seated slightly behind Carmichael on the stage were two middle-aged women, both tall and lithe and beautiful. They must be former ballerinas, she thought, perhaps judges in the competition, though she and Justin had apparently missed their introductions.

'It is an honour to be here in a room with so much talent,' Carmichael continued after the applause had died down. 'I truly wish we could accept all of you, for it is thanks to the efforts of young, passionate dancers like you that the Royal Court Ballet Company exists at all. It was nearly a century and a half ago that the company was founded . . .'

Justin leaned in and whispered, 'Everyone's so quiet.' A shiver ran up Vanessa's skin at the feel of his breath on her ear.

She inched her hand closer to his on the armrest, the darkness giving her confidence. 'I don't mind it,' she said, her voice hushed.

Justin narrowed his eyes. 'Neither do I. You know, if it weren't for Carmichael, it would almost feel like we're alone.'

'After what happened in New York, I'm not exactly the safest person to be alone with,' Vanessa said.

'Who said I wanted safe?'

Vanessa smiled.

The seats around them were filled with dozens of dancers their age, the reflected glow from the stage lights warming their faces.

'This is the thirtieth anniversary of the Royal Court competition, and our first time holding the auditions during the winter holidays,' Carmichael said, sweeping his arms wide. 'It is cause for celebration!' He clapped and stepped back into the shadows.

A single note filled the air, the pure tone of a violin. Two dancers appeared from the wings – a woman and a man, both young. They wore gold-embroidered coats over white leotards and tights, and as the music swelled, the man took up position behind the ballerina with his right hand on her hip. They raised their left arms in a delicate arch, their hands turned, their fingers lightly spread.

'*Don Quixote*,' Justin whispered. 'The *pas de deux*.'

And then it began. The dancers skipped lightly across the stage, his movements the perfect shadow of hers. He raised her into the air before gently setting her on her feet, and she made two quick, precise turns. And then back again, the woman performing elegant, perfect leg raises and swift, exuberant *fouettés*.

By the climax, as the man spun through one barrel turn after another, Vanessa had forgotten to breathe. They were perfectly graceful, seeming to expend no effort at all. *This is true beauty*, she thought.

The applause that greeted the end of the performance was deafening. All the students and coaches rose as the dancers clasped hands and bowed.

Then they melted soundlessly into the wings as Palmer Carmichael strode to centre stage again. 'Thanks to our two scholarship winners from last season.' He raised his arms, quieting the audience. 'The Royal Court was founded on the belief that real dancers are made, not born. We have designed this competition to find such talent when it is at its ripest, and pluck it and mould it before it rots.'

He looked delighted at the prospect, Vanessa thought. Something about Palmer was familiar, and it wasn't just that he was a choreographer. It had to do with the crooked curl of his lip, the shadow his brow cast over his face, the lilt in his voice – as if he were holding on to a secret. And his charisma, she realised. He had an animal magnetism that drew every eye in the room.

'Doesn't he remind you of Josef?' Vanessa whispered.

'A little, but so what?' Justin said. 'He's a choreographer. They're all like that.'

'There are ninety-six of you seated here today,' Palmer continued, gesturing towards the audience. 'In one week, there will be only two. The competition will last seven days, beginning now, and consists of three rounds, each separated by a day of rest and preparation. The first round, on Monday, is a traditional solo. Wednesday's round is a partnered dance. And the third round, next Friday, is a contemporary solo. We three judges will observe each of your performances and make our decisions by the end of each competition day. Sixty-four students will be eliminated in the first round.'

A murmur rose from the seats. Two-thirds of the dancers would be cut after day one?

'Twenty students will be eliminated in round two.' More loud whispers. 'And then, of the remaining twelve, two students will be offered a two-year scholarship position. We will announce the winners on the seventh and final day of the competition, followed by a press event.'

He gazed over the faces in the audience, as if he could already tell who would be cut. 'Many of you are used to being the very best. But here, you are surrounded by stars,' Carmichael said. 'We are looking for the sun and the moon. Nothing less. You will have the rest of today and tomorrow to prepare for the first round. I suggest you use that time well.'

Vanessa peered at the dancers around them. Beside each group sat at least one older person. They were coaches, Vanessa realised, as she watched some of them translating Palmer's speech for their students. But she and Justin weren't there with anyone from NYBA. 'Do we have a coach?'

'Maybe Enzo?' he said, shrugging. 'Or someone else from the . . .' He mouthed, 'Lyric Elite.'

'Over the next seven days, you will be working with dancers from all over the world who share your passion for the art of ballet,' Palmer said. 'I hope that even those of you who are not chosen will take away from this the unique experience of having performed among the best the world has to offer.'

Vanessa snorted. No one sitting in that theatre would be comforted by 'having performed among the best'. It was *be* the best or nothing at all.

'Shh,' Justin whispered, leaning towards her. Vanessa could feel him linger for a moment, his arm brushing against hers before he turned his attention back to the stage.

Palmer began naming previous winners, famous dancers who had begun their careers in the exact seats the students now occupied. Vanessa gazed around the room at her competitors.

A cluster of nine dancers and three coaches were sitting close to the front, wearing matching athletic jackets with block letters printed on the back in the Cyrillic alphabet – Russians, most likely. Beside that group was another team, all in expensive, well-cut uniforms bearing a school name that included the word *Académie* – clearly French. The Royal School of Ballet team sat near the back, the Union Jack emblazoned on their shirts. And then there were a few dozen smaller groups, each with a school coach, of just two or three dancers; some of the dancers looked vaguely Eastern European, others from further afield – maybe Asia or Africa. She overheard an occasional hushed comment in a language she didn't recognise.

'Do you see anyone else from New York?' Vanessa whispered.

'I don't think so,' Justin said, scanning the audience. 'We're the only ones. And I'm one of the few guys.' Of the ninety-six dancers sitting in the room, only about a third of them were male.

Vanessa felt a strange sensation: someone was staring at her.

She half imagined she'd spin and glimpse Zep standing in the shadows beneath the balcony, his metallic eyes roaming over her body, but when she turned she saw only a line of spectators – some older people who were probably parents or coaches, and a few people taking pictures, who might be with the press: a punk girl with dyed-black hair, a blonde woman in a garish pantsuit, a young man in a porkpie hat. Where was her mother? She had to be here somewhere.

And then a doe-eyed girl across the aisle blinked and said, 'Sorry!' her voice high-pitched and buoyant. 'I don't mean to stare!'

'You're American,' Vanessa said, relieved.

'I'm from the Midwest Grasslands School of Ballet.' The girl's face lit up. 'You may have heard of it. It's in Iowa.'

'Sure,' Vanessa lied. A dance academy in Iowa? The girl must be an amazing dancer to have been scouted from a nothing school like that.

'I'm Maisie,' the girl said, blushing furiously. 'Maisie Teller.' She had light brown hair and a round, rosy face that looked so young Vanessa could barely believe she was old enough for high school, let alone a competition like this one.

'I'm Vanessa Adler,' she replied. 'And this is Justin Cooke. We're from the New York Ballet Academy.'

'Wow!' Maisie said a little too loudly. A handful of dancers turned and scowled. Maisie lowered her voice. 'I've never been to New York but I've seen pictures. You're so lucky!'

'Maisie!' hissed her coach, a severe-looking white-haired man. 'Be quiet!'

'Sorry!' Maisie said. And then to Vanessa she whispered, 'This is already the best day of my entire life.' She turned her attention back to Palmer Carmichael.

Curious, Justin raised an eyebrow. 'Who is that?'

'A girl from Iowa.'

'She sounded . . . enthusiastic. And *loud*.'

'She's young,' Vanessa said with a shrug. 'She's probably really nervous –' she continued, when the girl in front of Vanessa spun round.

She was a lovely brunette with long lashes and a charming constellation of freckles beneath her left eye. Her hair was knotted into a loose braid. 'I couldn't help overhearing that you were from New York,' she said. 'I've only been there once, but I thought it was exceptionally beautiful. Especially in the autumn, with the colour of the leaves. It's not quite the same where I'm from in France.'

Vanessa thought of the canopy of trees over Central Park. She'd been gone only a day and yet a part of her yearned to be back in the city. 'It *is* beautiful, isn't it?'

The girl nodded. 'I am called Pauline Maillard.'

'Pauline?' Vanessa said, recognising the name. 'From the Paris Opera Ballet?'

Pauline smiled. '*Oui*. Have we met before?'

'No, I – I'm sorry. It's just that I've heard of you,' Vanessa said in awe. Pauline was a rising star on the international competition circuit. 'You toured with *The Sleeping Beauty*. *The New York Times* called you "astonishing".'

Pauline blushed. 'Oh, one day you are famous and everyone loves you; the next day everyone hates you. I try just to focus on my art and not pay attention.'

'That's probably why you're so good,' Vanessa replied. Not only was Pauline beautiful, but she seemed genuinely nice. Even though Vanessa knew the French girl was serious competition, she couldn't help but want to be her friend.

'And you are . . . ?' Pauline asked.

'Oh! I'm Vanessa – Vanessa Adler.'

'*Enchantée.*' Pauline smiled again. 'You are excited, yes? It is such an honour to be here.'

Vanessa nodded and said, 'Absolutely,' wondering what it felt like to be so happy, so grateful. Maybe that was why Pauline was so good. Because she truly loved what she did. Not that Vanessa didn't love to dance, but for her – especially now – it was complicated.

Each of the dancers around them had been scouted as the best in their school, the best in their country even. Watching them, Vanessa's chest tightened. She had felt this way before, years ago when she danced her first recital in front of her parents and Margaret. She could remember standing behind the curtain at her old dance school in Massachusetts, waiting for her cue, her heart pressing against her ribs as if her leotard were suddenly too small.

She focused on the stage again just as Palmer Carmichael clasped his hands together. 'I would like to finish with a short film about the history of the Royal Court competition,' he said, stepping towards the edge of the stage.

The lights dimmed. The curtains parted.

Then someone in the audience screamed.

Vanessa sat up, her body instantly rigid. In the projector's flickering light she saw a corpse dangling from a noose in the centre of the stage. Pinned to the front of the body was an enormous sign, its words scrawled in blood-red ink:

BREAK A LEG!

CHAPTER THREE

Frozen in fear, Vanessa stared at the body hanging above the stage, a sick feeling in her stomach. The dead girl's long black hair fluttered as her body swayed on the rope. Vanessa heard Justin say something, but his voice disappeared in the chaos erupting in the auditorium. She could sense his hand on hers, but all she could feel was her own heart, racing out of control.

The projector stopped and the house lights came on. Then she could see that the body was just a stuffed dummy in a tutu, a cartoonish lipsticked mouth on its white cloth face, its hair nothing more than a cheap wig.

A calm seemed to wash over the audience, followed by a wave of nervous laughter. A few seats ahead, two girls muttered furiously in a language Vanessa didn't understand, while, to her right, she could hear a boy's high-pitched giggle.

Pauline turned back around to Vanessa and sighed. 'They do this every year, I think. This prank. It's childish, no?'

'Yes,' Vanessa said, her heart still thudding. 'Childish.'

'Especially for such a prestigious competition,' Pauline said.

Onstage, Palmer Carmichael smiled at the audience. 'Scary, eh? We all know ballet is a competitive world – some of our students like to lighten the mood before the real work begins.'

'I don't think it's all that funny,' Justin whispered.

Vanessa couldn't help but agree with him. She listened halfheartedly as Palmer ran through a list of rules and regulations for the coming week. But all she could really think was: *If that's their idea of a joke, what else do they have in store?*

After the orientation, Vanessa and Justin wandered back into the lobby along with the rest of the dancers. Jennifer, the dorm manager they'd met earlier, sat behind a table next to a man whose nametag read *Wesley* – the boys' dorm manager.

'Form two lines,' he was saying, 'boys and girls. Please form two lines to get your room assignments.'

'I guess I'll see you later?' Vanessa said to Justin, who fell in behind two Polish dancers. The lobby was a bit chaotic – dancers and their coaches pushing every which way, rolling bags behind them and calling to one another in various languages. Vanessa felt like she was back in the airport.

'Text me,' Justin said with a blink of his blue eyes. Vanessa couldn't help but notice that even compared to all the other dancers, Justin was still one of the most handsome guys in the competition. 'Let's meet up in an hour?'

A girl with wavy blonde hair bumped into Vanessa's shoulder. 'Ow,' Vanessa said, whipping herself around. 'Excuse me.'

'You're excused,' the girl said, then pointed to the line. 'In or out?'

Not wanting to lose her spot, Vanessa muttered, 'In.'

Two minutes later, still waiting, she heard a familiar voice calling out her name. 'Oh, darling! Vanessa!'

Her mother strolled in, arm in arm with a tall blonde woman who, like her, had the posture of a former ballerina – spine straight, shoulders back. The woman must have been trained as a dancer. Either that or she was a princess.

'Dear! You will never *guess* who I ran into!' Vanessa's mother said. 'An old friend of mine, Rebecca Mainer.'

The blonde woman smiled, her blue eyes wide. 'I've been hearing so much about you, Vanessa. My daughter Emilie is here competing as well!'

'What a small world!' Vanessa's mother trilled. 'Rebecca and I danced together at the San Francisco Ballet about a million years ago. Doesn't it feel that way?'

Rebecca nodded, then tilted her head. 'I tell Emilie all the time – enjoy it while it lasts. Because before you know it, your knees will creak and you'll have babies, and dancing will seem like some faraway dream.'

'That's . . . encouraging,' Vanessa managed to say as the line kept moving.

'That's life,' her mother said. 'Anyway, Rebecca, I am so glad you're here. Stephen can't join us until the end of the competition – he couldn't get off work, you know – so I am thrilled, absolutely thrilled, to have a friend with me.' She shifted her attention to Vanessa. 'Dear, we're going to head back to the hotel and catch up. I'll call you later and we'll get dinner, yes?'

'OK,' Vanessa said. 'Have fun!'

Rebecca gave her a soft kiss on the cheek. 'I can't wait for you to meet Emilie. I hope you two will be fast friends. Or fast enemies!' She laughed. 'You know how we dancers can be.'

'Do I ever!' Vanessa's mother said. 'Goodbye, dear.'

Vanessa watched as the two of them glided across the lobby and out of the front entrance. She glanced back, trying to spot Justin, but she couldn't make him out – there were so many fewer boys than girls, and that line was moving a lot faster.

Finally she reached Jennifer, who looked exhausted but was trying to keep a positive expression on her face.

Jennifer handed Vanessa a thin packet with the name *Adler* written in black marker on the front. 'There's a map of the school in there in case you get lost,' Jennifer said, 'as well as your meal tickets and a schedule. Oh, and here's your key. Room 321.' She handed Vanessa a grey plastic rectangle the size of a credit card. 'You'll be sharing a room with one other dancer, and bathrooms are on each floor.'

Great, Vanessa thought. *A roommate.*

'Have fun,' Jennifer said in a fake-cheery voice. 'And good luck!'

The hallway on the girls' floor had crisp white walls, blond wood floors and warm incandescent lighting that made it feel like an extension of a dance studio. When she reached room 321, Vanessa slipped her grey key card into the lock.

Inside, the room had tall rectangular windows that looked out on to a panoramic view of the park. There were twin beds, two dressers, two desks and two closets, each equipped with a full-length mirror. Bland, but at least there was a nice view.

She closed the door behind her, seeing her suitcase resting at the foot of one of the beds. On the other side of the room sat a pile of patent leather luggage, enough for months of travel. What kind of person needed that much stuff for a seven-day trip?

Vanessa could hear voices in the hallway, girls chatting as they unpacked. She wandered across the room and quickly checked out the luggage tags. *Svetlana Chernovski*. The name was Russian, but the address was somewhere in England.

Suddenly the door opened with a bang.

'May I help you?'

Vanessa stood up and quickly stepped away from the luggage. She turned around to see a tall girl whose features were severe, her face possessed of a timeless beauty that would have looked right at home in some old 1930s movie. Her skin was as pale as milk, her cheekbones sharp and high, her lips a deep crimson. And then there was her hair, long piles of it – a rich, sensuous, wavy blonde.

It was the same girl who'd bumped into her in the lobby.

'Um, no – sorry,' Vanessa said. 'I was just trying to see who my roommate was.'

Svetlana sauntered over to her luggage and lifted one of the suitcases on to the bed. 'Well, I trust that now you have seen your fill. Please keep your hands to yourself.' Her voice had a tinge of a Russian accent, but her English was otherwise impeccable. 'I do not want you to steal my things.'

'I'm not going to –' Vanessa stopped herself and decided to try a different tactic. 'Hi. I'm Vanessa Adler. From the New York Ballet Academy.' She extended her hand. 'I guess we're roommates.'

Svetlana studied Vanessa's hand like it was a dead fish. She didn't shake it.

'That is nice. I hear New York is very fast-paced.'

'Um, I suppose . . .' Vanessa said.

'My friends call me Svetya,' the girl said. 'But you may call me Svetlana.' Her eyes travelled over Vanessa with a glint of amusement, taking in her worn sneakers and crumpled T-shirt. Suddenly Vanessa wished she had a piece of gum or a breath mint – the roof of her mouth felt sticky and sour, and she hadn't washed her face since yesterday. Her skin felt slick and oily.

Svetya – no way was she calling her Svetlana – couldn't be much older than she was, and yet something about the way she carried herself made Vanessa feel like a child.

Vanessa suddenly missed her old roommate, TJ, more than ever. 'OK then.' She lowered her hand and turned to her suitcase. She heard Svetya let off a quiet 'Hmmph!' as she began fussing with her own luggage.

Everything inside Vanessa's case was a mess. Her clothes were rumpled and strewn about, but even more distressing was what was nestled on top of them: her sister's pointe shoes, their pink satin worn around the edges.

They were all she had left of her sister really – besides memories and a partial journal she'd found back in New York. When she'd put the ballet slippers on after Josef and Hilda died, almost of their own volition they'd traced out the message *I'm still here.* Which is why Vanessa had agreed to come to London in the first place. Margaret was out there somewhere, and these shoes were Vanessa's only link to her.

Before she'd left, Vanessa had carefully packed them in a silk travel bag, tucked deep within her suitcase. Who had gone through her things and left them on top? Airport security?

Vanessa picked up one shoe, the inside sole imprinted with a faded indentation in the delicate shape of her sister's foot. She traced her thumb around the stitching, remembering all the times she'd watched Margaret tie the ribbons around her ankles.

'Those are nice,' Svetya said, craning her neck to see them.

'Oh, thanks,' Vanessa said. 'They were my sister's.'

'Pretty,' Svetya said softly, as if she were surprised that Vanessa had nice things. Before Vanessa could respond, there was a knock on the door. Was it her mother? Justin?

'Will you get that?' Svetya said. 'I have my hands full.'

Her hands were actually empty, but Vanessa chose not to say anything. Instead she walked over to the door and opened it.

There, standing in front of her, was Enzo.

'Hello,' he said, sweeping his black hair away from his forehead. 'Are you unpacked yet?' His looks were exotic and his voice had a strange lilt; unlike Justin or Zep, he was clearly not an American.

Vanessa thought of her still-full suitcase. 'Not exactly.'

'How about you, Svetya?'

Vanessa looked from Enzo back to Svetya, who was perched on her bed. They knew each other?

'Not yet,' Svetya said. She motioned to Vanessa. 'I have been a bit distracted.'

'Um, hold on a minute,' Vanessa said. 'How do you –'

'I'm also coaching Svetya for the competition,' Enzo said. 'So we'll all be practising together.'

'Great,' Vanessa said, hoping she sounded more enthusiastic than she felt. She was going to have to spend *more* time with this diva? 'I'm glad to know Justin and I aren't on our own.'

'Enzo was supposed to be coaching just me and Geo,' Svetya said. 'But then he added you and your American friend at the last moment. I'm not exactly pleased.'

'Svetya,' Enzo said in a stern voice, 'remember what I told you – focus on your own dancing and you'll be fine.' He paused. 'Vanessa, can we talk for a moment? Outside?'

'Sure,' Vanessa said, placing her sister's ballet slippers back inside her suitcase and grabbing her toiletry bag, with her toothbrush inside. 'Just give me a moment – I need to brush my teeth.'

'Thank God,' Svetya said from across the room. 'I could smell your breath from here.'

Five minutes later and her breath smelling – she hoped – fresher, Vanessa stepped into the hallway just outside the door to her room. Enzo was leaning against the wall, his hands stuffed into his pockets. His eyes were closed, as if he was in deep meditation. He was handsome in a dark, brooding way, Vanessa decided. The sort of looks her sister used to get moony about.

Vanessa cleared her throat. Enzo's eyelids fluttered open and he stared at her, his irises almost black.

'All clean?' he said.

'Something like that,' Vanessa replied.

He slipped one of his hands out of his front pocket, and with it a thin box of green Tic Tacs. 'That's why I always keep these with me.' He popped a few into his mouth. 'But enough oral hygiene.' He peered down the hallway – it had mostly emptied out from a few minutes earlier. Vanessa supposed all the girls were inside their rooms, unpacking, getting to know their roommates, who were probably much friendlier than Svetya.

'We couldn't speak properly in front of your mother,' Enzo said, 'and most of my communication has been with Justin. So I wanted to just . . . chat.'

'Chat,' Vanessa repeated softly. 'All right.'

Enzo tightened his lips. 'So you know why you're here, yes?'

That was a loaded question if she'd ever heard one. 'At the competition, you mean, or –'

'The demon you helped raise is on the loose,' Enzo said. 'That much you know.'

The memory of the nightmare from a few weeks earlier filled her: her angry helplessness as the demon possessed her. How, after Vanessa drove the spirit out, it devoured Hilda whole, burning her away into nothingness. Justin's body lying in a crooked heap. TJ, Blaine and Steffie, whimpering, shaking, speechless in horror. All while the dark pool of blood spread from under Josef's corpse, wider and wider until it seemed to swallow all the light in the room.

And then Vanessa remembered something even worse: her dream on the plane. 'But we left it behind in New York, right?'

Enzo's lips tightened into a frown. 'We believe it is now in London.'

Her stomach lurched. 'Did *I* bring it here?'

'Not exactly, though it probably followed you.' Enzo spoke softly but with great intensity. 'Understand, Vanessa, you are a target for the demon – a former vessel who still lives. No one before has played host to a demon and survived the experience. At the moment it's just a free-floating malevolent spirit, looking for a home in our world. You're the closest thing it has to a gateway.'

She leaned against the corridor wall, her knees weak. If it was here, waiting to use her as a portal, was she safe? Was anyone she cared for safe? 'I need to lead it away,' she said. 'My mom's here, Justin's here.' *My sister*, she thought.

Enzo shook his head. 'You are safer here than you would be anywhere else. The Lyric Elite will protect you, Vanessa. In fact, your deep connection to the demon may turn out to be to your advantage.'

'How?' Vanessa asked.

Enzo paused, glancing down the corridor to make sure they were still alone. 'The Royal Court Ballet has a dark faction,' he said. 'They are like Josef but worse, and I have reason to believe that they are working to summon a demon and harness its power for themselves. I have been trying to uncover the identities of these sinister members of the Royal Court for years, to no avail. But now . . .' He trailed off.

'Now what?'

'Now we have you,' Enzo said. 'A secret weapon.'

'I'm not a weapon,' Vanessa said. 'I'm a person.'

'You misunderstand me,' Enzo said. 'If Josef told this dark group about you, they will do their utmost to have you win the Royal Court competition. Your ties to the demon will be . . . *very* attractive to them.'

'Is that why you asked me to London?' Vanessa asked. 'So you can use me as bait with this dark faction and uncover its members?'

'I would never do anything to compromise your safety, Vanessa. Or Justin's. But by the same token, you must help us protect you. Be extremely wary. If you feel any . . . contact by the demon, let me know immediately.'

'Why?' She felt sick at the realisation that her dream hadn't been a dream at all. 'How can you possibly help?'

He gave her a grim look. 'There's a book the Lyric Elite has heard rumours of called the *Ars Demonica*. It contains rituals and instructions that will help us control the demon.'

'A book? You're going to drive a demon away with a book?'

'It's not just any book, Vanessa, as you'll see soon enough. But for now, let's keep any discussion of the demon between the two of us.' He handed her a slip of paper with a room number on it. 'There is more to discuss, much more, but I'm saving some of it for our first practice. Until then, get some rest. You're going to need it.'

Enzo turned and walked down the hallway. She was about to call out to him, to tell him about her dream, when her phone buzzed.

She slipped it out of her back pocket. It was a text from Justin. *Meet me in the stairwell, 5th floor. 5 minutes.*

She thought about dropping off her toiletry bag in her room, but she didn't feel up to seeing Svetya again. Vanessa scanned the hallway and located the stairwell door. Then she was off.

Justin was waiting for her at the top of the stairs, on the landing. He said something to her, but she barely registered his words. She couldn't shake her conversation with Enzo. *What had she got herself into?* she wondered, dread swelling within her.

'Vanessa?' Justin said, placing one hand on her shoulder.

'Sorry,' she said, coming back to the present.

'So . . . we're finally alone.' He grinned. 'Sit.' He looked as if he had just showered; his hair was wet and matted to the sides of his head. He was wearing a white T-shirt and a pair of green mesh shorts. His feet were bare.

He dropped down on the landing and sat cross-legged, patting the space directly next to him. Vanessa sat down too and leaned against the white brick wall. The sight of him calmed her, made her feel safe. He reminded her of home, she realised.

'How's your roommate?' Justin asked, his voice echoing in the quiet stairwell.

'Terrible. Her name is Svetya.'

'She sounds Russian.'

'Maybe originally,' Vanessa said. 'But I think Russia expelled her or something.'

Justin leaned back against the wall beside her, his smooth arms flexing beneath the cotton of his shirt as he ran a hand through his hair. Realising she was staring, Vanessa quickly looked away.

'I'm rooming with this guy named Geo,' Justin said, a glimmer in his eye. 'He's pretty nice, I guess; we didn't talk much.'

'He goes to the same school as Svetya.'

'Oh?' Justin said. 'And you know that how?'

'Enzo came to see me. Did you know he's our coach? And they're training with us – Geo and Svetya?'

'I knew that Geo was,' Justin said. 'Enzo found me earlier and told me. But I didn't know he had a friend.'

'Well, they might train together,' Vanessa said, 'but I doubt she and Geo are friends.'

Justin inched closer, pressing his leg against hers. 'Why's that?'

Vanessa's cheeks flushed with warmth. 'Svetya isn't the kind of girl who has many friends.'

'Fair enough.' Justin shook his head lightly, and droplets of water fell on Vanessa's shoulder.

'Hey! Watch it,' she said. 'You're like a dog after a bath.'

'A dog, eh?' Justin raised an eyebrow.

'You know what I mean,' Vanessa said.

'Sure.'

She could feel the warmth coming off his skin as, silently, he placed his hand on top of hers, interlacing their fingers. He cupped the other hand behind her neck, and Vanessa felt herself moving towards him, her lips closer to his. All she could think about was their first kiss, and now they were about to have their second . . .

A vision burst into her mind like fireworks. Her dream, dancing with Justin, the demon taking over his eyes, his mouth, his body. *Your kiss will bring me home again, my love*, it had said. She tried to tell herself that it was just a nightmare. The demon had never entered Justin; it had never been interested in him. But what if there was some part of the demon still lurking within *her*, buried deep beneath her skin even after she'd forced it out? Sometimes she imagined she could still feel its tickle of heat within her. She had tried to ignore it, and yet she wasn't completely convinced. In her dream, the demon had devoured

Justin. It seemed so strange, such a premonition, that it frightened her. What if the demon *had* left a shard of itself inside her? And what if kissing Justin would somehow put him – and her – in danger?

She yanked herself away as if she'd just touched a hot coal.

'What's wrong?' Justin's eyes were wide, confused. He inched closer, but Vanessa pulled back. She looked around at the floor, the stairs, the door – anywhere except at him.

'Please,' she said, 'don't.'

'Don't what?' Justin asked. 'Touch you?'

Vanessa nodded.

'Why? What did I do wrong . . . ? I thought –'

'It's not you,' Vanessa said. 'It's me.'

Justin laughed. 'What, are we filming a movie for MTV or something? Even you can come up with a better line than that.' He paused, and she could tell he was trying to figure out her motives. 'Do you . . . not like me?'

Vanessa shook her head. 'Justin, it has nothing to do –'

'Because I thought you liked me. I mean, I thought we liked each other –' he began to say, before cutting himself off. 'Oh,' he said, looking at Vanessa as though seeing something in her that he hadn't before. 'I understand now. You're still stuck on Zep.'

She trembled, remembering Zep's nightmarish face melting into Justin's, her heart racing to the beat of his name. 'No,' Vanessa said. 'That's not it at all. Just the thought of him frightens me. I promise you, it has nothing to do with him.'

'Then what is it?' Justin said, his voice cracking. 'I'm not good enough for you?'

'Of course you are,' Vanessa said. 'You're a great guy. It's just more complicated than that.'

Justin frowned. 'How?'

She told him about her dream, about the demon's promise. 'If I kiss you, whatever part of it is still in me . . . it could hurt you. And I can't be responsible for that.'

There was a long pause as she watched him take in her words. And then he started to laugh.

'Seriously?'

'This isn't funny,' Vanessa said. 'I'm being honest with you.'

'I know,' Justin said. He took a deep breath and said, more calmly, 'but Vanessa . . . that's crazy talk.'

'After everything we've been through, now you're going to tell me that I'm crazy?' She stood up, suddenly feeling claustrophobic. 'You're an ass, Justin Cooke.'

She turned, about to press open the door, when Justin's warm arms wrapped themselves around her. 'I'm sorry,' he whispered. 'You're not crazy.'

Vanessa could feel the muscles of his chest against her back, the sweet warmth of his breath on her neck. 'Thanks,' she said. 'And you're not . . . an ass.'

He chuckled softly. 'The demon is not going to hurt you. Not while I'm around.'

She let out a long sigh. 'But it's so close –'

'We don't know where the demon is, Vanessa.' Justin gave her a gentle squeeze. 'And mark my words – at the first sign that it's here, in London, well ... I'll make up some crazy excuse to your mom and we'll hop on the first plane back to New York.'

Vanessa froze. There was no way she could leave London – the Lyric Elite were here, and they were the only ones who could help her find her sister.

'I don't want to leave London,' she said softly.

'I'll do whatever is necessary to protect you,' Justin murmured, softly kissing her neck.

'Justin!' she said, spinning around in his arms. She wanted to tell him that the demon *was* in London, Enzo had said so, but she couldn't. She wanted desperately to kiss him, but she couldn't do that either. Not now. Not until the demon was destroyed.

'The demon possessed me, and I survived,' Vanessa said stiffly, breaking away from Justin's arms. 'There is some sort of . . . link between us. I can feel it. And I can't risk putting anyone I care about in danger.'

'So what are you saying?' Justin asked.

She stared into the clear blue eyes of this boy who clearly liked her. And who – if she was going to be honest – she liked back. 'I'm saying . . . we need to be just friends for now. OK?'

'That's ridiculous,' Justin said. 'I don't understand –'

'Please,' Vanessa said. 'If you care about me at all, you won't question me on this.'

Justin still looked as if he didn't quite believe her, and it made Vanessa sick that she was hurting him this way. 'OK?' she whispered.

Justin looked away. 'I guess.'

The silence between them was deafening. Vanessa pushed the bar on the door leading back into the hall. 'I'll see you at rehearsal.'

He nodded. 'Later.'

And with that, Vanessa climbed down the stairs, along the hallway to her room. Alone.

Back inside room 321, Svetya was nowhere to be found. Which was probably a good thing, because Vanessa still hadn't unpacked, and her chat with Justin had unnerved her. She pressed her back against the closed door. She had wanted Justin to kiss her, more than anything, but she had to be careful. She couldn't let anyone else be hurt because of her, especially not Justin. She was trying to protect him . . . even though, right now, it didn't feel that way.

One of Svetya's shoes was lying in the middle of the floor. Frustrated, Vanessa kicked it and it hit the wall with a satisfying thud. She sighed, then picked up the shoe and set it back where it was. Piece by piece, the demon was taking her life away from her.

With new resolve, she set her toiletry bag on her bed and unzipped her suitcase. There, staring back at her, should have been Margaret's ballet shoes.

Only they were gone.

Two And A Half
Years Earlier

From the Diary of Margaret Adler
March 2

It was just after four in the morning when I woke up, startled.

The engines had fallen quiet. After six days of that steady vibration in my bones, its sudden absence was like the loudest alarm clock.

Erik's voice came from the upper bunk. 'We've stopped.'

'Is that OK?' I asked. I pictured us adrift somewhere in the North Atlantic, bearing down on an iceberg, about to pull a Titanic.

I had only gone up on deck once since we'd departed from Trenton, New Jersey, and I hadn't enjoyed it. The sea hadn't been romantic at all – just a cold, never-ending plain of white-capped grey – and all of the sailors were running around or shouting at each other in Portuguese, smears of motor grease ground into their overalls.

'Of course it's OK,' Hal said with a yawn from his bunk. 'It means we've arrived. Lady and gentleman, welcome to dear old Blighty.'

'Blighty?' I asked. 'Is that the city we're in?'

Erik laughed. 'No, we should be in Southampton. "Blighty" means "England."'

Hal switched on the overhead light. 'It's what British soldiers in World War Two called England when they got homesick.'

Homesick. I had to blink away tears. Maybe it was Hal telling me earlier that I could never contact Vanessa or Mom and Dad, but at that moment home seemed further away than ever.

I swore to myself then – and I repeat my vow here, on paper – that I will find a way to talk to Vanessa again. Somehow I will get word to my family that I'm OK.

I owe them that much.

It was surprisingly simple to leave the boat. We just had to dodge some of the sailors and head down a railed gangplank to the dock, a wide road made of cement and asphalt. Street lights led the way to a bright, low building.

'We have to pass through customs,' Hal explained. 'Everyone, be cool.'

That early in the morning, no one was in a rush to help us, and it was only after the third time Hal explained that we were students who had booked a cheap passage to England aboard a freighter that someone took our papers.

The customs agent looked a bit like my grandma if my gran were built like a sofa. She raised her eyebrows. 'You're eighteen?' she asked me.

'Yes, ma'am,' I said, trying to stand taller. It was obvious that no matter what Hal had put on my fake passport, I still looked fifteen. I needed to find some way to come across as older than my years. 'You going to take all day with that?' I went on. 'I'm dying for a cigarette.'

The customs agent just scowled and stamped my passport. The machine made a satisfying thunk against the page, and I was officially Margot Adams.

Handing it back, the woman said, 'You kids look younger all the time, but you never get any smarter, do ya? Tobacco will kill you. Shift along now.'

And just like that, we were outside on an empty street. Though it wouldn't be empty for long. Already up and down the road, shutters were being raised with a rattle – businesses opening up for the day.

'What was that all about, crazy girl?' Hal asked. 'Are you trying to get us arrested right off the boat?'

Erik laughed. 'No, that was smart. Just enough to bother her, but not enough to get us into trouble.'

Hal's shrugs must be contagious. I shrugged and said, 'I guess so.'

'Well, whatever it was you were doing, you got us past her,' Hal said.

And there on the street, Erik took my hand in his and gave it a gentle kiss. 'Now we're even,' he said, as my fingers fell from his.

'Who's paying for all this?' I asked as we took our seats on the train, facing each other across a table. Outside the window, the country-side passed by, neat rows of buildings glowing gold with the rising sun, burning off the morning mist.

Hal shrugged and said, 'Erik's people.'

Erik said, 'It's complicated and hard to explain, but I have access to money. Not a ton of it, but enough to get us over here and to pay for a few months' rent on a flat.'

'A flat?' I asked. I admit it, diary: I had dreams of some cosy apartment like the ones I'd seen in movies.

'It's not much money, so it's not much of a flat,' Hal added. 'A room, more like.'

'A room?' I repeated. Clearly they had discussed this without me. I wondered what other surprises they had in store. How much do I know about Hal and Erik, really?

'More like a room with a cubbyhole,' Hal said. 'It was the best I could do. But it should be hard for the people you're running from to trace us.'

'Don't worry,' Erik said. 'It will only be for a short time, until we've found some way of making money and blending in.'

'And I'll only be there for a few days,' Hal said. 'Just long enough to rest up before moving on.'

Hal had told me he'd taken a year off to travel the world on the cheap, couch-surfing in the homes of hacker friends and getting around in the most thrifty ways possible – which was how he knew to book the freighter.

'The room we're letting is above a pub called Barre None, not far from the Royal Court,' he went on. 'I wanted someplace where the two of you would blend in, and the woman who runs it is a former dancer. She calls herself Coppelia.'

'Calls herself?' I asked.

He shrugged and ran a hand through his dishwater-blond hair. 'I don't think it's her real name. But it doesn't matter. Everyone says good things about her. I trust the online community.'

A former dancer. *I don't doubt that Hal's online friends are trustworthy, but the dance world is small. Can we trust someone who doesn't even give out her real name? Can I even trust Hal? Why is he so devoted to Erik?*

'At least you'll always have a place where you can eat,' Hal said.

'Good,' Erik said, 'because I'm starving. I didn't think I'd miss having breakfast on that merchant ship, but if we don't get food soon, I'm going to have to eat one of you.'

'Eat Hal,' I said. 'He's got more meat on his bones. I'm pretty scrawny.'

Erik's smile was for me alone. 'But you're so much tastier-looking.'

I laughed and looked away, embarrassed but for some reason bursting with joy. He always seems to know how to make me blush.

Flat *is kind of an overstatement. Even* room *is pushing it. When we got there, Barre None wasn't open yet, but this Coppelia woman met us at the door. She had that faded beauty of so many former ballerinas – perfect posture, with her white hair pulled back into a messy bun.*

She took in the three of us and said to Hal, 'You must be Henry Greene.'

'I prefer to be called Hal,' he said, nervously ducking his head.

'Henry it is,' she said, not bothering to introduce herself to me and Erik. Then she turned and led us down a dim hallway and up four flights of stairs, her long skirt stirring up dust until it tickled my nose.

At the top was a worn-looking wooden door. The woman unlocked it and started downstairs again, saying, 'I'll be sleeping until two, so see you don't ring my bell until then.'

We stood in the doorway and beheld our new home.

It is an attic room, mostly unfinished. It stinks of woodchips and mothballs. There are two big beds with sagging mattresses pushed under the eaves. Erik and Hal dragged those out and pushed them to opposite ends of the room. 'We'll take one,' Erik said, 'and we'll let you have the other.'

'Obviously,' I said.

With loose planks on top of a bureau and a vanity without a mirror, they created a desk. Almost immediately, Hal produced three laptops from his bag, plugged in an adapter and a power strip, then hooked up all the computers. 'This is how I make my living,' he said, plopping himself into a rickety old wooden chair and hooking up a glowing blue plastic thing. 'First thing to do is set up our internet access. Second thing is . . .'

Erik held up a sheet of paper, 'Second thing is to see if he can get us registered for this.'

'What is it?' I asked. He gave me the sheet. It was a notice of a scholarship programme for the Royal Court: two dance students each year get a free ride with their company. Provided those two students beat out ninety-four other dancers. 'Sounds difficult,' I said. 'Plus you have to be affiliated with a dance school.'

'You are one of the best dancers of your generation,' Erik said, sitting down beside me and taking my hands. 'You will have no problem winning one of those two positions. Me, we shall see. And as for needing to be affiliated with a dance school . . . Hal? Can you do something about that?'

'Already on it,' he said, hunching over one of his laptops.

For the first time in a long while, I breathed a sigh of relief. God only knows what my parents are thinking right now, or Vanessa, who's only in middle school and too young to understand *what's truly going on. I may be in a strange city, with boys I barely know, but at least I can continue to dance. It's what got me into trouble in the first place, but maybe – just maybe – ballet can still be my saving grace.*

CHAPTER FOUR

'See you later, darling!' her mother called out to her after their too-long lunch. 'Good luck! Not that you'll need it. The Adler women are born stars.'

'Right, Mom,' Vanessa said. 'I'll keep that in mind.'

'But that doesn't mean that you don't have to practise,' her mother added with a raised eyebrow.

Vanessa rolled her eyes. 'I know, Mom. Don't worry. I've got it covered.'

'I know you do, darling. And –'

'– you'll be proud of me, no matter what happens,' Vanessa said, completing her mother's sentence. 'But you'll be even more proud of me if I win.' She'd heard her mother say those words many times, and while they usually made her anxious, their familiarity was almost comforting.

Her mother squeezed her shoulder. 'That's my Vanessa.'

Vanessa pushed her way inside the entrance to the White Lodge, waving goodbye to her mother. She dug her phone out of her pocket – it was 2.50 p.m. She had ten minutes to get back to her room, change into her dance clothes, and meet Enzo for their three o'clock rehearsal.

No way she was going to be on time.

If only her mother had had less to say about Rebecca, her long-lost ballet friend from San Francisco, maybe their lunch would have clocked in at under two hours.

'Rebecca and I were the stars of that company,' her mother had said, picking at her Caesar salad with grilled chicken (no dressing, no croutons). 'She danced Cinderella, and she was marvellous.' Her mother paused. 'But then I danced Giselle *and* Juliet in the same season.'

Vanessa had nibbled at her sandwich, half listening, half watching the clock. All her life she had known how high the bar was for her and her sister. It didn't matter how well they danced; if they weren't the stars, their performances would always just be mediocre.

'Sure, Mom,' Vanessa had said. 'Sounds incredible.' She'd realised a long time ago that her mother's nostalgic excursions were just another way for her to reinforce the expectations she had of her daughters. She closed her eyes, thinking about Margaret's missing shoes. Svetya must have taken them, but where were they – and why would she have stolen them?

Back in her room, she slipped into a white leotard, then pulled on a loose-fitting pair of shorts and her hoodie. She grabbed her dance shoes and a bottle of water, threw them into a bag and glanced at the slip of paper Enzo had given her earlier.

Rehearsal Space B1.

Could he have been any less informative? There must be rehearsal rooms in the building, but she had no idea where they were. Vanessa took out her phone again – 3.05 p.m.

Great, she thought. *Just great.*

After asking five different people, Vanessa found the wing of the building with the rehearsal spaces. There were four floors of dance studios, but none was labelled B-1.

Then Vanessa spotted an EXIT door. Did *B* stand for *basement*?

She had to push hard on the door before it opened, its hinges squealing, to reveal a dusty corridor, the walls a drab grey, the ceiling low. A faint smell of old grease hung in the air. The corridor led her beneath a string of dingy lights until she reached a spiral staircase that descended into darkness.

She touched the railing. Her fingers left clear marks in the thick dust.

Down she went, the metal steps ringing beneath her feet, to a dank basement passageway lined with steam pipes and mossy brick walls.

She shivered. Something about this place made her uneasy. It reminded her of the basement practice room back in New York where Josef had rehearsed *The Firebird*. The damp air felt thick in her lungs.

She turned a corner and found herself in an alcove facing a set of ancient double doors. She pushed them open. This was their dance studio?

Enzo was standing in the middle of the room.

'Ah,' he said, waving for Vanessa to enter. 'Finally.'

Cautiously Vanessa stepped inside. Some of the elements were familiar – a warm-up barre, walls covered with mirrors, a sprung wooden floor suitable for dancing.

But everything was old and rundown. The mirror on the far wall actually had a crack running down it like a vein, and the other mirrors were smudged with handprints and dust. The wooden floor was scuffed a dull brown and the floor-boards squeaked under their weight. *We can't dance here*, Vanessa thought. This had to be a joke.

'Welcome to your practice space at the Royal Court,' Enzo said. 'Not glamorous, I know. But I requested this space. Nobody uses it any more, so it's perfect for us.'

At the word *us*, Vanessa realised that Justin, Svetya and another boy – Geo, she assumed – were already there, warming up. Justin was wearing black tights and a grey tank that exposed the muscles in his arms. Svetya was wearing a navy leotard, her right arm arched over her head in a deep stretch. Geo wore a white T-shirt and black tights, though he didn't fill them out the way Justin did. He was tall and skinny for a dancer, with a shock of orange hair that made him look like a human carrot.

'Vanessa,' Enzo said, 'you've met Svetya, and this is Geo.'

Geo stood up from the floor and stuck out his hand. 'Hullo,' he said in an English accent. 'Nice to meet you, Vanessa.'

Vanessa shook his hand, then dropped her bag and took out her pointe shoes. Justin wasn't looking at her. He was focused on Enzo. He must still be upset about their conversation in the stairwell. That was understandable, but she wondered how long he was going to be mad.

'As I was saying before Vanessa arrived,' Enzo said, 'you four are here for a special reason: we recruited you.'

Vanessa glanced at Geo, then Svetya. Did they have experience with demons as well?

'There is a dark faction within the Royal Court,' Enzo said, 'dancers who in the past have identified themselves as *necrodancers*, who use the power of dance to unlock evil forces. The Lyric Elite came into being to stop them from plying their evil craft. That is where you four come in. At least one of you needs to win the competition and then let yourself be recruited by this group. We need inside information.'

'*Win* the competition?' Vanessa asked in disbelief. 'That's practically impossible – there are so many good dancers here, and ninety-four of them are going to be losers. I –'

'Speak for yourself,' Svetya said. 'I am no loser.'

'Why doesn't the Lyric Elite just go after these necrodancers on their own?' Justin asked.

'Because we don't actually know who in the Royal Court is part of the dark company and who isn't,' Enzo admitted. 'We've had dancers try to infiltrate the group before, but they never got past the audition process.'

'So after this, will we officially become part of the Lyric Elite?' Geo asked.

'Let's not get ahead of ourselves. First comes your training,' Enzo said. 'It is essential to the secrecy of our mission that you tell no one what we are here to accomplish. Vanessa and Justin, that means you are to tell people only that you represent the New York Ballet Academy; Svetya and Geo, as you know, you are representing the Royal School of Ballet. Should the name of the Lyric Elite ever come up in conversation, you must pretend ignorance for your sake as well as ours. I will be your coach for the duration of the competition.'

'You couldn't book us one of the newer rooms?' Svetya asked, gazing up at the bare bulbs dangling from the ceiling, one of which flickered and burned out. 'The Bavarian school team is working in a beautiful windowed studio on the first floor.'

'We needed somewhere we could rehearse unobserved. The work we'll be doing is not exactly . . . conventional.' Enzo pointed to a corner of the studio, which was filled with old furniture. 'Justin, Geo – can you stack those so they're out of our way?' He turned to Vanessa. 'And can you or Svetya run that broom across the floor? And wipe down the mirrors, would you? You'll find hand towels in that duffel bag.'

Vanessa gaped at his sexist attitude, but no one else seemed bothered. The boys headed towards the furniture. Svetya leaned against the wall and began texting, barely acknowledging Enzo's request. Vanessa walked over to her and placed her hands on her hips. *Don't make a scene*, she reminded herself.

But Svetya didn't pay her any attention whatsoever – not even when Vanessa tapped one foot against the floor.

'Excuse me,' Vanessa said.

'Hmm?' Svetya said without looking up.

'What did you do with my sister's shoes?'

Svetya raised an eyebrow. 'What do you mean?'

'My sister's shoes,' Vanessa said. 'They're missing.'

'Girls!' Enzo called from across the room. 'Is there a problem?'

'No!' Vanessa called back. She picked up one of the brooms.

'Honestly, I have no idea what you're talking about,' Svetya said. She locked her phone, then placed it in her bag and picked up a broom as well.

'You admired them, and now they're missing, and I really –'

'Vanessa,' Svetya said, cutting her off, 'this conversation is over.'

Then she walked away, broom in hand. Vanessa was sure her roommate was lying, but she would have to prove it. Meanwhile, she had to get to work.

Cleaning.

When they had finished with the chores, they gathered at the centre of the room.

Enzo clapped his hands together. 'Now we begin.'

He fiddled with the waistband of his sweatpants, then yanked them off. Underneath, he was wearing a pair of white tights that left nothing to the imagination.

'*Rowr*,' Svetya muttered.

'You are all here because you know what it feels like to dance perfectly,' Enzo said. He straightened his back, extended one arm and began a complicated step. It was a deliberate series of movements, each one slowed down as though he were moving underwater.

'You all know that when you dance perfectly, it can sometimes make the room spin and fade.' He flitted across the room in a strange slow-motion cabriole, his ponytail gently whipping across his face. 'It makes the floor seem to shift and the walls close in on you.'

Vanessa's breath caught. All this time she'd thought *she* was the only one who experienced strange things when she danced. Apparently that wasn't the case. Had this happened to Justin too? Why had he never told her?

'It makes your chest swell with heat,' Enzo continued. 'Your veins pulse with fire, your eyes burn with light.'

When he said those final words, Vanessa could have sworn Enzo's eyes met hers. But he was moving so rapidly that his entire body became a blur, and then he disappeared.

A collective gasp filled the studio.

Vanessa spun round, as did the others, searching for him.

'But none of you knows how to *harness* that power,' Enzo said from the furthest corner of the studio, bringing his arms to his sides.

Vanessa blinked. Had she just seen what she thought she had? He had travelled across the room so quickly it was almost as if he'd been moving invisibly. But that couldn't be possible. Could it?

'We call that step *le flou*, "the blur,"' said Enzo, walking towards them, 'when you move so quickly, with steps so perfect that you become virtually invisible.'

'Perfection is not enough,' he said, slipping across the room in a slow *glissé*. 'To elevate yourselves above the mere level of motion, you need to *master* the dance. Harness its power and use it to bend the light around your bodies, to mould the room around your shape, to make the floor shift at your direction!'

He twirled once, twice, his body swaying as if he were about to fall, and disappeared again, reappearing behind them, mid-pirouette. 'When you are able to do that,' he said, 'anything is possible.' He traced his left toe up the inside of his right leg, and leaped into a *petit jeté*. There was a tiny blur in the air, and again he was gone.

The only trace of him was a soft patter of footsteps across the wooden floor. Vanessa turned to follow them, but the sound seemed to bounce throughout the room, echoing off the walls in a dissonant jumble.

Then Enzo reappeared right in front of her, landing in first position, his ponytail slightly loosened, his heels tucked together as if he had never left. It was impressive – magical even – but would a fancy dance step really save Vanessa once the demon caught up with her?

As if sensing her unease, Enzo said, 'Trust me, mastering this will help you.' He looked around the room. 'But for now, we will work on your solo dances for Monday.'

The rest of the afternoon was gruelling. Not even Josef had worked them this hard, Vanessa thought. Svetya and Geo were brilliant dancers, better than anyone she'd seen back at NYBA. Their form was incredible and, best of all, they looked as if they enjoyed dancing. Svetya actually came to life – her eyes brightened, and her smile seemed to take up half her face. Vanessa could imagine being friends with the girl who danced like that.

Plus, she needed a friend right now. Aside from a few passing gestures – an accidental glance in the mirror, a nod as they caught their breath on a water break – Justin barely acknowledged her existence. Vanessa couldn't help but notice how he averted his eyes every time she tried to make contact with him, how he positioned himself as far away from her as possible.

There was a time limit of two minutes and forty-five seconds for the first round of solo competitions, and they had all chosen dances that would showcase their individual strengths and increase their odds of advancing to the next round. Enzo already had their musical selections on his iPod, which he hooked up to a small set of speakers, working with each of them in turn.

Vanessa had chosen one of the routines that Margaret had done before she'd gone to NYBA; she'd picked it as soon as she'd seen Tchaikovsky's *The Sleeping Beauty* on the approved repertoire list. If Vanessa could pull off even a *tenth* of what Margaret had been able to do that time, there was no way the judges wouldn't pass her to the second round.

Just after six, Enzo let them go. 'Our next rehearsal will be tomorrow morning at nine o'clock sharp.' he said. 'I strongly suggest you spend some time this evening practising. Goodnight,' he added, as they all filed out; then he locked the room and disappeared down the hallway.

'And you?' the waitress said. 'What do you want?'

What do *I want?* Vanessa wondered. If only she knew.

She turned her attention to the menu, but she was distracted by Justin, who was sitting across the booth, talking to Svetya, his voice soft, as though the rest of the table didn't exist. It didn't help that every time Vanessa looked at her roommate, she was struck anew by how beautiful she was. Vanessa watched Justin whisper something to Svetya, then laugh, and she suddenly wondered if she had made an incredible mistake.

After rehearsal, the four of them had joined a group that was heading off for dinner at a nearby restaurant in the Richmond neighbourhood, a place called Barre None. Geo said it had been a favourite of local dancers for decades. Vanessa wasn't sure she wanted to go, but her only other prospect was dinner with her mother or in the cafeteria, alone.

'It's delicious,' Geo promised. 'Everyone at our school loves to go there after classes and not eat.'

Vanessa laughed and decided to tag along.

On the walk over, Svetya and Geo had chattered on about school and rehearsal, while Justin and Vanessa walked together through a light drizzle, not saying much of anything. Between the overnight flight and the long practice, Vanessa was exhausted, and she wasn't sure what to say to Justin. It was awkward walking beside him as if he were a stranger. But what could she say? She'd told him the truth and either he didn't believe her or he was punishing her for pushing him away.

No, better to say nothing.

Barre None, at least, was warm and inviting, its walls crowded with framed programmes and posters and even worn pointe shoes that had belonged to famous dancers. A black-and-white photograph of Margot Fonteyn in an arabesque hung beside a photograph of Rudolf Nureyev suspended mid-leap, the light reflecting off his bare chest. Facing it was a huge print of Mikhail Baryshnikov soaring so high he looked as if he was flying.

Beneath Baryshnikov sat Justin, pushing his hair out of his eyes and grinning as he said something to Svetya.

Vanessa shifted in her seat. She hadn't come here to fall in love with Justin, and yet now that she saw him laughing with stupid Svetya, his eyes so wide, so eager, she was consumed with jealousy.

The waitress tapped her pen against her order pad. 'All right, honey, I'm putting you in for a goat's cheese and walnut salad. How does that sound?'

To Vanessa's surprise, it sounded perfect. 'That's great.'

'I thought so,' the waitress said, winking. 'And you, dear?' She turned to Svetya, who was telling a long story with gestures, her lacquered fingernails flitting about her face, her features bewitching.

Vanessa pointed to the title on the menu: *Barre None*. 'What does that mean?'

The waitress chuckled. 'It's a pun on the phrase *bar none*, which means "without exception". The Royal Court is the best company of dancers, *bar none*.'

Svetya let out a low laugh. 'Indeed,' she said, handing the menu to the waitress. 'I'll have the gravy and chips platter. Hold the salad.'

Geo let out a deep laugh. 'One day this is going to catch up with you.'

The waitress pressed her lips together. 'Very well then,' she said, and looked around the booth. 'And for the boys?'

After everyone had ordered, and the waitress had disappeared, Vanessa looked around the restaurant. A few tables away was Pauline, the ballerina from Paris, sitting with a noisy group. All around them were clusters of dancers, eating and laughing and chattering about the competition and what they would be performing.

'I said, are you OK, Vanessa?' Justin tapped her shoulder.

'Sorry, you guys, I'm just . . . tired,' she said.

'There is absolutely no need to apologise,' Geo said, running his fingers through his orange hair. 'You two flew halfway across the world to be here. Svetya and I? We rolled out of bed this morning, and here we are.' He took a piece of bread from the basket in the centre of the table. 'So . . . who are you?'

Justin laughed. 'What do you mean?'

'I mean, we're all training with Enzo for a reason. And you two –' he pointed to Vanessa and Justin – 'were late additions. They don't even have your head shots up in the lobby. But you didn't blink when Enzo did his magical blur step. So why are you here?'

Vanessa looked at Justin. What should they say? They couldn't talk about Hilda and Josef, and she certainly couldn't talk about the demon.

'Well?' Svetya said.

'I guess you'll have to wait and see,' Vanessa said.

Geo laughed. 'Svetya doesn't like to wait for anything.'

Just then the waitress arrived, filling the table with a savoury mess of food.

'In the nick of time!' Svetya said. 'I am so hungry I could eat my own head.'

Vanessa didn't realise how hungry she was until her salad was in front of her.

'I'd never even heard of the Lyric Elite until about three months ago. Enzo pulled me aside after one of our student recitals,' Geo continued. 'Svetya and I were dancing *Romeo and Juliet* – the Prokofiev version.'

'A Russian composer,' Svetya said proudly. 'There is nothing like them.'

'Anyway,' Geo said, 'we were in the middle of the balcony scene, and as I was lifting Svetya I felt myself getting . . .

light-headed. I was so involved with the dance that suddenly I couldn't even see. I was ... I don't know ... enveloped by the music. All of the colours in the room seemed distorted and very bright, and, well –'

'What Geo is trying to say is that he dropped me,' Svetya said, turning to Geo and smacking him lightly on the back of the head. 'Lucky for you I didn't hurt myself.' She dipped one of her chips into the gravy on her plate, then popped it into her mouth. 'My Juliet was glorious, by the way.'

But Vanessa was much more interested in Geo's story. 'That sort of thing,' she said, 'it's happened to me. Sometimes when I'm dancing really well, it's almost like ... I'm taken out of my body and into a different plane.' She laughed and stared into her salad. 'I know that sounds crazy, but –'

'No,' Geo said. 'It's not crazy. I promise.'

He looked at her with affirmation in his eyes, and for the first time since she'd arrived in London, Vanessa was glad to be there.

'So,' Svetya said impatiently, 'you two were *partners*?' Her eyes darted back and forth between Vanessa and Justin as if the thought were unbelievable.

'No,' Vanessa said, just as Justin said, 'Yes.'

Svetya curled a lock of blonde hair around her finger. 'It can't be both,' she said, sounding amused. 'Which one is it?'

Vanessa felt her face grow hot as Justin shrank back in his seat.

'Actually, it can be,' Justin explained, sounding uncomfortable. 'We didn't start out as partners, but we were at the end of the semester.'

In a way they *had* been partners, Vanessa thought. While she'd been obsessed with Zep, Justin had been looking out for her, gathering information on Zep and Josef, bursting into the studio just before the demon would have taken her soul. If it hadn't been for him, she wouldn't be here at all.

'He's right,' Vanessa said, staring at Justin. 'I had another partner before, but he, um, turned out to be a bad match. Justin came in at the end and caught me from a fall. A fall that could have ended my career.' Vanessa willed Justin to look at her, but he wouldn't. 'I don't know what I would have done if he hadn't shown up.'

Look at me, she pleaded again, silently, waiting for Justin to meet her eye. When he finally did, he merely gave her a stiff nod before turning away.

'That's a nice story and all,' Svetya said, pulling her masses of wavy blonde hair into a loose bun. 'But let's talk about me. After one of my performances last fall, Enzo was waiting. At first I thought he wanted me to sign his playbill. You know, like a fan –' Geo groaned – 'but instead he told me there was more to dance than I'd been taught. He told me I could learn things my teachers never imagined. That he would help me.' Svetya stared at Vanessa. 'And he did. I *earned* my way into this competition – I placed first in all of the preliminaries. I'm here to win.'

Vanessa stumbled for something to say in response. 'That's nice,' she replied. 'I'm glad you and Enzo have such a nice relationship.'

Svetya rolled her eyes. 'Enzo is just my coach. He's not my type. He's too involved with himself,' she said. 'You can tell by the way he looks at himself in the mirror every time he walks by. I want a man to look at *me*.' Svetya's gaze drifted to Justin, who straightened in his seat.

'I'm sure that when any man looks at you, he sees the same thing I see,' Geo said.

'What is that?' Svetya asked.

'Someone to run away from.'

Svetya swatted his arm playfully. Vanessa pushed her plate aside and let her gaze drift along the walls of the restaurant, scanning the photographs of ballet companies, some of which stretched back decades, until a face jumped out at her.

Vanessa gasped. 'Excuse me,' she said to the group. 'I have to . . . go to the bathroom.'

She stood up. Instead of heading for the ladies' room, she walked over to the photograph, which was on the opposite wall. It was a portrait of the Royal Court Company: a black-and-white shot of the entire dance troupe, the dancers' lean figures outlined in simple black leotards and tights as they gazed into the camera.

And there in the centre of them all was a girl, her lips arranged in a haunting smile, the light glinting off her eyes as if she were holding on to a secret.

Margaret.

CHAPTER FIVE

Margaret's pale shoulders were luminous, her figure like a white outline frozen into the wall. The photograph was labelled *The Royal Court Ballet Company* and dated two and a half years earlier.

Had Margaret been in London all along? Was she here now?

Vanessa's mind tumbled back to her family's kitchen, the feel of the cold metal chair against her legs that night nearly three years ago when the New York Ballet Academy had called to inform them that Margaret had run away. Disappeared. Posters went up all over the city; the police and private detectives had searched everywhere, but no leads were ever found, no sliver of evidence on which to hang hopes that her sister was alive.

Had Margaret been in the Royal Court all this time? Why hadn't she told her family?

A hand on Vanessa's shoulder startled her.

'Sorry!' Geo said when she jumped. He nodded to the others, who were all putting on their coats. Vanessa's jacket was draped over his forearm. 'The restaurant is closing.'

Behind him, Justin was chatting with Svetya as the two of them wove slowly through the tables towards the door.

'Is everything OK?' Geo asked, concern in his voice.

Vanessa glanced back at the photo of Margaret. Geo seemed nice enough, but she barely knew him – she couldn't tell him about her sister. 'I'm fine,' she said quickly, taking her jacket from him and pulling it on. 'Thanks.'

Outside, Justin and Svetya were wandering down the pavement, chatting and laughing about God-knows-what, their voices ricocheting off the darkened storefronts. The weird London misty not-quite-rain filled the air.

Vanessa jogged forward and touched Justin's arm. 'I need to show you something,' she said.

He must have read the disquiet in her face, because he turned to Svetya and said, 'Will you give us a minute?'

Svetya glared at Vanessa but said nothing.

Vanessa waited until Geo had got a few steps ahead of them and was walking side by side with Svetya, out of earshot. 'Sorry to interrupt.'

'You weren't interrupting,' Justin said. 'What's wrong?'

Vanessa lowered her voice. 'I saw Margaret.'

'What?' Justin said, alarmed. 'Where?'

'On the wall in the restaurant, in a photograph of the Royal Court Company. I'll show you.' Vanessa started back towards the restaurant, but Justin didn't move.

'Vanessa, wait!' he called out.

'It was *her*,' Vanessa insisted. 'When you see the picture –'

'I believe you,' Justin said carefully. 'But the restaurant is closing. The photograph will still be there tomorrow. We'll come back right after rehearsal. I promise.' The misty dark around him glowed with the light from the street lamps. A damp tangle of sandy-coloured hair fell loose over his forehead. 'We just got out of the strangest rehearsal we've ever had, and we have to wake up bright and early tomorrow morning and do it again. And then we have to win this competition. That's enough for our first day in London.'

'You don't understand,' Vanessa said. Why couldn't Justin see how *big* this was? How had Margaret ended up in the Royal Court Company? And where was she now?

Justin looked over his shoulder at the others, in the distance.

And then it dawned on her. 'You just want to go back and flirt with Svetya.'

'Is that what you think?' Justin's face went blank. 'I'm only interested in you, Vanessa. Demon or no demon. But Svetya *is* a dancer with the Royal School of Ballet. It's basically a feeder into the Royal Court Company. Maybe she knows something about the dancers who – the ones who are like Josef. It doesn't hurt to be nice.'

What he said made sense, and yet Vanessa couldn't help herself from saying, 'And she's very pretty.' She wasn't sexy like

Svetya; she didn't have pouty lips or curves that made boys turn their heads. Justin was three years older than she was. Vanessa was just a freshman. What did he see in her anyway?

'She is, but so what?' Justin leaned so close their foreheads almost touched, the familiar smell of his skin filling the air between them. 'That's not why I'm here,' he whispered. 'I came here for you.'

She knew she should back away; she shouldn't let Justin get close. The demon's voice from her dream echoed in her mind: *Your kiss will bring me home again, my love.* But staring at Justin now, at the flecks of light that seemed to dance inside his eyes, at the perfect slope of his nose and the arch of his lips, she couldn't deny that she wanted him to like her because . . . well, she liked him.

She more than liked him actually.

He'd come here for her. That was romantic, wasn't it? But she didn't feel safe knowing that the demon was here in London, and she didn't want anyone to get hurt because of her. Especially not Justin.

'We're together in a foreign city,' Justin said. 'A very cold and damp foreign city. For just a little while I want to enjoy it. With you.' He pushed her hair back from her face, his hand lingering for a moment on her cheek. 'Be here now,' he said. 'With me.'

She looked back towards the pub, and for the first time all night she noticed the beauty of the London skyline, how the old buildings were jumbled together with the new, creating something spectacular and almost otherworldly. 'OK,' she whispered.

The fog of his breath mingled with hers, so close it tickled her lips. He slid his fingers down her cheek, and for a moment she didn't care about the competition or the demon or her nightmares. She let him pull her towards him, her body melting into his, as drumbeats floated on the wind from somewhere up ahead.

'Come on,' Geo hollered from a block away, yanking her back into reality. 'Let's see what's happening!'

Vanessa caught herself and stepped back, realising what she had almost allowed herself to do.

'We shouldn't lose them,' she said, and squinted into the distance as Geo and Svetya ran ahead.

Justin brushed the hair from her face. 'No,' he whispered. 'We shouldn't.'

The street ended at the river, with a flight of steps that led from street level down to a flat area alongside the water. In front of a row of darkened boats, a ring of firelight flickered with the shadows of street performers.

'Hurry up, slowcoaches!' Geo cried.

Without hesitating, Justin took Vanessa's hand in his own, and they ran, catching up to Svetya and Geo, who lingered at the edge of a large crowd.

'Everything's good, yeah?' Geo asked them.

'I forgot my scarf at the restaurant,' Vanessa said quickly. 'But I'll go back for it tomorrow.' She arched her neck to see over the crowd of onlookers. She could just make out a series of torches lying in a circle on the pavement, their flames flickering in the wind. A troupe of dancers flashed through the dim light, thumping their feet against the pavement. 'What is this?'

'Nobodies,' Svetya said, dismissing them with a wave of her hand. 'Amateurs.'

Vanessa had seen street dancers before, but nothing like this. There were seven of them, five men and two women. In spite of the cold, the men were shirtless, and all seven wore brightly coloured harem pants and leather sandals. They circled the pile of torches, their hands linked, stepping in perfect synchrony. A wider ring of torches highlighted their performance space. A man stood in the back, beating a tall teak drum.

Watching them made Vanessa shiver and push her hands deeper into her coat pockets. 'How can they stand the cold?'

'Keeps them moving, I guess,' Justin said.

As the drumbeat picked up again, the dancers pistoned their legs up and down in unison. They chanted across the piled-up torches in a call-and-response that got faster in time with the drumming.

Then suddenly the dancers were clapping and turning cartwheels over the flames, leaping into the air and flinging themselves back the way they'd come, as if gravity couldn't hold them.

A lean, muscular man climbed on to another dancer's shoulders, resting his feet on either side of the man's head. Then he leaned down and replaced his feet with his hands, kicking his legs in the air.

'Bloody perfect!' someone in the crowd hollered as the audience clapped its approval.

'I've never seen anyone dance like this,' Vanessa said, awed. 'It's more acrobatics than anything else. But . . . wow.'

'You guys go ahead,' Justin told Svetya and Geo. 'We're going to stay and watch.'

After the others had gone, Justin slipped deeper into the crowd, pulling Vanessa with him until the outer ring of torches were flickering at their feet.

One of the women swept by, her arms clinking with bangles and bracelets, her skin glistening through holes in her raggedy pants. She stopped and picked up the two torches in front of Vanessa, then twirled them around her body. Her black eyes lingered unblinking on Vanessa's for a moment, blank and depthless like a wild animal's gaze.

Then the woman arched her neck and raised the torches above her head. With a swift bend of one arm, then the other, she plunged the fire into her mouth, swallowing the flames with a hiss. Behind her, the others did the same.

In a moment there was only one torch left, sputtering alone on the pavement.

Silence, followed by applause and catcalls from the crowd.

Justin's breath was warm against the back of Vanessa's neck. 'What did you think?' His cheeks were flushed pink with cold, his blue eyes as wide and clear as a winter morning.

'It's like nothing I've ever seen,' she told him. 'Thanks for making me stay.'

Justin let out a laugh. *Making* you stay? If only I could. Every time I look at you, I think how devastated I'll be when you finally decide to leave.'

80

The drumming began again, and the audience cheered, their claps and shouts echoing into the London night. Behind Vanessa, the torches had been lit again – she could see the fire-light's reflection in Justin's face, could hear the chanting from the circle.

Gently she ran her fingertips down the rough calluses of Justin's palm, imagining him grasping her waist, his fingers tangling in her hair, his lips pressing against hers. She turned back to the dancers.

Justin wrapped his hand around hers and pulled her close, until she could feel his chest rising and falling behind her. She leaned into him, and for the first time in a long while she felt her worries about Margaret and the competition extinguished by his touch. If only life were simpler and they actually could be together . . .

A man strode into the centre of the circle, his bare chest gleaming in the torchlight. His bronze skin was streaked with paint and sweat, his head shaved except for a thick braid that hung down the centre of his back. He held the single torch in front of him.

'We need a volunteer,' he said. 'Are there any dancers in the audience?'

Before Vanessa realised what was happening, Justin had raised her hand into the air. 'No,' she told him, pulling away. 'I don't want to –'

But it was too late. The bare-chested man had already whisked her into the circle, his hand closing around her wrist.

'You'll have fun!' Justin called. 'I promise!'

All around her, Vanessa heard drumming, chanting, the sound of the dancers' bracelets clinking together as they circled her. The pungent smell of their sweat filled the air. A part of her wanted to leave, to run back to Justin, but another part suddenly felt free.

'Just follow me,' the man whispered over the music. 'You'll be fine.'

The thump of the drums grew louder, taunting, coaxing her to keep up. She straightened her spine and watched as the dancers tossed the torch over her head, their voices calling out for her to catch it.

She let her feet take over, allowing herself to be carried away by the rhythm.

With every flash of firelight overhead, she spun, following the torch, her feet propelling her around the other dancers, her hair whipping across her face. Her moves were wild, unchoreographed. There were no steps to learn, no positions to hold – only the stamping of the dancers around her, and the drums reverberating through the ground like a heartbeat.

Her body moved almost without her knowing, and she found herself leaping up just as the torch passed over her head, the flames flickering like glowing locks of hair. Her fingers wrapped around the handle.

The crowd roared its approval. Someone screamed, 'Nice catch!'

Landing, she swung the torch and tossed it to one of the dancers.

The crowd applauded again, and she laughed and swung herself back into the dance. She was actually having *fun*.

As she did, she met Justin's gaze. Flushed with exertion, she threw her jacket to the ground, letting the cold breeze hit her skin.

'Come on,' she called to him. 'Dance with me!'

Justin stepped forward and grasped at the thin fabric of her shirt, his hands circling around her back. She let her body soften into his, letting his hand guide her back into a low arch. The crowd sounded watery, as if echoing from a parallel world. The night around her melted into light and faces, the expressions of those around her hollow and foreign.

All except one. Justin's.

There were more cheers. Vanessa laughed and looked up at the sky. Her heart was racing, life pulsing through her veins. She felt free and joyous. This was what it should be like to dance. This was what she loved. The dancers flitted on all sides like sparks around a flame. She let the wind carry her, her long hair tangled around her face, her feet finding their way back to Justin while the crowd whistled and whooped.

She leaped up and caught the torch again, then waved it in a circle, illuminating the faces of the other dancers. As she spun, faces in the crowd came into focus: a young bearded guy in a porkpie hat; a mother and father with kids on their shoulders; two teenage girls linking arms and –

She dropped the torch. The crowd went silent. The dancers around her slowed.

'What's wrong?' Justin asked, taking her hand.

One of the other dancers, her face streaked with paint, picked up the torch and approached Vanessa. 'Are you OK?'

But Vanessa barely noticed, for in the flicker of the torch-light, someone else had caught her attention: a pair of familiar metallic-grey eyes.

Across the circle, he still looked just as beautiful as he had in New York. And just as dangerous. He could be here for only one reason: the demon.

'Zep,' she said to Justin. 'He's here.'

'Where?' Justin followed her gaze just in time to see Zep turn away, fading into the crowd. Without another word, Justin ran after him.

Vanessa grabbed her jacket and followed, dodging well-wishers in the audience. Far away, she could see Zep fleeing up the steps, Justin close on his heels, horns honking as they dived in and out of traffic. One car swerved, its tyres squealing.

She bolted after them. The cold bit at her lungs, each breath seeming to whisper, *Zep. Zep. Zep.*

Justin had almost caught up to him when a double-decker bus pulled away from the kerb, its headlights casting yellow cones of light across the road. Zep leaped and pulled himself up on to the back.

Vanessa caught up to Justin, and together they watched as the old-fashioned tourist bus sped away down the street, Zep hanging off the outside and looking their way with haunted eyes as he was carried away into the night.

CHAPTER SIX

By firelight, three men huddled over a tarnished lamp, swirls of black tattoos on their arms, a heavy book written in a foreign language open between them. Its cover was cracked brown leather, its yellowed pages covered in strange symbols.

The three men chanted, their voices a low rumble.

We invite you in. Enter our vessel. Take our offering. Make the stars fall until the night is black and bitter. We are yours. Enter our vessel. Take our offering.

The lamp on the floor was familiar somehow. She watched it tremble as its metal handles began to glow. The lamp shimmered, the air around it warping with heat, the glow reflecting off the men's faces until, with a metallic shriek, it burst.

An unbearable white-hot radiance swept over the three men, instantly incinerating them. A burning figure rose from the ruins of the lamp, too bright to look at directly, as if it were made of molten metal.

It had no face, but Vanessa could feel it studying her. She felt naked under its gaze.

You belong to me, it said, smiling, *as I belong to you. And soon we will be one again.*

Vanessa opened her eyes and sat up.

Outside, the first signs of dawn reflected off heavy grey clouds.

She raised her hand to her mouth, remembering. She could still see its eyes like coal, relishing her presence.

Across the room, Svetya murmured something.

'What did you say?' Vanessa asked her roommate.

'I asked if you had a nightmare.'

'Sort of,' Vanessa said. She could still see the lamp rattling on the ground, could hear the men shrieking as they were burned, could feel in her bones the demon's threat: that they would soon become one.

Svetya threw off her covers and slid out of bed. Wearing nothing but a tight pair of shorts and a camisole, she sat on the wood floor and spread her legs wide.

'What are you doing?' Vanessa asked, turning on her bedside lamp.

Svetya bent down towards the floor until her cheek was touching the wood. 'Stretching,' she said, sitting up. 'We have practice in a few hours.'

'Oh,' Vanessa said, surprised. 'Do you get up this early every morning?'

'Yes,' Svetya said. 'Every morning for at least two hours before class. Which is why I looked ace in the studio yesterday and you looked like you couldn't tell your arse from your elbow.'

'What?' Vanessa fired back. 'I didn't look . . . like whatever you said. I was jet-lagged.' She watched in silence as her room-mate leaned forward over one leg, then the other.

'I know about you,' Svetya said, reaching her arms forward. 'You don't get pleasure from dance. I can tell.'

Vanessa wanted to be offended, but Svetya had a point. She'd been so distracted by thoughts of the demon that she hadn't thought much about what she needed to be doing: practising so she could win the competition.

Svetya's voice interrupted her thoughts. 'Is Justin your boyfriend?'

'What?' Vanessa said, flustered. 'I – I don't – no.' *Not yet*, she thought to herself.

'He makes me laugh,' Svetya said. 'I like that.'

Vanessa fidgeted with her sleeve, remembering how Justin had laced his fingers through hers, the feeling of his voice against her neck, the way he'd pushed her out into the ring of street performers without asking, because he knew she'd have fun.

'I know what you mean,' she said softly. Last night, with the street performers, Justin had reminded her why she had fallen in love with dance in the first place. She held on to that feeling as she slipped out of bed.

It was time to get to work.

An hour later, armed with their bags of gear, Vanessa and Svetya walked to breakfast. Both wore leotards beneath their clothes, Vanessa in tights and leg warmers, while Svetya had opted for tight black jeans that hung low on her hips, her blonde hair coiled into a tight bun.

'You should cut your hair,' Svetya said as they crossed the marble floor of the lobby.

Vanessa looked at the end of her loose braid. 'Why?'

'It's too long. It makes you look young.'

'Thanks.' Vanessa sighed. 'I'll keep that in mind.'

They pushed through the doors into the bright chatter of the dining hall. It was a vast room with exposed wood beams in the ceiling and a wall of long windows. The tables were crowded with colourfully dressed students. Dancers on the larger teams wore matching jackets printed with their school name, and everyone wore leotards and leggings in browns, blacks, pinks and blues. The boys leaned back in their chairs and scoped out the competition. The girls spoke in nervous whispers, their eyes darting around the room. All of them were wondering who could leap the highest or spin the fastest, who would be cut first.

Vanessa knew because she was wondering the same thing.

Svetya didn't seem bothered by the people staring at her. She picked up a plate as if no one were watching and began spooning up scrambled eggs, bacon and hash browns, plus some items that Vanessa had never seen before.

'What's that?' Vanessa asked, pointing to something that looked like a burnt piece of sausage.

'Black pudding,' Svetya said.

'Like chocolate pudding?' Vanessa asked.

Svetya laughed. 'Definitely not. It's made of congealed blood. Want to try some?' She used tongs to pick up a piece and held it out towards Vanessa.

'Um, I'm going to get some fruit,' Vanessa said. 'I can never dance on a full stomach.'

Svetya just shrugged and put it on her own plate.

Vanessa wandered over to a table stacked with large bowls of fresh fruit and yogurt on ice. A lone banana rested at the top of the pile. She reached for it, but a hand smacked hers out of the way.

Vanessa spun around to find a girl standing before her. She had short caramel-coloured hair, red lips – and her understated designer clothing fitted perfectly.

'Sorry! Last one!' the girl said in a posh accent. She gave Vanessa a fake smile, peeling the banana as she walked away.

Vanessa stood there for a moment dumbstruck, watching the back of the girl's jacket: *The Royal School of Ballet*. She was English. This was her home turf.

'I cannot believe that,' Vanessa said to no one in particular, when she felt a hand touch her arm. She turned, half expecting to see the girl again, but instead found herself face to face with Maisie Teller.

'Vanessa?' Maisie said in her cheery Midwestern tones. Her light brown hair was pulled into an upbeat ponytail and tied with a ribbon. She looked bright-eyed and well rested. 'I just saw the Banana Incident. She's my roommate, Ingrid. She's not . . . nice. Here,' she said, and handed Vanessa the banana from her own tray.

'Oh, no – you don't have to do that,' Vanessa said.

'Don't worry,' Maisie said. 'I had two already.'

Vanessa raised an eyebrow. 'You're sure?'

Maisie nodded. 'I'm like a bottomless banana pit.'

'Thanks,' Vanessa said, and made her way towards the tables. Maisie scurried beside her. 'She's a fierce dancer,' Maisie said. 'Ingrid, I mean. She has a tattoo of Margot Fonteyn on her butt. I saw it.'

Vanessa saw Ingrid lean over a table and whisper something to another girl. 'Exactly how amazing is she?' Vanessa asked Maisie.

'I found one of her recitals on YouTube. She's *super-amazing*,' Maisie said. 'Like, if she wasn't so mean I'd *totally* ask her for some tips. She's one of the better dancers here –' Maisie stopped for a second, then lowered her voice – 'though Evelyn Giles, who also goes to RSB, is supposed to be the best.' Maisie looked down and sighed.

'Evelyn?' Vanessa repeated. 'Which one is she?'

'The one sitting next to Ingrid. With the mole above her lip.'

Evelyn Giles was lovely, her skin flawless, the mole somehow adding to her beauty. Vanessa watched as Ingrid whispered in Evelyn's ear, and the girl's perfect lips curled into a smug grin.

'So where are you guys rehearsing today?' Maisie asked, interrupting Vanessa's thoughts. 'And who are your coaches? I didn't see them at orientation.'

'Just in one of the studios,' Vanessa said. 'And, um – we have one coach,' she added, 'named Enzo.'

'Which studio?' Maisie asked with what seemed like genuine interest. 'I would *love* to see you practise one day. Maybe we could practise our solos together?' Maisie blinked rapidly. 'I would *love* your input –'

'Oh, um, yeah. Maybe . . .' Vanessa said. She spotted Svetya sitting by a window, picking at her breakfast. 'Well, I – I have to go. But I'll see you later, OK?'

Maisie nodded enthusiastically. 'Later? Great! I *totally* understand. You're really busy. So am I. I'll just find you after rehearsal.'

Vanessa nodded. 'That would be great,' she said, forcing a smile. 'Thanks for the banana.' And before Maisie could say anything more, she walked towards Svetya's table.

'Who was that girl?' Svetya said. She had already wolfed down most of her breakfast. 'She's even more pathetic than you.'

'She's from Iowa,' Vanessa said, as if that explained anything.

Svetya nibbled on a piece of bacon. 'What is Iowa?'

'Never mind,' Vanessa said. 'I think I know who –'

But Svetya cut her off. 'Less talking, more eating, Adler,' she said. 'We're already late.'

Vanessa barely had a chance to gulp her milk and peel her banana before Svetya took her arm mid-bite and pulled her out of the dining hall, down the back staircase and through the dusty rear corridor.

'Do you think anyone's inside yet?' Vanessa said, as they stood in front of the double doors of their studio.

Svetya raised an eyebrow. 'Let's find out.' She pushed hard on the doors and they swung open.

The room wasn't any more inviting than yesterday, though it was cleaner. The others were already inside; Enzo must have come by at some point and unlocked the doors for them. Geo was stretching at the barre. He nodded to Svetya and Vanessa. 'Morning, guys.'

Svetya strutted over to Justin, who was warming up by the mirror, and began to stretch. 'Hello, Justin.'

'Hey, Svetya.' He gave her a tiny wave, then turned towards Vanessa. 'How'd you sleep?' he asked, but before she could answer, Enzo came into the room. The mirrors offered multiple views of his muscular body. His dark, handsome gaze drew everyone's attention.

Vanessa and the others waited silently.

Enzo slipped off his sweater, his shoulders bulging beneath his leotard. He tugged on a pair of ballet shoes and walked to the centre of the room.

'Let's get started. We've got a lot to cover today.' He clapped his hands. 'First, I'm going to show you how to perform the blur step that you saw yesterday. *Le flou.* It requires a unique kind of choreography.'

Enzo placed his feet in first position. 'To the untrained eye, you seem to move invisibly. But in truth, you just dance blindingly fast from one point to another.'

Enzo disappeared, reappearing twelve feet away near the double doors. Despite having seen him perform the blur the previous day, Vanessa still gasped. Really, it was like magic.

'The trick is to fix a point in the room in your mind,' he explained. 'You imagine going through the steps before you begin to move. If you've learned the steps to the point where you don't need to think about them, then to see a place is to go there. You merely *will* it to be so.'

Enzo set his gaze on the centre of the room and raised his hands. There was a flurry of footsteps like the patter of rain, and suddenly he was standing among them.

Vanessa waited for him to explain more, but he only clapped. 'What are you waiting for?' he said. 'Begin!'

Vanessa watched as Geo set off across the room, his steps perfect but completely visible.

'I can see you!' Svetya told him in a teasing voice, but he only grumbled and tried again, going back the other way.

Vanessa searched the room, choosing a spot to aim for, when she spied Justin in the corner. Seeing him there, practising his steps alone, put her mind at ease. She would go to him, she decided.

She imagined her body moving towards his, the way her feet would sound against the wood in a *piqué*, how her arms would rise above her as she reached out for him. He would turn to her, surprised, arms ready to catch her if she stumbled.

But she wouldn't, and he'd rush to her, rapt, his hand brushing against hers in a flush of warmth. She smiled, and before the image left her head, she *willed herself there*.

And time stopped.

Or almost. Vanessa turned her head, spotting as she spun across the room, her feet falling into place without any effort. Everything around her had slowed. She could see the others, their movements ponderous and slow.

And before she realised it, she was there beside Justin. The room rushed towards her in a roil of noise and light, as suddenly everything was crisp and precise and normal speed again.

'Vanessa?' Justin said, holding out an arm to steady her as she fell out of position. 'But you were just –' He stared across the room. 'You *did it*.'

Vanessa smiled, hardly able to believe it herself.

'Huh!' Svetya said from the barre, sounding annoyed. She closed her eyes to try again.

They practised until everyone had sufficiently learned the steps of the blur. Geo was the last to master it, his legs disappearing but his body remaining visible, as if his torso alone was zooming through the air.

'Enough!' Enzo said with a clap. 'Practise and perfect this step, because it could one day get you to safety.'

Geo muttered under his breath and took a swig from his water bottle. They were all exhausted, their muscles burning, their legs seized with cramps. Vanessa took off her shoes and examined the bandages on her toes. They were worn thin, the red blisters on her feet visible through the gauze. Wincing, she pulled her shoes back on and wrapped the ribbons tighter.

'Up, up, up!' Enzo said.

Everyone groaned.

'No time to rest.' Enzo snapped his fingers. 'That was just the *first* part of the day. Now it is time for the *second*. You all need to rehearse the traditional solos that you will be performing tomorrow.'

Each of the dancers once again claimed a different part of the studio. Vanessa settled in the dusty corner by the stacked chairs, where she could see the reflections of the others dancing in the mirrors.

By the door, Geo's leaps carried him through the air, his long legs crossing in a *sissonne*, his steps so meticulous that he seemed weightless.

Beside him, Svetya traced a *rond de jambe*, her arms languid and slow as she arched her body forward and scratched at the floor like a cat. She looked feral, vengeful, as she crept across the floor, her entire being a study in *adagio*.

And then there was Justin.

He'd transformed himself into a villain, his shoulders rolling forward as he swooped his torso down into shadow. Then he lifted his face to the light and became a prince, marching in a stalwart *pas ballonné*.

In a flash Vanessa returned to her dream on the plane, when he'd spun towards her, his face transfigured by the demon inside him, a hellish fire filling his eyes and mouth. It was all too easy to imagine Justin possessed by the demon, lost to her forever. She'd do anything to stop that from happening.

Forcing her gaze away, Vanessa focused on preparing for her solo from *The Sleeping Beauty*. But as she placed her feet in third position, she felt a tingle creep through her body.

Fatigue, she thought, trying to shake it off and focus on her steps. But, as if summoned by her thoughts a moment ago, a strange whisper distracted her.

My love, it said, speaking low in her ear, filling her with a dry heat. *Let me in so that we can again become one.*

Vanessa swallowed, her mouth parched. It was *here*, somehow. She shut her eyes tightly and swept her right leg behind her in a sharp arabesque, toes off the ground, focusing on the choreography for her solo. She would not let it into her head.

As her foot came down on the boards, she had a sharp memory of Margaret executing the same move when she herself was twelve and Margaret about to leave for NYBA.

Is that what you want? said the whisper in her mind. *She is near. I can take you to her. Just let me in.*

Vanessa felt her chest constrict, her knees buckle and she fell in a heap on the wooden floor.

Justin rushed over. 'Vanessa,' he said, helping her sit up, 'what happened?'

The presence in her head began to fade. Vanessa gasped in a lungful of air and coughed. She was about to answer Justin when she heard one last whisper.

Kiss me. I can take you to her.

Vanessa found herself staring into Justin's eyes. She coughed again, and he handed her a bottle of water.

'Sorry, everyone,' Vanessa said, taking a drink and getting slowly to her feet. 'Just a bit dehydrated.'

'I don't believe that,' Justin said. He stood beside her, his face etched with concern.

'I'm fine,' she insisted. 'Just a little light-headed.'

Before Justin could say anything more, Enzo snapped, 'Vanessa, take five and hydrate yourself. And you three, start again from the top.'

When Enzo finally let them go late that afternoon, Vanessa's legs burned and her feet were sore and raw. A part of her wanted to go back and investigate the picture of Margaret she'd seen last night . . . but a bigger part was exhausted from rehearsal. Right now all she could think about was her bed, and how badly she wanted to curl up beneath the covers and rest. She checked her phone and was relieved to see a text from her mother, saying she and Rebecca would be out for the evening, going to dinner and a show. One less thing to worry about.

She, Justin, and the others walked to the cafeteria in the main hall, but lunch was long over.

'We could go to Barre None,' Geo said to Vanessa and Justin. 'You guys wanna come?'

Svetya patted her stomach. 'Make up your minds quickly.'

Justin frowned at Vanessa. She could tell he was worried about what had happened to her in rehearsal.

'Come on,' Svetya said. 'You need to eat something before tomorrow. It's not good to dance on an empty stomach.'

'Vanessa,' Justin said, 'maybe we should just stay here and talk.'

But Justin was the last person she could talk to about the demon. If she let it in, it might help her find her sister, but at what cost? How did she know that the demon wouldn't destroy her, as it had those men who'd tried to summon it? And Hilda. And Josef. Would it destroy Justin as it had in her dream?

'I don't want to stay here,' Vanessa said, avoiding Justin's eager gaze. 'Food is exactly what I need. Let's go.'

TWO AND A HALF
YEARS EARLIER

From the Diary of Margaret Adler
May 16

*Hal has proven to be a talented hacker — he snuck our names
on to the audition rolls for the Royal Court scholarship
competition.*

*This is what I've been working towards my whole life: dancing
with the best on an international stage. That I could cross the ocean
to another country, take up a new identity and still have the
opportunity to dance? How many people get two shots at making
their dream come true?*

*But even though the Royal Court competition should be
dream-like, in real life it's more like a nightmare. All because of
the lead choreographer, Palmer Carmichael.*

It's not just that he sort of looks like Josef. (He's got the same smoky mix of European swagger and overly precise English.) That's not reason enough to find him scary, and yet I do.

'What is it?' Erik whispered during the orientation.

But I only shook my head.

Outside, my anger kept me from opening my mouth during registration, which was probably for the best. Erik handled everything perfectly.

'Our school encourages self-actuation,' he explained to the registrar.

'Self- . . . ?' the woman asked, cocking an eyebrow.

'The training at the–' Erik glanced at the name Hal had created – 'Mass Arts Center relies heavily on the dancer learning to self-coach, so that he or she has a fuller understanding of the decision points involved in any piece of choreography. For example, consider the mad scene in Giselle. The pointe work demands . . .'

He went on like that for a while, saying crazy things about footwork and concentration and even throwing in weird bits of math, parabola this and secant that. It would have been funny if so much hadn't been riding on the registrar's letting us move on without a coach. The woman's eyes glazed over. Erik spoke so well and easily that he distracted me from my dislike of Palmer, and I found myself smiling.

Erik rescued me, maybe even saved my life. He has cared for me, looked out for me, made sure that Josef can't find me. And now he's found a way for me to continue as a dancer.

'Enough!' the woman said, raising her hands. 'Yours is an unconventional education, I gather. Please don't tell me any more about it. Ever.' She signed our forms and said, 'I'll be curious to see you perform on Monday. Good luck.'

We left the White Lodge and trudged over the muddy grounds of the park, back towards our room above Barre None. Grey mist hung in the air, like rain that couldn't make up its mind to fall.

'I knew this would work out,' Erik said as he grabbed my hand and squeezed.

'What now?' I asked, feeling weirdly giddy.

'We rehearse,' he said.

'Where?'

'Leave it to Hal,' he said, shaking his head, so drops of water flew from his hair. 'If anyone can find a place for us to practise, it will be Hal.'

We had only two days to rehearse once we got into the Royal Court competition, but we made them count: ten hours each day, with breaks for stretching and what Erik calls 'focused rest'.

We rehearsed in a small space at the back of a local gym, just down the street from Barre None, but a different world.

A lot of the men there speak other languages, and the place smells funky. If my mother could see it, she'd flip out. I can't imagine what the muscle-bound guys there think when Erik and I glide through their workouts and into the empty room past the boxing ring, his arm through mine as though we're high-school students sneaking beneath the bleachers at night. No one says anything, though. They just watch until Erik has unlocked the doors and we've gone inside.

Our room is small — maybe twelve feet square — but it's enough. We move around the space as though our bodies are an extension of one another's, his always daring mine to get closer, move faster, jump higher. And when I finish my steps, breathless, he wipes the sweat from my lip, his touch so tender I can't help but believe that he loves me.

Erik hadn't mentioned Giselle by chance: he's intent on my mastering a solo from it for the first round of the competition, and the duet for the second. For the third, my contemporary solo piece, he proposed Balanchine's Concerto Barocco.

As hard a taskmaster as Josef was, I think Erik may be even tougher.

Erik pushes me, and when I fail, it almost seems to hurt him, to disappoint him personally. The glint in his eye fades, and suddenly the room feels cold and empty. Even the lights seem dimmer, as though the shadow of my poor performance has cast us both into the darkness. I can tell he feels it too.

So I try harder.

I don't want to fail him.

When we returned to the room the night before the competition, we were surprised to see Hal still there. His bags were packed and waiting by the door, but he didn't seem to be going anywhere.

'What's going on?' Erik asked. 'Worried you'll miss us?' He went over and ruffled Hal's hair.

Hal pushed him away. 'Don't worry, I'll be out of here soon enough. But . . . I found out some information you guys might want to know.' He frowned.

Erik flopped on to the bed he shares with Hal. He looked so exhausted that I worried about how he'll perform tomorrow. We've been pushing ourselves hard. Maybe too hard.

'I was trying to tie up loose ends before I go,' Hal began, 'looking into some of the folks at the Royal Court to make sure I leave you in good hands and all, and . . .' He paused and stared at me before shifting his gaze to the floor.

'What is it?' I said. 'Just spit it out.'

'Josef wasn't the only one of his kind,' Hal said.

I winced at the mention of my old choreographer.

'Dark dancers like him have infiltrated all the great troupes of Europe. The Ballets Russes, the Royal Swedish Ballet, the Bolshoi, the Paris Opera.'

'Did you find any proof?' Erik asked. 'Anything to let us know for sure that we're in danger.'

Hal shook his head. 'No. It's just a hunch. And I feel like I should stay here until –'

'We'll be fine, Hal,' Erik said. 'London is my home turf. You can stick around if you want, but no more of this crazy talk. Especially not before a big day like tomorrow.' Standing up, Erik came over and rested a hand on my shoulder, and I felt some of the tension inside me dissipate.

Hal looked as if he was about to say something, but instead he shut down his computers and wished us both good luck for tomorrow morning. 'Not like you'll need it,' he added.

Erik smiled. 'Thanks.'

As I got ready for bed, I couldn't seem to shake Hal's concern. What if he's right?

The next morning, just before our audition, Erik came over, bent down, tipped my chin up and gave me something I didn't know I needed.

A kiss.

I was so surprised that I didn't have time to be nervous, though my lips somehow knew what to do. They melted into his, and I could no longer tell if it was his hands or mine that were trembling.

'Are you OK?' he asked me afterwards, his face inches away from mine.

The sweet taste of coffee and sweat still lingered on my tongue.

I shook my head no but said, 'Yes,' and then, 'Do it again.'

And he did.

Then he broke away and stepped back and said, 'I'm sorry. I guess I shouldn't have done that. You don't look so happy now.'

'No,' I told him. 'It was nice! I'm just . . . I have to be thinking of my solo.'

'Of course,' he said, and he rushed away to the boys' changing room as the first audition began.

What a day this is. It was only a kiss, but now I know: I love Erik.

I can only hope he loves me.

CHAPTER SEVEN

Where r u?

Vanessa read the text message on her phone.

'What's that?' Svetya said as she slid into the booth. The four of them were at the front of Barre None, far from Margaret's photograph. Yet Vanessa could still make out her sister's pale outline across the room. 'A message from your secret lover?'

'If by secret lover you mean my mother,' Vanessa said, 'then yes.'

Svetya stuck out her tongue. 'Eww.'

Vanessa quickly texted her mom that she was out having a bite to eat, then put her phone away.

'Want me to take your coat?' Justin said.

'Thanks,' Vanessa said, and slid in beside him, glancing up at the stained-glass lamp that hung over the table.

Justin flashed her a tight-lipped smile, and Vanessa wondered what he was thinking. A memory of his hands on her body during the buskers' dance the night before made her flush – they had been so close, almost like boyfriend and girlfriend.

Until she'd seen Zep, which had reminded her of why they couldn't be together.

After they ordered, the four of them sat in uncomfortable silence. 'So,' Svetya said, 'are you nervous?'

'I –' Vanessa started to say.

'Because you should be.' Svetya took a sip of water. 'There are a lot of talented dancers here. Especially girls.'

'Vanessa is talented,' Justin said defensively. 'Extraordinarily so.'

'Perhaps,' Svetya said, tossing back her hair. 'We shall see.'

For a second, Vanessa thought of all the different girls she'd seen just that morning – Ingrid, the rude dancer who had stolen her banana, and her friend Evelyn. Not that stealing a banana was a criminal offence, but still. And then there was wide-eyed Maisie Teller and the beautiful French girl, Pauline. How good were they?

'I'm just surprised nobody has, like, smashed someone's toes or thrown poison in someone's face,' Geo said. 'Ballerinas are mean. Thank God I'm not a girl.'

'You couldn't handle being a girl,' Svetya said.

Geo smirked. 'Probably true.'

'Evelyn Giles will definitely advance,' Svetya continued. While she was speaking, a waitress with her hair in a braid came to take their order. Vanessa was starving, but she didn't want to eat anything heavy the night before a competition. So she ordered a salad with grilled chicken.

'And so will Pauline Maillard.' Svetya took another sip of water, then pursed her lips. 'Ingrid too, I bet. And there's supposed to be an amazing Swedish dancer named Oola who's been flying under the radar.'

'Is Ingrid always so mean?' Vanessa asked Geo and Svetya. 'You guys go to school with her, right?'

'She's horrid,' Geo said. 'One time, during a rehearsal for *Romeo and Juliet*, she tried to trip Svetya.'

Svetya laughed. 'She was dancing the nurse's role and was mad she wasn't cast as Juliet. But no one trips me. My eyes are very fast. Seriously. They move more rapidly than most people's, so I can see things coming.'

'That's . . . odd,' Justin said.

'Most gifts are,' Svetya said casually. 'But yes, Ingrid will do anything to win. She's definitely one to watch.'

Geo listened quietly. His eyes lit up when the waitress brought their food, and he quickly dug into his chicken wrap. 'The question we *should* be asking,' he said, 'is which dancer is now best positioned to win the competition?'

'So who is it?' Justin said. 'Who's supposed to be the best dancer here now?'

Vanessa shrugged. 'Who knows? There isn't an official ranking or anything.'

Svetya patted her lips with a napkin. In front of her was a burger half the size of her head. *She must have an amazing metabolism*, Vanessa thought. 'Not until tomorrow,' Svetya said. 'Perhaps then it will be me.'

'Not if you keep eating like that,' Geo said.

'Touché,' Svetya said, then took another bite of her burger.

Later, after they'd finished eating and paid the bill, Justin and Vanessa hung back. 'You guys go on,' he told the others. 'We'll catch up with you later.'

Svetya's gaze lingered on them with an air of disapproval, but she said nothing. Once she and Geo had left, Vanessa led Justin to the back of the restaurant and showed him the photograph.

When he saw Margaret posing with the Royal Court Company, the colour drained from his face. He whistled softly. 'It's really her,' he said.

He was right, and yet he wasn't, Vanessa realised. Something about her looked different, changed. Though Margaret looked the same as she had when Vanessa had last seen her, the mysterious glimmer in her eye was new.

What had happened to her sister?

On the walk back, they tried to piece Margaret's story together.

Three years ago, Josef had recruited her for the lead role in the New York Ballet Academy production of *The Firebird* – including *La Danse du Feu*, a strange and unearthly dance that would call forth a demon, the same role he'd cast Vanessa in last fall. But, before the performance, Margaret had disappeared, leaving the school without telling anyone.

As far as Vanessa knew, Josef hadn't raised a demon through Margaret – but somehow this demon knew her sister. How was that possible?

Sometime afterwards, Margaret must have got to London and joined the Royal Court Company. Had she won the same competition Vanessa was competing in now? If so, why hadn't she and Justin heard about it? Had Margaret been recruited by the Lyric Elite? Wouldn't Enzo have mentioned it if she had?

'There must be other ways into the Royal Court that we don't know about,' Justin said. They were strolling down a narrow pavement on a quiet picturesque street lined with brick townhouses. It all felt faraway and strange to Vanessa, like a movie set. She wished intensely that she were behind the doors of one of those houses, doing something simple like watching TV, instead of out here in the cold worrying about demons and cut-throat dance competitions. Maybe that's why Margaret disappeared – maybe she too had longed for a more ordinary life.

'I don't see how she could have joined the Royal Court without anyone recognising her,' Vanessa said.

'People weren't looking at the Royal Court,' Justin said. 'A student in New York disappeared, and a dancer joined a company in London. No one would think to connect the two. Besides, maybe she changed her name.'

Vanessa shivered and crossed her arms. Justin was right, she thought. 'But why join the Royal Court?' she said. 'Why not just disappear some other way?'

'We keep thinking of her as this weak girl, running for her life,' Justin suggested. 'But that isn't the Margaret I remember.'

'Me neither,' Vanessa agreed. 'The Margaret I know would never stop dancing – no matter what.' They paused in the amber glow cast by a lamp post. 'Maybe she was seeking the dark faction, just like we are.'

Justin was silent, and Vanessa felt she might have finally hit upon the truth.

The curtain swung shut.

A girl ran off the stage in tears, shoving past Vanessa as she headed towards the dressing rooms.

'Another one bites the dust,' a raven-haired Canadian girl said with a snicker.

But Vanessa only turned back to her stretching. They were just a few hours into the competition, and she had already seen eight contestants leave the stage crying that morning.

Vanessa leaned down and pulled into a deep hamstring stretch. All around the backstage area, dancers cluttered the floor, their bodies so close they were practically sprawled on top of one another. They kneaded their pointe shoes into submission and stuffed them with lamb's wool. The air was thick with the smell of talcum powder, hairspray, perfume and sweat, and, underlying it all, the sweet, earthy scent of rosin.

The male dancers leaned against the walls and spilled out into the hallway. They gently pulled their necks to the left and right, shook out their limbs and arched their backs in long, low stretches.

Hushed whispers hung in the room, punctuated only by the snap of a leotard strap and the soft clink of bobby pins falling to the floor.

From beyond the curtains, one of the judges called the next name.

The other dancers quietly watched a slender girl from Spain slip off her cardigan and walk towards the stage, nervously patting her bun before stepping through the curtain.

Vanessa wrapped each of her toes in new bandages, covering the red, swollen skin with white gauze. Music drifted in from the speakers on either side of the stage, and the Spanish dancer took her position. Vanessa moved to where she could watch the girl's solo as she laced the ribbons of her shoes up her ankle.

She was a lovely dancer. Her frame had a lightness to it that made her look almost ethereal. And yet, as she continued, she seemed a little too stiff, too controlled. She glided across the floor in a cabriole, then lifted herself *en pointe*, shuddering with the effort, and raised one leg into the air.

Vanessa coiled her hair into a tight chignon and pinned it to the back of her head. The girl's leg wasn't steady or straight enough, she thought.

Svetya sat a few feet away, sipping a can of Diet Coke. She must have seen the mistakes too, for she turned to Vanessa and faked a yawn.

But Vanessa ignored her roommate and focused on the dancer. She made a mental note of every mistake the girl made, reminding herself that she couldn't afford any errors. Now that she knew her sister had joined the Royal Court, every step Vanessa took on that stage could bring her one step closer to Margaret.

Vanessa had to be great. No, not great – *excellent*.

But dancing here wasn't like her classes at NYBA, or the minor dance contests she'd entered back home. Just being in the same room as the judges unsettled Vanessa.

From backstage, she could just make out the three judges sitting in the front row, the stage lights reflecting off their faces. She studied them through the gap in the curtains.

Palmer Carmichael sat in the centre of the row, his mouth pursed in a severe frown as he watched the Spanish dancer. He squinted at her through horn-rimmed glasses, grimacing every time her foot thumped against the floor too heavily. He turned to Apollinaria, sitting next to him, and muttered something in her ear.

But Apollinaria Marie, a retired principal ballerina whom Vanessa's mother had described as 'as brilliant a dancer as she is a terrible person', waved him away and leaned back. Even in the dim lighting, her skin seemed to glow.

Becky Darlington, the third judge, sat on the other side of Palmer, her posture prim and upright. She was the only source of warmth in the room, eagerly watching each competitor, jotting down notes on her clipboard.

Any one of them could be in league with the necrodancers.

Beyond the curtains, the music stopped.

'Thank you,' Becky said, averting her eyes as the Spanish dancer walked offstage. Looking down at her clipboard, she read out the next name on the list.

'Vanessa Adler.'

Vanessa stood and glanced at Justin, who was warming up beside her.

'Show 'em what you can do,' he said with a smile.

Vanessa smiled back. She paused for a moment behind the curtain and took a deep breath, then stepped out into the spotlight.

At centre stage, Vanessa closed her eyes and remembered Margaret's long-ago performance.

Then she straightened her back, raised her arms in front of her and lifted her chin to the light. The opening bars of Tchaikovsky's *The Sleeping Beauty* suite floated through the speakers, and on cue, she began to dance.

With each step, she tried to channel Margaret. When she extended her leg behind her in a low arabesque, she imagined her sister, the light playing off her pale cheekbones as she slowly lowered her toe and slid it around her body in a *rond de jambe*. With every *jeté* she tried to mimic Margaret's lightness of step.

But something was off.

Out of the corner of her eye, she saw Apollinaria yawn. Palmer frowned, tapping his fingers on his clipboard, then leaned over and whispered something in Apollinaria's ear. She nodded and began to examine her fingernails.

Suddenly she realised what she was missing: herself.

She wasn't like Margaret and never could be. Vanessa was fiery and bold, her body demanding the attention of the audience in a way that Margaret's slight frame never could. Her sister had been a superb, world-class dancer, but Vanessa could never be that by trying to mimic her. Vanessa had to let loose and be the dancer only she could be.

Go big or go home.

The music slowed until she was tiptoeing, adagio, across the floor. She felt the hard wood scrape against the soles of her shoes. As the sound of a harp trembled through the room, Vanessa arched her neck, like a princess waking up from the deepest slumber. Languidly stretching her arms, she thrust herself upright and into a *grand pirouette*.

She felt herself awaken as she twirled, could sense the judges' attention snap back to her, though she didn't dare look at them. Her mother was somewhere in the audience, and Vanessa knew she was silently cheering her on.

And then she felt it – a tremor, so the walls seemed to quiver. A warping of the floor beneath her. A thickening of the air. She felt a hot breath fight its way up her throat, passing through her lips in a dry exhale.

Yes. Yes. Yes, said the voice only she could hear, a voice like the hiss of dying embers. *You are here, my love*, he said, sounding pleased. *And so am I. And so is your sister.*

Her body felt hot, as if she was being pricked by a thousand pins. Margaret? Could she really be here, somewhere in the audience? Vanessa's limbs seemed to lead her, instead of the other way around. She could actually feel the demon manipulating her like a puppet: it straightened her legs, made her arms reach out on either side, bent her spine into a soft curl.

Higher! its voice whispered. *Faster!*

She floated across the stage in a series of *tours chaînés*, her toes barely touching the floor. Its heat fluttered within her, sending a whisper of fear through her mind. Why was it helping her? What did it want? But she quickly pushed those thoughts away. Everything felt right, her steps falling into place, her body graceful, almost weightless.

Margaret, a voice in her mind seemed to whisper, as though Vanessa and her sister were one being. *Are you here?* Vanessa asked. She could feel Margaret answer, her essence inhabiting her as she lifted her arms, the heat of the demon kissing her skin like the warmth of her sister's touch. Vanessa raised herself on to her toes, her feet trembling, before she thrust herself into a *fouetté jeté*, turning once, twice, three times, her arms reaching upwards like the petals of a flower.

The room brightened, the lights beating down on her shoulders, until she could see nothing except a blaze of brilliant red that seemed to scorch the entire stage as she raised one leg for the grand finale. And she leaped in a final *jeté*, taking a deep breath and landing, softly, centre stage.

Slowly the room around her solidified until Vanessa could see again, but the audience was in shadow. Was Margaret out there somewhere?

Through the glare of the overhead lights, the faces of the

three judges seemed frozen. Vanessa waited, unsure what their silence meant. Even the dancers backstage had gone completely still. Had her performance been that bad?

Or that *good*?

Vanessa lowered herself in a graceful bow. Then she walked offstage, willing her hands not to tremble as she let a dry, hot breath escape her lips.

What just happened?

Backstage, Vanessa wiped the sweat from her forehead, still thinking about her performance. If Margaret was really in the theatre, certainly her mother would have spotted her. No, this was just the demon toying with her, trying to trick her into giving in, inviting him in for good.

But she would never do that.

Just then, Maisie ran to her side. 'OMG!' she said, her eyes brimming with tears. 'You're *so* good and pretty and perfect.'

'Oh, um, thanks,' Vanessa stammered.

'You're going to win – I just know it,' Maisie said, and then lowered her voice to a whisper. 'I'd do anything to be as talented as you.'

'Oh, no – I'm just a . . . regular girl,' Vanessa said. Maisie gave her a confused look. Before Vanessa could say anything else, another girl brushed past, knocking her shoulder hard.

Ingrid. She wore a tight black leotard and was so impeccably made up that she looked almost like a doll.

'You think you're good,' Ingrid whispered, her voice high and sweet like candy, 'but *good* won't keep you around in this competition.'

Vanessa felt anger stir within her. She narrowed her eyes. 'If you want to win so badly, why don't you go out there and dance better than me?'

'I'll do more than that,' Ingrid said, whispering in Vanessa's ear. 'I'm going to destroy you. I'm going to wipe the stage with your broken body. *Nobody* is going to stop me. Mark my words,' she finished, and stomped away.

Fortunately Vanessa didn't have too much time to think about Ingrid, as her mother swooped in and gave Vanessa a suffocating hug. 'Darling, you were glorious!'

'Mom,' Vanessa managed to get out, 'did you see anyone . . . familiar in the audience?'

Her mother loosened her grip and took a step back, staring at Vanessa with pride. 'I sat next to Rebecca, if that's what you mean.'

'No,' Vanessa said, 'I –'

'Honey, *really* – you were divine!' Her mother beamed, looking radiant. 'Your *jetés* were so full of life, and, oh, I am so proud of you.'

Vanessa forced a smile. Her mother was so enthusiastic and happy that she didn't have the heart to mention Margaret.

'Thanks, Mom,' Vanessa said. 'But I won't know until later if I'm moving on to the next round.'

'*Of course* you're moving on, dear. Don't worry about that. You were wonderful! Do you want to come out for a celebratory tea?' she asked, fixing the neckline of her lavender dress.

'Sure, Mom,' Vanessa said. 'That would be nice.'

'Mother–daughter time! Wonderful!' Her mother took out her guidebook and said, 'There's a funky old dancer's hang-out nearby called Barre None. We could go there.'

All the joy Vanessa had been feeling drained away. She couldn't let her mother anywhere near that photograph of Margaret and the Royal Court Company.

'Can we go somewhere fancier?' Vanessa said. 'I really want the whole British experience. I haven't even had a crumpet yet.'

Her mother's eyes widened with joy. 'I know just the place. You're going to love it!'

Inwardly Vanessa sighed with relief. 'I bet I will,' she said.

CHAPTER EIGHT

Dusk had fallen, and a narrow cone of light shone down from Vanessa's desk lamp. On any other evening its warmth might have felt nice; now it only reminded her of the demon's fiery presence during her performance.

Dancing seemed to make it easier for the demon to contact her. But why? She couldn't trust what it told her about Margaret, and until she found her sister, she'd need to find a way to block it out. She wished more than anything that she could talk to Justin about what was going on, but if she did, he might try to get her to leave the competition. And she couldn't do that, not now that she knew her sister was so close.

Vanessa shivered and looked over at Svetya, who was sitting on her bed, putting on make-up while reading a magazine.

They were supposed to meet Geo and Justin in an hour to celebrate, since all four of them had made the cut.

Diverted from Barre None, her mother had taken her to a fancy tea at a hotel called the Berkeley. They rode there in a roomy black taxi, while her mother went on and on about Vanessa's performance. At the hotel, the maître d' gave them a prominent table looking out on a wealthy street called Wilton Crescent.

'Why look, Vanessa,' her mother said as they sat down, 'it's begun to snow. It rarely snows in London, I'm told.'

White flakes slowly sifted out of the afternoon sky, filling the air.

'It's pretty,' Vanessa said, and meant it. And she realised that she was happy to be here with her mother, watching the snow fall in London, about to have tea and scones with clotted cream. 'Thanks for bringing me here, Mom.'

Her mother smiled a warm, easy smile. 'There's no place I'd rather be,' she said, and reached over to squeeze Vanessa's hand.

Despite herself, Vanessa felt at ease.

But now she was back at the dorm, and the memory of the demon made it hard to keep hold of her earlier festive mood.

Vanessa turned back to the eerie blue glow from her laptop.

Dear Dad,

There was too much to say, and Vanessa knew her mother had spoken with him, like, constantly.

How are you? Everything here is great. London is beautiful, though I haven't had a chance to see much of it. There's so much to learn, and I spend most of my time in the studio, rehearsing. So far my work has paid off, because I made the first cut in the competition.

Vanessa paused, rereading the last sentence. Something was missing – excitement. She added a couple of exclamation points.

Two-thirds of the dancers were sent home after today's solo competition. I can't believe I'm still in the running. There's so much talent around me that I sometimes wonder how I got here. I wish you could have been in the audience.

Vanessa imagined her father reading the email in his home office, squinting through his reading glasses. The house would smell of warm apple crisp, her father's winter speciality.

I miss you, and I'm even a little homesick. I can't wait to see you.
    Love, Ness
    PS Stop worrying. I'm fine.

She clicked *send*, and was about to start a new email to her friends at NYBA when her roommate noisily threw her magazine across the room.

'So, how did you do it?' Svetya asked. Her blonde hair was tied up with a silk scarf.

'Do what?'

Svetya raised an eyebrow. 'Your solo. I have never seen you dance like that. Normally you dance like a Christmas pudding, but today you were a sugarplum.'

Just a few hours earlier the judges had posted the list of dancers who'd made it to the next round. Pauline Maillard had placed first among the girls, and Evelyn Giles was second. Vanessa had come in number three, and Svetya was fourth. 'You're just sore because I did better than you.'

'Sore?' Svetya said with a bitter laugh. 'Yes, my feet are sore – but not because of you, right? Besides, I don't want to be number one – not yet.'

'Oh? Why not?'

'Because that makes you a target. It's like that movie *The Hunger Games*. You must hide some of your strength until the final round.'

Vanessa cocked her head at Svetya, who was now standing in the middle of the room with her arms crossed. 'So, you're saying you could have done better but held back?'

Svetya bit her bottom lip. 'That's exactly what I'm saying.'

There were lots of ways Vanessa could have responded to Svetya. 'OK then,' she said finally.

Vanessa had been comforted by seeing Justin's name at number three on the boys' list. To her distress, Ingrid had made the cut too, at number five among the girls. She turned back to her computer, to compose an email to Steffie, Blaine, TJ and – she'd typed *Elly* too. Her finger hovered over the *delete* key, not wanting to press it. But of course she had to.

She scrolled down and began to type.

Hi guys,

I'm here in London, safe and sound – at least for now. It's night-time here, but it's still light out where you are. I'm rooming with this girl who just compared me to a Christmas pudding – seriously!! – and I'm not entirely sure, but I think she has the hots for Justin. Rooming with her makes me miss you guys even more. Can you believe that I actually miss the dining hall at NYBA? Pathetic.

On Sunday night, Justin and I saw Zep in a crowd. Justin chased him through the streets, but he ended up getting away. Honestly, I can't even begin to tell you how freaked out I was. I have no idea why he's here, what he's doing, what he wants. After what happened back at school, I swore to myself if I ever saw Zep again I would hurt him for what he did to Elly. What he did to all of us. But now that he's here, I'm just . . . scared. I think he and the demon might be connected in some way, though I don't know how.

And if that isn't enough, the real shock was that I saw a photo of the Royal Court Ballet Company from a couple of years ago and Margaret was in it! Can you believe that?

Which brings me to you three. I need to ask a favour.
I need to find out more about the Royal Court. If you
can find any old rosters or recruiting brochures among
Josef's things or in the library, that would be great.

Margaret is alive. I'm sure of it. She might even be
here, in London. I'm going to win this competition and
get to the bottom of this, and I don't care what I have to
do or who I have to step on to find her.

Vanessa was surprised by the intensity of the words she'd just typed. When had she become so determined? So ruthless? She felt that familiar heat in her head, but this time it wasn't because of the demon.

Love, Ness, she wrote, then clicked *send* and closed her laptop, noticing a small brown gift box that she hadn't seen earlier.

She glanced at Svetya, who was busy fixing her hair, then picked up the box and turned it over in her hands. The contents shifted.

Wondering if Ingrid or some other dancer had left it for her as a warning, she eased the lid off with a pen.

Inside was a glossy photograph of Lincoln Center at night, the spray from its fountain glittering in the lights. A postcard. Beneath the picture, the caption read: *The New York Ballet and The Metropolitan Opera House, New York, New York.*

Vanessa traced the card with her finger, imagining herself strolling there with Steffie, TJ and Blaine, laughing, their faces pink from the cold. She flipped the postcard over.

Scrawled on the back in blue ink, the colour of Justin's eyes, was: *Thought you might need a taste of home. Congratulations! xx Justin*

Vanessa could almost hear him speak the words aloud as she read them. Beneath the postcard was a Hershey's chocolate bar, a can of Diet Coke and a straw. She smiled to herself and popped open the can. She rarely drank soda, but she could make an exception tonight.

Stripping the paper from the straw, she slipped it into the can and took a sip, letting the fizz tickle her tongue. It reminded her of the past, of summer, Vanessa sipping on a Coke while her mother gardened and her father grilled burgers in the back yard, Margaret lounging in a lawn chair by the sprinkler, her long legs glistening with sunscreen. How had Justin known this was exactly what she'd needed?

Vanessa stared out the window into the London dusk. Outside, the lights from downstairs stretched over the snowy front lawn in long yellow bars.

Someone was standing in the snow.

At first she thought it was a trick of the light – just the shadow of a passer-by on the lawn – but as she stared into the dusk, the figure didn't move. Someone was there, staring back at her.

It was a young man, his body little more than a silhouette. Was he actually looking at her, or just facing the building? Vanessa pressed her hand to the glass. To her surprise, the boy lowered himself into a slight bow, gesturing to the white sprawl of the park. He looked back at her once, then strolled away into the dusk.

Vanessa sat back, unsure what to do. She stared at the open box on her desk, the sweet postcard.

Justin.

A ripple of excitement travelled up her skin as she reached for her coat.

'Where are you going?' Svetya said. 'We're not supposed to meet them for another thirty minutes.'

'I have an errand to run,' Vanessa said, pulling on her boots. 'I'll meet you all at the restaurant.' Before Svetya could ask any more questions, she was out in the hall.

The first thing Vanessa thought was that the lawn was so quiet she could hear birds rustling in the trees. The second thing she thought was, *Man, it's cold.*

Pulling up her collar, she ventured off the path and across the lawn, to where she had last seen the boy. The snow was ankle deep. Where did he go? And then she saw it. A message written in the snow just a few feet away:

Step into me

Leading out of the words was a trail of footsteps.

Vanessa shivered. The phrasing reminded her of the demon. But that was silly; Justin was just trying to be romantic and cute. Should she turn back? They couldn't be together right now because of the demon, and she couldn't risk kissing him, but couldn't she enjoy one moment of fun?

She lowered her foot into the first print, then stretched her other leg to reach the next. Justin's steps led through a thicket of naked trees, ice crackling beneath her feet like strange music. The bridges and lamp posts of the park were frosted with snow. She eased down a short hill, her feet sliding, her toes numb from the cold.

At the slippery peak of a footbridge, the prints stopped.

She searched the snow on the bridge, first in front, then behind, but there were no other footsteps. Where had he gone?

Confused, she looked up. Beyond the bridge, the park was a pristine white, the stars in the sky like spilled glitter. She looked down again and saw a figure on the path below the bridge, his hair blowing in the wind, his eyes the colour of metal.

Her smile fled.

She was wrong – it wasn't Justin beckoning to her. Even though it was freezing, the boy stood with his jacket open, the tails of his scarf loose by his sides. The wind seemed to whistle his name.

Zeppelin Gray.

At his feet a second message had been written in the snow: *Give me a second chance*

Vanessa's throat tightened with anger. How could he even ask for such a thing?

She kicked away the snow in front of her. It was *his* footprints she'd been walking in, not Justin's. She'd been tricked. A chill ran up her spine, and it wasn't because of the cold – the last time she'd been with Zep, he had delivered her to Josef.

Zep was a killer. He wasn't to be trusted. And she was sure he was here because the demon was here in London.

So why was he asking her for a second chance?

Vanessa looked up from the snow, but Zep had already backed into the shadows and vanished.

She was alone.

CHAPTER NINE

After Vanessa had followed Zep into the park, she'd run back to the White Lodge, arriving just as her roommate and the others were leaving.

'Where were you?' Justin had asked. 'You look as if you've seen a ghost.'

She hadn't known what to say; she'd known only how happy she was to see him. 'Thank you,' she'd said, trying to push the strange encounter out of her mind. 'For the gift. It was ... perfect.'

Justin had smiled easily, but he didn't take her hand. 'Any time.'

Together the four of them had walked to Barre None, complaining that it was the only place nearby. 'I would give anything to be closer to the centre of London,' Geo said.

'I would give anything for you to go away,' Svetya said.

Inside, Justin picked out a table in the back corner, and they each took a seat.

Vanessa had just finished ordering when she felt someone tap her shoulder. She whipped around, and there was Pauline with one of the boys from her school.

'Congratulations!' Pauline said, leaning down to kiss Vanessa on one cheek, then the other. 'For making the first cut! All of you!' She waved, and Justin and Geo waved back, but Svetya suddenly seemed fascinated by her menu.

'Congratulations to you too,' Vanessa said. 'You're in first place!'

'For now,' Pauline said, brushing some of her hair behind her ears. Again, Vanessa noticed the interesting pattern of freckles beneath Pauline's left eye, and decided it only made her more beautiful. 'Oh, how rude of me.' Pauline turned to the boy at her side. 'This is Jacques. We are going to be dancing the partner round together.'

Jacques gave them a tiny nod.

'Here,' Justin said, scooting his chair closer to Vanessa. 'Why don't you sit with us? We just ordered.'

'Thank you,' Jacques said, taking a seat. 'We would love to.'

'Thrilling,' Svetya muttered under her breath.

Everyone made small talk, and Vanessa felt a sudden warmth as Justin gave her knee a squeeze. 'Hi,' he mouthed to her.

'I can't believe they take your head shot down immediately after you're cut,' Pauline said, resting an elbow on the table. 'What is the rush? They could wait a few days.'

'No, it is better this way,' said Svetya. She pursed her lips. 'They are losers.'

Geo shook his head. 'It wasn't our talent that got us our ranking,' he said, staring into his drink. 'It was the mistakes of the others.'

'I agree,' Pauline said. 'That one dancer from the British team didn't even make it through his first few steps without stumbling.'

'Some girls in the hallway were saying the main stage is cursed,' Jacques said.

Svetya crossed her arms. 'It is not cursed. They just didn't dance well.'

'I felt *something*,' said Geo, pushing his hair away from his eyes. 'It was very odd. I walked out on to the stage and took my position. The floor felt fine then, but when I started dancing, it suddenly felt strange.'

Beside him, Sveyta let out a laugh. 'It is your *legs*. They are too long for your body.'

Justin laughed, then turned to the others. 'Well, at least there are fewer of us now,' he said.

'*Oui*,' Pauline said, batting her long lashes. 'And it is exciting to see our names in a press release!'

'Press? Where?' Svetya said.

Pauline pulled out her iPhone and showed them all.

'Ingrid's still in the competition,' Vanessa said softly. 'She bumped into me after I finished my solo and said she was going to destroy me.'

Jacques laughed. 'Really?' he said. 'She said that?' No one else seemed to find it funny.

'Why didn't you tell me?' Justin asked.

Vanessa fidgeted with the tablecloth. 'I'm telling you now.'

'Don't let it bother you,' Geo said. 'Last year she told me she was going to put out my eyes with a fork and sell them on the black market.'

'That's frightening,' Pauline said, putting her phone away. 'But she wouldn't really do something like that. She meant it like a metaphor, I'm sure. You know,' she went on gently, 'my grandmother had a saying: "Enemies can be turned into friends through generosity." Perhaps with a little bit of kindness, Ingrid will surprise you. In the meantime, all you can do is be careful.'

'Or stop dancing so well,' Justin said.

'Maybe it's the demon,' Jacques said with a grin.

Vanessa could feel Justin's muscles tighten beside her. 'Excuse me?' he said.

'What?' Jacques said, shrugging. 'You've never heard of the dancing demon?' He said it like it was a joke, something he'd made up on the spot.

'No,' Justin said. 'I haven't.'

'It's an old legend,' Jacques explained. 'Many dancers, especially those in our grandparents' generation, believed that if you danced a very demanding ancient choreography, you would conjure a demon. It sounds silly, but people used to take it very seriously. To her dying day, there were certain ballets my grandmother would never watch because she was certain they were derived from old demonic rituals. Crazy, right?'

Vanessa forced herself to laugh. 'Yeah.'

While the others joked about dancing demons and stuffed themselves as a reward for making it to the next round, Vanessa noticed an older woman clearing dishes by the bar. She had long greying hair and wore a flowing skirt that swished about her ankles, with an oversize sweater that hung loose around her thin frame. Vanessa wondered how long she'd worked here. Two years? Longer? Maybe she had seen Margaret come through Barre None, just like Vanessa and her friends.

Vanessa wiped her mouth with a napkin and stood up. 'I – excuse me.'

She made her way through the restaurant towards the bathroom. Then, looking over her shoulder to make sure no one from her table was watching, she turned and walked over to the woman in the long skirt.

Vanessa watched as the woman ran a rag around the rim of a glass.

'You pay at the front,' the woman said, barely looking up.

'Actually, I wanted to ask you a question,' Vanessa said. She took a tentative step forward. 'Have you worked here for a long time?'

The woman sighed. 'Long enough,' she said in an accent that fell somewhere between Cockney and upper class. 'I own this place.'

Vanessa hadn't seen that coming.

'You can call me Coppelia,' the woman said, smiling warmly. Even though her face was weathered with age, Vanessa could tell that she had once been quite beautiful. She wore almost no make-up, with only the slightest hint of red on her lips, and her grey hair was tangled with strands of white, falling nearly to her waist. 'It's not my name,' the woman continued, 'but I've been called nothing else for twenty years.'

Vanessa shook her hand, which was damp from the rag. 'I'm Vanessa.' She looked up at the wall of photographs, her gaze resting finally on Margaret's face. 'I just wanted to ask you about one of the dancers.'

'That could take all night, dear. There are hundreds of them, and my memory isn't what it was.' She blinked, and studied Vanessa as though she were a painting. 'Not like when I was your age, running around the Royal School of Ballet.'

'You were a dancer?' Vanessa asked. Nothing about the woman's wild hair, long Bohemian skirt or the baubles she wore around her neck made her look like a ballerina. And yet, as Vanessa studied her, she noticed the way she held her chin up and her shoulders square: her dancer's posture had never left her.

Coppelia put her hands on her hips. 'Well, don't sound so startled, dear.' She stacked a handful of glasses on the shelf behind her, then began to wipe down the countertop. 'I was in the London Ballet for years,' she said. 'Until I was twenty-five. And I would have had a few more ahead of me, if it hadn't been for *La Sylphide*.' She frowned, as if the memory still bothered her. 'Halfway through rehearsals, I stumbled on a landing and fractured my ankle. That was the end of that.'

Vanessa thought back to all the times she'd faltered in a spin or rolled an ankle landing from a leap. 'What did you do?'

'I went to physical therapy and tried to get my rhythm back, but my ankle was never the same. Even now, it still hurts when I stand on tiptoe.' Coppelia glanced at a photograph on the wall behind her, where a young woman stood at centre stage, her taut body pointed in a brisk pirouette. *That was her*, Vanessa realised.

'After I stopped dancing, I took over my father's restaurant.' Coppelia ran her hands along the wooden bar. 'You should have seen it before,' she said with a chuckle. 'It used to be called Right Said Fred, like the old Bernard Cribbins song, but I changed that and everything else, made the place my own.' She motioned to the ballet paraphernalia on the walls. 'If I can't dance any more, I can at least surround myself with the things I love.' She swept her hands forward to indicate Vanessa. 'Including all the young dancers who come here. You remind me of better days.'

Vanessa pointed to the photograph of the Royal Court Ballet Company. 'This girl,' she said, 'her name is Margaret Adler. Do you know anything about her?'

Coppelia squinted at the photograph. 'No,' she said. 'Not Margaret, I'm sure of that.' She stroked her chin. 'She called herself Margot.'

Margot? Vanessa's mind raced. In Margaret's bedroom back home, she'd hung a poster over her bed of Dame Margot Fonteyn balancing in a beautiful arabesque, a white tutu fanning out from her hips. Margaret had always adored her more than any other ballerina. 'Oh, right,' she said. 'That was her stage name.'

Coppelia studied Vanessa, a curious look on her face. 'Your friends . . .' she said.

'What? No, we're not friends,' Vanessa said, and then realised the woman wasn't talking about Margaret.

Justin and Geo were waving to her from across the room. Geo dodged around a few tables and was suddenly right beside her.

'Ready to go?' he asked. 'Svetya was hoping you had fallen into the toilet, and sent me to flush you away.'

Vanessa turned her back to the photograph. 'I'm sure she did.'

'Don't worry though,' Geo said. 'She's just jealous of you.'

Justin and the others were standing by the cash register, putting on their coats and scarves.

Vanessa turned to Coppelia. 'Thank you.'

'Any time,' Coppelia said, picking up her rag again as Vanessa followed the others back through the door and into the night.

Svetya and Justin were already half a block ahead, walking so close together that she kept bumping him. Justin stepped away, but Svetya grabbed his arm to pull him closer, looking up at him with her smoky eyes and whispering in his ear. After a moment, he replied, then turned until his eyes found Vanessa.

Embarrassed that he'd caught her watching, Vanessa lowered her head.

Justin walked back to join the main group. 'You OK?' he whispered to Vanessa, matching his pace to hers.

Vanessa felt her shoulders relax just because he was by her side. 'I think so.'

They dropped back from Svetya, Geo and the others, meandering along the pavement together. Vanessa wanted to tell him about Coppelia and how she'd remembered Margaret but called her *Margot*, but instead she and Justin walked in silence.

They took the long way around to the dormitory. Narrow brick townhouses lined the kerb above winding streets, their windows framed with quaint black shutters, the glass glowing with velvety yellow light. The city was beautiful in the snow. The fall of white covered up the gutters and grime, blanketing everything in clean, unblemished perfection.

Every so often their arms brushed each other. 'Sorry,' Vanessa said, as she pulled away from him for the third time.

'You don't have to apologise,' Justin said, drawing closer. 'I like it.' And then, without warning, he slipped his fingers through hers.

'Too cold not to hold hands,' he whispered.

Vanessa was so startled by his touch that it took a moment for her hand to melt into his. Would he try to kiss her? She wanted him to stop walking, to pull her into the shadows and press her against the cold brick of a townhouse. To taste his lips, feel his breath mingle with hers, feel his arm inch up her waist, making her skin prickle with goosebumps.

And yet she knew that she shouldn't – couldn't – want any of those things.

In two days, he would be her partner in the *pas de deux*. Justin was the only one at the competition who knew what had happened in New York, who knew the demon was real. She wanted to tell him that she was even more certain now that it was here, in London, and it was in her head. She wanted to tell him it had promised to bring her to Margaret, and that it had helped her dance, but she was afraid how he'd react.

And really, she wanted Justin to kiss her. But did the demon want that too?

Vanessa was about to try to explain this to him when, to her surprise, Justin said, his voice gentle, 'Don't worry, it's just a walk. A walk with a friend.'

They drifted down the cobblestones, the icy night pushing them closer together. Justin stepped from one stone to the next, letting them guide him like marks on a stage. Vanessa followed, her shoulder bumping his, their legs tangling until they were both laughing. When a car approached, its head-lights bouncing through the night, Justin pulled her out of the way, the wind blowing her hair into her face. He brushed a stray lock away from her eyes.

'You're cold,' he said, touching her cheek.

Before she realised what she was saying, she whispered, 'Then warm me up.'

Justin leaned forward, his hand buried in her hair as he pulled her into a kiss. Only just before his lips touched hers, he moved his head just slightly so they landed on her cheek instead. His hands wrapped around her waist as he pulled her to him. 'I know you're afraid of kissing me,' he said, 'but when you're ready . . . I'm here.'

They stood like that, pressed together like puzzle pieces, for a few minutes. When they finally parted, he whispered into her hair, 'I like this dance.'

Vanessa smiled, allowing herself this one moment before she pulled away.

'I thought it was just a walk,' she whispered.

'It is,' Justin said, and stepped back, but didn't let go of her hand.

Vanessa walked beside him, feeling the rhythm of his body next to hers, the comfort of knowing he understood. She wasn't alone. And as they strolled beneath the lamp posts, their hands laced together, the snow catching in their hair, their eyelashes, Vanessa felt that, maybe, everything was going to be OK.

Two And A Half
Years Earlier

From the Diary of Margaret Adler
May 17

Tragedy.

It's so much worse than I could have imagined.

Not my dancing. I don't know if it was Erik's kiss, or my anger at that pompous Palmer man, or the intense two days of rehearsals, but I danced ~~well~~.

No, I danced magnificently.

The moment the music began for my solo, I stopped thinking. I stopped worrying about Josef finding me here in London, about what I was missing in my old life and if I'd made the wrong decision to come here. I even stopped thinking about how much

I missed my parents and Vanessa. For the almost three minutes of my solo, I just danced. I was Giselle.

And I remembered why I love ballet so much in the first place.

I never feel more alive than when I am on the stage. There is something about being connected to an art form that is nearly as old as time itself, and dancing to music that hundreds – no, thousands – of ballerinas have danced to before me.

As soon as I heard the familiar opening notes, I fell into position, and the dance possessed me.

Every turn, every leap, was perfect, as though I barely touched the wooden stage.

When it was over, the judges actually stood up and applauded, which has to be against the rules. Aren't judges supposed to appear impartial?

I wish my family could have seen me.

But enough about me. I'm just happy that I didn't let Erik down. I want him to be proud of me. He says he is, but it's hard to know how seriously he means it, because even though I made the first cut . . .

He did not.

Oh, he danced well. I thought he danced better than a lot of the boys who didn't get cut. He performed an excerpt from Prince Siegfried's solo in Act One of Swan Lake. I've always found this particular moment haunting – the prince arrives at his twenty-first birthday and is told by his parents that, because of his age, his marriage is going to be very quickly arranged. The prince is afraid of all his future responsibilities, so he flees the castle, heading to the wood.

Erik did wonderfully, I thought, and truly seemed to capture a sense of longing and discovery as the prince. He even looked like one, his muscles golden in the spotlight, his dark eyes glinting as he searched the room, finding me. But that Palmer man wasn't impressed, and with his cold, bored voice he read the list of sixty-four dancers who did not need to return for the second audition. Erik was one of them.

Erik has been in a black mood ever since. He congratulated me and told me he's proud, but I know inside he is hurting. I can almost feel his disappointment as though it's mine. If only I could bear some of his burden. I know if it were me, he'd want to bear mine.

Erik has done so much for me already. The only way I can help him is to dance well enough for both of us. *And to win.*

CHAPTER TEN

The next morning, Vanessa slid out of bed and wrapped the comforter around her like a shawl. She stood for a moment staring out the window at the frozen lawn beyond the White Lodge. The sun was above the trees, which cast long blue shadows across the snow. It was beautiful.

Svetya's bed was already made – she was probably downstairs getting breakfast before the morning's rehearsal. There'd be no fight for bananas today, not after the cafeteria had been cleared of over half the students.

The competition had got cut-throat, brutal. It was all too much. Vanessa shook her head, dropped the comforter on to her mattress and made her way to the bathroom.

No matter what, today was going to be a long, long day.

The others were already warming up.

Justin was splayed on the floor in a grey sweatshirt and loose-fitting pants, stretching. Geo stood in front of the mirror a few feet away, wearing a white tank and a pair of navy blue tights, his hair combed back and still wet from the shower. From the barre by the door, Svetya watched his form as he practised their upcoming *pas de deux*, correcting the shape of his legs and the curve of his back as she slowly lowered herself into a *grand plié*.

Vanessa let out a sigh of relief. At least she wasn't *too* late – Enzo hadn't shown up yet. She sat down and unzipped her bag, taking out her pointe shoes.

Justin and Svetya came over from the other side of the room. 'Everything OK?' Justin asked.

'I slept through breakfast,' Vanessa said. To Svetya, she said, 'Why didn't you wake me up?'

'I'm not an alarm clock,' her roommate pointed out. 'I'm your competition.'

Vanessa didn't get a chance to reply to that, because Enzo entered the room.

Justin and the others stopped talking and went back to their warm-ups, but Svetya remained at Vanessa's side.

'Can I ask you a question?' she said, her voice low so only Vanessa could hear.

Vanessa sighed. 'If I say no, will that stop you from asking anyway?'

'No,' Svetya said. 'So my question is: are you with him or not?'

'What are you talking about?'

'*Justin*,' Svetya said.

Vanessa frowned, not sure what to say. She watched Justin's reflection in the mirror as he ran through his warm-up. She studied his hands, remembering how warm they had felt when he had slipped his fingers through hers last night. She thought about how much she wanted him, and how much better off he would be without her.

Vanessa turned to Svetya. 'No,' she said. 'I'm not with him.'

'Good.' Svetya wagged a finger in Vanessa's face. 'I do not want to hear you crying in our room when I take away the only handsome straight boy still in the competition.' Then she went back to the barre, her hips swaying seductively.

'May I have your attention?' Enzo said, his long hair in a ponytail, his thighs flexing beneath his tight black pants. 'Congratulations. You should all be very proud of yourselves. It is not easy to get past the first round of the Royal Court Competition . . . Most talented young dancers never do.' He paused for a moment, then added, 'Tomorrow is day two.'

'The *pas de deux*,' Geo said.

'Yes,' Enzo said. 'The duet. You four are lucky. Some dancers, their partners have been cut. They still dance with their eliminated teammates, though for such a dancer to win the competition is extremely rare.

'The *pas de deux* is much more difficult than it appears from the audience,' Enzo went on. 'Two dancers means twice the number of possible errors, twice the likelihood that one performer will outshine the other and throw the dance off-kilter. It is the true test of a dancer's *esprit de corps*. It's about teamwork.' He clapped his hands. 'Everyone, pair off!'

Vanessa and Justin walked over to an empty corner of the studio. She took a sip of water and then offered the bottle to Justin.

Before they'd left New York they had chosen a *pas de deux* from *Onegin* and had each practised on their own. This would be the first time they'd danced it together.

They took their positions, and Vanessa began by bowing her head in sorrow, gazing away from Justin as if he were her estranged lover.

It was difficult to practise without music, but Vanessa practically knew the accompaniment by heart. Apparently, so did Justin. On his cue, he crept towards her, begging for her forgiveness. She swept away, avoiding his gaze. They danced around each other, inching forward, recoiling, unable to start their conversation.

Slowly they came together, Justin's arms careful as they grazed her body. His breath was a whisper against her neck, his fingers a tickle of heat along her spine. She felt herself get lost in their movements as their legs tangled, her body stirred awake by a fervor she hadn't felt since the raspy warmth of the demon had filled her lungs.

Vanessa had danced with Justin at NYBA, when he'd been cast as Zep's understudy for *The Firebird*, but the way he'd danced then had been nothing like *this*. She could feel his anger in his motions – his *sissonne* quicker, his *ballonné* kicks higher, his *tours chaînés déboulés* so perfect he could have been floating.

Vanessa met him halfway, her heart pounding as she moved beside him, then thrust him away like a scorned lover. She felt his hand slide up her thigh, making her body tremble.

'Your duets have to be perfect!' Enzo shouted. 'Complement each other! Do not let yourself be the weaker of your pair! Dance through the pain.'

Vanessa kept waiting to feel the familiar blur of the room, the dizzying sensation of the ground shifting beneath her feet, followed by the demon's heat fluttering inside her. It frightened her that she wanted him, that she felt she needed him, but she couldn't help herself. It was exciting to feel that invincible.

But the sensation never came.

Justin lifted her by the waist, her legs extended wide as she floated through the air, weightless. He set her down and she stepped away, letting all her emotions spill out, twirling, spreading her arms wide over her head like a flower blossoming at the first sign of sun.

And with one last gasp, it was over.

Vanessa held her final position a moment longer, breathless but beaming, her leotard damp with sweat. She had never danced this well, not without feeling the room warp and collapse in on itself or the dry heat of the demon pressing against her skin. Smiling, she turned to Justin, expecting him to be as satisfied with their performance as she was, but instead he walked away, his face hard and unreadable.

'What's wrong?' she asked, her smile fading. 'We were great!'

'We were *too* great,' he said, a hint of apprehension in his voice. 'If you keep dancing like that, you're going to get hurt. You'll be a target for girls like Ingrid.'

Vanessa let out a startled laugh. 'If the worst I have to fear is a bitter ballerina,' she snapped, 'then the dark dancers will be a cakewalk. So back off. You're not my father, and you're not my boyfriend. Got it?'

After a moment, Justin's hurt expression turned to bitterness. 'Thank goodness for that,' he said. 'You and your last boyfriend were a perfect match.'

And with a blindingly quick step, he disappeared, his body blurring as he whipped through the room and out the door, the only remaining trace of him a quick brush of air.

CHAPTER ELEVEN

'What happens if we really capture it?' the woman asked.

She stood in a group of five, all young except the one in the centre. He was craggy and white-haired and wore a tattered purple blazer. An orange crest on the breast pocket read: *Chatswyrth*.

The older man hefted a fat leather book and said, 'This tome also tells how to banish it.' Then he began to read. The words were strange and unnerving, a series of scratchy noises that sounded as if they were clawing their way out of his throat. As he spoke, his face trembled, his jaw parting as if he were being gagged. He clenched the book, his knuckles white, his eyes straining.

The young people froze in place.

Through his spectacles, the white-haired man's eyes glimmered as if something inside him were trying to elbow its way out. *You think you can control me, call me to do your bidding?* said the demon, speaking through the man, his voice a gasp of hot air. The man's lips began to crack, his face contorting as though something behind his skin had collapsed.

He went to the young man nearest him and reached inside the boy's open mouth. There was a terrible sound and then the man withdrew his arm as the boy fell to the ground. In the man's hand he clutched something red and pulpy.

As the white-haired man's skin brightened and burned away in a blinding light, he looked up.

Vanessa, he said, *I offer you my heart.*

Vanessa sat bolt upright in her bed.

The sounds of the dream faded, until all she heard was the night wind sighing through the window. Her heart was pounding; her hair was matted to the back of her neck. As the horror of the dream – vision? – faded, one sentence kept echoing through her head.

'*This tome also tells how to banish it.*'

The heavy volume in that man's hands was the book Enzo had told her about. The *Ars Demonica*.

Across the room, Svetya shifted in her sleep. The clock on her nightstand blinked 4.00 a.m. The sun wouldn't rise for another few hours.

Vanessa rubbed her eyes – the rest of the day had gone by so quickly after her fight with Justin: a quick lunch with Svetya and Geo, more rehearsal, with Justin stiff and unhappy by her side, and then a long, tedious dinner with her mother, who talked so much that Vanessa didn't have to do anything but sit there and play the dutiful daughter.

'Of course you *can't* get cut. Your father will be *devastated* if he arrives here on Saturday and you haven't won the scholarship,' her mother mused at one point.

Vanessa guessed that was supposed to be encouragement. 'I'll try not to be eliminated,' she said. Privately she thought her father would be proud of her no matter how she performed.

'But in the meantime, I'm enjoying the single life! I just saw a show in the West End with Rebecca, even though her poor Emilie got cut.' And then, in a loud whisper, her mother couldn't help adding, 'Deservedly, I thought! Did you see her shoddy form?'

'Do you ever run out of opinions?' Vanessa muttered.

Her mother narrowed her eyes. 'Excuse me? There's no need for attitude like that. Not when the stakes are this high.'

Vanessa let out a chuckle. If only her mother knew how high the stakes really were.

'What, exactly, is so funny?' her mother asked.

Vanessa didn't have the energy to battle it out with her tonight. 'Nothing,' she said. 'That's the problem. It's all getting so serious.'

Her mother's irritation faded into concern. She pursed her lips. 'You're just tired, darling,' she said. 'I'm sorry I snapped at you. It's my nerves! These competitions really take it out of me.' She dabbed her lips with her napkin, then added, 'Finish your salad. You look like you need iron.'

It wasn't even nine by the time Vanessa had got back to find her room empty. She was relieved not to have to deal with Svetya, but on the other hand, her roommate was probably off somewhere trying to seduce Justin.

Vanessa was still mad at Justin for trying to control her. And surely he was still mad at her – she hadn't been particularly nice to him. Though nice had never been a quality that either of them had looked for in the other. After all, when she'd first met him hadn't Vanessa thought that Justin was an arrogant jerk? And hadn't he thought the same of her? She'd thought that was what Justin had liked about her, that she wasn't like the other girls, that she was harder, stronger and maybe a little more dangerous.

I offer you my heart.

Vanessa shivered, throwing off the comforter and untangling her legs from the bedsheets. Her dream, that white-haired man, the others . . . The demon wanted her – she was the only person who had managed to host it and survive – and when anyone else tried to summon it, it murdered them. She had to sever her connection to this thing. She knew she should tell Enzo, but what about the demon's offer to lead her to Margaret? What if Enzo's friends in the Lyric Elite banished the demon before she found her sister? For now, she'd just have to continue dancing with it until she got what she wanted.

Vanessa slid out of bed and opened her laptop, squinting as her eyes adjusted to the light from the screen. *Chatswyrth*, she typed. The crest on the man's coat. Why did the name sound familiar?

Immediately Google responded with a page of links – all for the Chatswyrth Arts Academy, which had apparently closed in the nineties after an explosion had burned out the entire ground floor and destroyed much of the main building. Among its faculty had been two long-ago winners of the Royal Court competition.

She clicked on a map. The school had been in London too, closer to the city centre. Somewhere inside it, maybe, was the *Ars Demonica*.

'Gotcha,' Vanessa whispered.

Justin's room was almost exactly below Vanessa's, its tarnished brass 213 nailed to the centre of the door.

Vanessa stood in the quiet hallway and wondered whether she should knock.

She didn't want to ask Justin for help. There was a good chance he would turn her away after what she'd said to him, and besides, it was four thirty in the morning. He would definitely still be asleep.

But she couldn't do this alone.

Vanessa fixed her ponytail and tugged on the sleeves of her navy cable-knit sweater. She'd thrown on a pair of jeans and the only sneakers she'd brought with her, the scuffed-up, white New Balances she'd worn on the plane.

She pressed her ear to the door and, when she heard nothing, gently tried the knob, surprised to find it unlocked.

Inside, she could see the outline of two beds, each with a person curled beneath the covers. On one side of the room she recognised Geo's red hair and pale forehead, his arm dangling over the side as he let out a thunderous snore.

Vanessa tiptoed to the other bed.

In the dim moonlight she made out the contours of Justin's body under the comforter, his messy hair strewn about his face, and his lips, murmuring something: '*Vanessa*.'

Was he dreaming about her? She stepped back, feeling guilty. What if he woke up and was still mad at her? Quickly, before she changed her mind, she touched his arm and whispered, 'Justin.'

No response.

She gently shook his arm and repeated, '*Justin*. Wake up.'

For a moment he was completely still – then his eyes snapped open. 'Who's there?' he began, when Vanessa pressed her fingers to his lips.

'Shh!' she said. 'It's me.'

'Vanessa?' he said, his voice soft.

Across the room, Geo mumbled something.

Justin sat up and rubbed his eyes. 'What are you doing here?'

'I had a dream,' she whispered.

He yawned. 'You came down here to tell me about a dream? What time is it?'

His voice was creaky from sleep; his muscles strained against his white cotton T-shirt as he pushed off the covers. Unable to help herself, she gazed at his bare arms, wondering what it would feel like if he were to wrap those arms around her right now. To slip beneath the covers and curl up beside him in the bed and forget everything she'd just seen in her dream.

'It's a little past four thirty,' Vanessa whispered.

'I was having a dream too,' he said in his deep baritone. She could smell the thick scent of sleep clinging to him, could see the soft prickle of stubble along his jaw. 'It was about you,' he said, his eyes roaming over her. 'And now –'

A voice made him freeze. On the other side of the room, Geo muttered in his sleep. They waited until he turned on his side and let out another long snore.

'Get dressed,' Vanessa said finally. 'I'll tell you everything outside.'

'Now?' Justin said. 'Can't it wait?'

She shook her head. 'Mine was more than just a dream, Justin. It was a nightmare. Or a vision.' She paused. 'About the demon. It's in London.'

'OK,' Justin said, snapping awake. 'That got my attention.'

They barely looked at each other as she led him down the stairwell and into the dimly lit entrance hall. There, in front of the wall of old portraits, Vanessa told him about what she thought were glimpses through the demon's eyes, about the latest vision and Chatswyrth, about the book that could banish the demon. 'If we can get that,' she finished, 'maybe we can get rid of it.' Though even she had to admit that seemed nearly impossible. Every time her mind drifted back to that awful scene, all she could think of was how the man's face collapsed as the demon inhabited him, the way his eyes seemed to glow with a life not his own.

She turned and scanned the wall of portraits. 'There,' she said, jabbing her finger at a group photograph from the early seventies. In the centre was a young man with perfect posture, his long hair braided and pulled over his shoulder. Along the bottom edge of the picture, the winners of that season's competition were listed: Richard Waite, Chatswyrth Arts Academy. 'That was the man in my dream. Or vision. Whatever you want to call it.'

'Nice hair,' Justin said, leaning in to look at the picture. 'But go back a second. You've had visions like this before? Why didn't you tell me?'

'I thought maybe they were only dreams,' Vanessa said. 'I'm telling you now, aren't I?'

'I don't know why,' Justin said, clearly still hurt from their fight. He was fully awake now; his earlier sweet, groggy, gentle expression had all but faded away. 'I'm not your dad and I'm definitely not your boyfriend, remember? Why come to me for help now?'

Vanessa winced. 'I'm sorry I said that, Justin. It was hurtful. It's just . . . it's hard. I don't know what I feel any more.'

'It's hard for me too.' He reached out and touched her hand. 'I like you, Vanessa.'

'I like you too,' she said, and once the words were out of her mouth she knew they were true. 'But what this demon is doing

157

to people is horrible.' She withdrew her hand from his. 'It sees into me somehow, and I see into it. Like it's part of me. Until I know it's gone, I'm scared of hurting you.'

He nodded and said, 'OK. I'll just park my heart until – what? Are you OK?'

Vanessa leaned against the wall and took a deep breath. 'Like I told you, it pulled out someone's heart and . . . offered it to me.'

Justin pulled her into his arms and hugged her, hard. 'Right now, this is bigger than us,' he said softly. 'Whatever else is going on, we're still friends, right?'

'Right.' Vanessa nodded against his shoulder.

Justin yawned. 'We have about four hours until the start of the competition. We'd best get moving.'

As their cab wound its way through the streets, Vanessa wondered what they would find in the old Chatswyrth building if that was where the old man had killed that boy – or if that had even really happened. She watched through the windscreen as a ring of lights appeared over the skyline. 'What's that?' she asked the driver.

'That's the London Eye,' he said. 'A honking big Ferris wheel that was part of the big millennium celebration. Actually not all that far from the address you gave me.'

A few minutes later, the driver parked in front of an old brick building, its walls tagged with graffiti, its few uncovered windows cracked or missing. A chain-link fence surrounded it, with NO TRESPASSING signs every few feet. Chatswyrth Arts Academy.

'Can't fathom what two American kids want at this address at this time of the morning,' the driver said.

'A friend lives nearby,' Vanessa said, handing him a wad of bills as she and Justin got out of the cab. 'Thank you.'

The night was cold, but she'd been running on so much adrenalin that she hadn't truly felt the chill until now. She shivered.

On an upper floor of the derelict building, Vanessa could just make out a faint flickering of orange flames dancing off the pane of an open window. 'There,' she said, pointing.

Justin followed her gaze. 'Are you sure you want to go in there?' he said. The collar of his peacoat was flipped up, his scarf wrapped tightly around his neck. 'If the demon is still there –'

'I don't want to turn back,' Vanessa said, walking towards a gap in the fence. 'Not when we're this close.'

'Maybe we should have called Enzo,' Justin said. 'He could've . . .'

But Vanessa had already pushed through the fence and into the yard. Justin followed her.

The two of them carefully picked their way over the broken pavement, which was overgrown with weeds and littered with trash and shards of glass. Something stirred in the shadows and ran off.

Justin yelped. 'Sorry!' he whispered. 'I think that was a cat. I *hope* it was a cat.'

The front door was boarded up, a big x drawn across the wood with spray paint, as if the whole place had been condemned. Vanessa rattled the plywood, then shoved the door open with her shoulder.

'Whoa,' Justin muttered. 'Intense.'

Vanessa shrugged. 'Seems like something they'd do on *Law and Order: SVU*.' Then she stepped into the building, Justin close at her heels.

'Hold on,' Justin said. Vanessa could hear him fumbling in his pocket, and then there was light. '*Voilà*, the flashlight app,' he said, holding up his iPhone.

Cautiously they moved forward through an entry hall, the ceiling dripping with rusty water, the floor tiles cracked and covered in puddles.

Down a corridor was a vast room lined with wooden benches, a drained swimming pool at its centre, filled with garbage. Wrinkling her nose at the smell, Vanessa followed Justin along the side of the room.

Justin wrapped his hand around hers and swept the light from his phone across the room. 'There's a stairwell,' he whispered, and she saw a mildewed old EXIT sign.

The two of them mounted the stairs hand in hand, avoiding missing steps and mounds of trash. At the top, they emerged into a hallway.

A faint light flickered beneath a door at the far end.

Justin paused, his palm against Vanessa's. Around them the building groaned and creaked. 'I *think* it's safe,' he whispered. 'Careful now.' Together they walked quietly down the hall to the closed door. Justin reached out and rested his hand on the tarnished metal knob. 'Ready?'

She nodded, and Justin pushed it open.

Vanessa braced herself for something awful – for the man or one of his students to attack them, or even for the demon to rush at her, to press her mouth open and force tendrils of fire deep within her. *Your kiss will bring me home, my love* . . .

But inside, all was still.

Justin tried the light switch by the door, but nothing happened. 'Thought it was worth a try,' he said, shrugging. He raised his phone higher and let out a low whistle at the sight before them.

It was an old lecture hall, tidier than the rest of the building, as if someone had been keeping it clean. The illumination came from a small fire burning in a trash can by the far wall.

In a charred circle at the centre of the room lay four heat-blackened bodies in poses that suggested agony – arms shielding their faces, legs knotted together.

'Oh my God,' Justin whispered. 'You've been *dreaming* about this?'

'Not this exactly,' Vanessa said, wondering what had happened here after she'd woken up. In the centre of the burned bodies stood a man's figure, his body arched as if in pain, arms outflung, his skin and clothes entirely grey, as if he had been cast in cement. His features were contorted in an agonised expression. She gazed around the room, paralysed with fear, wondering if the demon was lurking somewhere beyond the cold concrete.

Justin inched forward. 'This is the guy? Looks like a statue.' He reached out and touched the man's shoulder.

The figure seemed to shiver, then disintegrated into a pile of ash. Justin jumped back, waving the dust from his face. 'Gross!'

'That used to be a person,' Vanessa said, feeling a wave of nausea.

'Do you think the demon is still here?' Justin asked.

Vanessa closed her eyes and tried to sense any hint of its presence, but there was nothing. 'I don't feel it,' she said.

'You don't *feel* it? You can feel when it's nearby? How long has this been going on?'

'It's complicated,' she said. 'Let's just find the *Ars Demonica* and get out of here.' She scanned the floor, trying to avoid the inert bodies, until her eyes rested on the spot where she had seen the book in her dream.

It wasn't there.

'It's gone,' she said. But who could have taken it? The only survivor had been – 'The demon,' she whispered. 'But he couldn't have taken it.' She looked to Justin. 'Right?'

'I have no clue.' Justin shook his head. 'If that guy was the host, it doesn't look like the demon got all that far using his body.' He leaned in, and then whispered so quietly she could barely hear it, 'Someone else is here.'

Then he whipped around and kicked, his leg slicing through the air so quickly that it was a blur, connecting with something: a figure that crumpled to the ground at Vanessa's feet.

Before she could look down, she felt an arm wrap around her neck.

CHAPTER TWELVE

Vanessa tried to free herself, but the person behind her was too large, too strong.

A strangely familiar voice sounded. 'What'd you go and do that for?'

The figure at their feet rolled away and stood up, Justin's light reflecting off her face. Round, full cheeks dotted with a single freckle just below her left eye: Nicola Fratelli. She shook the dust out of her thick brown hair. A red mark on her forehead revealed where Justin's foot had connected.

The arm around Vanessa's neck slid away. 'Is that any way to welcome old friends?' a voice said from behind her.

'Nicholas?' Vanessa said, turning. She wrapped him in a hug, her arms barely reaching around him. 'You idiots!' His chest was hot and sweaty against her cheek, but it didn't matter. Just knowing he and his twin sister were here, that she and Justin weren't alone, made everything more bearable. 'What are you guys doing here?' Then it dawned on her. 'Are you part of the Lyric Elite now?'

Nicholas and Nicola Fratelli were seniors at NYBA and friends of Justin's. They'd been the ones who'd tried to contact the Lyric Elite to stop Josef and Hilda, which eventually resulted in Enzo showing up at NYBA – though too late to do much of anything. The Fratellis joked around a lot, but they were deadly serious about fighting the dark dancers.

Nicholas exchanged a look with his sister. 'The Lyric Elite?' he said. 'Never mind them.'

Vanessa frowned. 'So . . . they didn't want you as members?'

'Apparently,' Nicholas continued, 'we aren't good enough dancers for them. Or so that Enzo guy told us –'

'When did you meet *him*?' Vanessa asked.

'When he was at NYBA, remember?' Nicholas, like his twin, wore a black long-sleeved T-shirt and black jeans. Even his sneakers were black. 'We asked to audition for the Lyric Elite.' He let out a sigh. 'But he never even let us try out. He blamed us for the mess at school, which is ridiculous.'

'They only wanted you, Vanessa. And pretty boy here.' Nicola flicked her wrist towards Justin. 'You, we understand. After all, you were *possessed by a demon*. No one else who's alive shares a connection to it. But Justin?' She turned to him. 'What's so special about you?'

Vanessa studied Justin, the light from his phone casting his face in shadow. There were so many things about Justin that she didn't know. Their conversations always focused on *Vanessa* – on her problems and her goals. How incredibly selfish.

Nicholas rolled his eyes. 'Never mind that for now,' he said. 'We've got news.'

'*Big* news,' Nicola chimed in. 'Zep is here.'

'We know,' Vanessa said. 'We've already seen him.'

'What?' the twins said nearly in unison, looking shocked. They turned to Justin, who nodded in confirmation.

'You've *seen* him?' Nicola said.

'Once,' Justin said. 'I chased after him but couldn't keep up.'

Twice, Vanessa wanted to say, thinking about Zep's message to her in the snow. But she still hadn't told Justin about that, and now – in front of the Fratellis – didn't seem like the right time to bring it up.

Nicola continued, 'We think there are some shady dancers like Josef in the Royal Court Company. We think that's why Zep is here. He's working with them.'

'Or trying to,' Nicholas said.

'That's what I was thinking too,' Justin said, though that was news to Vanessa.

'Or,' Vanessa suggested, 'he's here for the same reason we're all here tonight: the demon.'

'So,' Nicola said, tracing a question mark into the soot on the floor with the toe of her shoe, 'that's why you came here – the demon?' She didn't seem fazed by the twisted, blackened bodies in front of them. 'You guys must have a pretty tight competition schedule. Don't tell us you were just out for a 5 a.m. stroll.'

'We were looking for something,' Justin said.

'Us too,' Nicholas admitted. 'We've been in London for about a week, tracking potential necrodancers. We followed this bunch here, hoping they'd lead us to –' He gestured and Nicola picked up something from the floor.

'This,' she said.

She held out the heavy volume Vanessa had seen in her dream. Thick, arcane letters embossed on its faded leather cover read: *ARS DEMONICA*.

Vanessa stared at it. 'That book. Yes.'

Nicola raised a thick eyebrow. 'How did you know it was here?'

Nicolas turned to his sister. 'That doesn't matter,' he said. 'Anyway, good luck reading it,' he told Vanessa. 'It's in Latin.'

'Latin?' Vanessa whispered, her heart sinking.

'That's no problem for us, because we happen to know Latin,' Nicola said. 'Our parents were big on classical education.' She cracked open the book and added, 'These pages, for example, detail a ritual used to entrap and banish a demon.'

'The key to any entrapment is that your demon has to be invited into a vessel,' Nicholas explained.

'Which is me,' Vanessa said softly. 'So I just let it have me?' She could still remember how it felt the first time she'd summoned it: the way its breath coiled up her throat, the way her chest heaved and her sight went red. The way she had lost herself.

'No!' Nicola said. 'There's a way to do it with a vessel that's not a person.'

'You can do what's called a binding initiation,' Nicholas explained, 'which means that the demon doesn't have any choice in the matter. It just gets dragged into your body. The binding initiation is supposed to force the demon to do your bidding, but that doesn't usually end so well.' He gestured at the bodies around them.

'The demon gets really angry, so it eats your soul,' Nicola continued. 'Only arrogant people try the binding initiation.'

Vanessa looked at the mound of ash on the floor. If that man could read the *Ars Demonica*, then he knew what he was getting into. He'd been thirsty for power.

'And then there's what's called the *lesser invite*,' Nicholas said. 'You welcome the demon into yourself – or into that other vessel, really – but it doesn't *have to* accept. If it wants you, it joins you, and you work in more of a partnership.'

'At least, in theory,' his sister added. 'I mean, it's a demon, not your granny, and it could potentially eat your soul anyway, but it might be cool enough to hang out in your body without burning you to a crisp.'

Justin coughed. 'That's reassuring.'

'Which is where you come in, Vanessa,' Nicola said with a tight-lipped smile.

'As it happens,' Nicholas said, furrowing his brow, 'we're not joking. With the lesser invite, it helps if the demon actually wants to be joined to a particular host. And that, my dear Vanessa, is why you're so popular. You've proven that you can host the demon and survive.'

'So when you do it again –' Nicola said.

'No way,' Justin said, at the same time as Vanessa said, '*If I do it again.*'

'Right,' Nicola said. 'Once the host – you – is possessed by the demon, you just have to send it back where it belongs.'

'I just send it back where it belongs?' Vanessa said in disbelief. 'How? Do I just ask it politely to leave?'

Nicola sighed. 'The only way is to destroy the vessel with the demon trapped inside.'

'What?' Justin said sharply.

Vanessa's words caught in her throat. 'I – I don't think I like this plan.'

'There's a way to trick it though,' Nicholas said, 'so that we get rid of the demon without having to kill anybody.'

'It's complicated but doable,' his sister said. She thumped the book. 'This will explain how. But we're going to need your help, Vanessa.' She put a hand in her pocket. 'So what do you think?' Nicola asked. 'Are you in?'

Vanessa walked over to the windows and looked out. The sky was brightening. The sun was rising over the city, its rays gilding the shadowy spokes of the London Eye. Somewhere out there was her sister.

She could return to the competition and hope she won, and then . . . what? Join the Royal Court? Rely on Enzo to protect her?

Or she could take matters into her own hands for once. Margaret had fled to London and started a completely new life, even changed her name. Couldn't Vanessa become braver, stronger herself? Though she hadn't meant to, she had brought the demon into this world. It was her responsibility to get rid of it.

'I'm in,' Vanessa said softly.

Behind her, Justin sighed, as if he'd been hoping she'd refuse. 'Is this what you really want, Vanessa? We can quit the competition and leave London. Your mom won't care, and you'll be safer at home.'

But he was wrong, and not just about her mother. The demon was a part of her. Eventually it would either take control or destroy her trying. 'Running away won't stop it,' she said. 'It'll just come after me until I give in. I'd rather do something about it instead of just waiting around.'

Justin looked at her as though he finally understood. 'I hear you,' he said. 'But you're not doing this alone.'

Just then, something vibrated in Vanessa's pocket. Her phone's alarm, reminding her that it was already seven thirty in the morning, and the first dancers went on at nine.

'Crap,' she said to Justin, flustered. 'We're going to be late for the competition!'

TWO AND A HALF
YEARS EARLIER

From the Diary of Margaret Adler
May 18

I'm in the final twelve!

I did it!

Actually, we *did it, because even though he was cut, Erik danced the duet from* Giselle *with me. He was there every beat, every step, and it is only thanks to his dedication that I have made it this far.*

A real dancer gets used to her partner's hands on her body – on her hip, at her waist, splayed out against her stomach during a lift. Awareness of her partner's touch is the last *thing a dancer should be thinking of. Instead, her partner should almost be an instrument, something she relies on in order to perfectly execute a step.*

I know *that. That's how it has been all my life. Until now.*

My teachers always told me not to let my heart get in the way of my feet. But today my heart and head were both *part of my dancing. And far from ruining things, it only made me better.*

Maybe this is the secret to becoming great. Not love of dance, as my mother says again and again. But plain and simple love.

Erik, Hal and I celebrated in the back booth of Barre None. While we ate our salads and bread (all we could afford), a century's worth of sour-faced old ballerinas glared down at us from the walls.

'She was magnificent, Hal; you should have seen her,' Erik kept saying, and then Hal would stuff a roll into his mouth and nod. That Erik could be so happy for me amazes me. If I was the one who'd been cut, I'm not sure I would have enough self-confidence to cheer Erik on, let alone *dance with him in the actual competition.*

But that's one of the things I appreciate about Erik. Above all, he believes in ballet as an art form. And he believes I am good.

It's funny that he uses the word art, because to me, that's exactly what he *is. When he walks in the room, people can't help but look at him. That's how magnetic his presence is. And his eyes. God, his eyes. They're so dark, and yet they seem to glitter onstage. When they meet mine, it feels like a spotlight focusing on me, and when he turns away, the whole world seems to go dark.*

Hal just sort of groaned and rolled his eyes when Erik complimented me, but I knew he was happy for me too. Everything went on like that until Erik said, 'She was the best on that stage by far. No wonder Josef was so dead set on using her.'

I couldn't help myself, diary; I gasped.

It's so stupid. *We never said we couldn't talk about Josef. So why did I find it hard to breathe at the sound of his name?*

Erik knew immediately what he'd done. His hand found mine on the table. 'I'm so sorry,' he said. 'There's no way he'll ever find you here. You're safe.'

I nodded.

'I won't let anyone use you, Marg – Margot,' he said. 'You're not a puppet in some crazy occult mass. You're a girl, and a great dancer, and I love you.'

Hal coughed loudly and said, 'Guys, I am sitting RIGHT HERE. Do you mind?'

And I couldn't help myself: I burst out laughing.

So did Erik, and then Hal, and the three of us didn't say another word about Josef or demons or love the whole rest of the night.

I can't remember when I've felt so happy.

The next morning, though, was another story.

Before Erik and I went off to the practice space, Hal turned and sat astride his desk chair and said, 'I meant to tell you two something last night.'

'Unless it's about how you've hacked the Royal Court roster and can change the scores for the dancers,' Erik said, 'I don't want to know.' He hefted his backpack, full of toe tape and towels and rosin.

'Funny you should say that,' Hal said. 'Because I have, actually, hacked into the Royal Court servers.'

'Brilliant, Hal,' I said, dropping cross-legged on to the floor. We have only the one chair.

'No computer is safe from his wily ways,' Erik said.

'Stop, you two – this is serious.' Hal rubbed a hand through his dishwater-blond hair, and I could see that he was really concerned. He wouldn't meet my gaze.

'OK,' Erik said. 'What's the problem?'

'See, cracking their server took forever.' Hal shot us a cryptic smirk. 'It was easier getting all of us on the dole via the government's network.'

'Maybe they're really protective of our identities?' I asked.

'I don't think this is about protecting students,' Hal said. 'But I wasn't sure, so I just kept digging. It wasn't easy, but –'

'We get it, Hal,' Erik said. 'You worked hard to find something out. You always do. But can you just tell us what you found?'

'Fine.' Hal licked his lips. 'I am certain there are dancers like your friend Josef in the Royal Court.'

I froze. 'That can't be,' I said.

'What evidence do you have?' Erik asked.

'I hacked into some of their emails.' Hal shrugged.

'And?' Erik said, but it was as if he already knew the answer.

'There are exchanges with Josef at NYBA.' Hal looked at me. 'I'm sorry.'

'That doesn't mean anything,' Erik said. 'It makes sense that they would be in contact with Josef. He's the lead choreographer at one of the pre-eminent ballet academies in the world.'

'Sure,' Hal said. 'But why all the security? I couldn't even read the emails; it was all I could do to verify the sender and recipient. Why such hard-core, military-level encryption? What are they hiding?'

'Maybe they're just careful,' Erik said.

'Careful is one thing. This . . . This is something else.' Hal drummed his fingers on the chair back. 'I think you guys should drop out. I've got a really bad feeling about this.' He leaned forward, pressing his hands to his temples. I'd never seen him so distraught.

Erik's laugh startled me. 'Drop out? Are you kidding? After how beautifully Margaret – Margot – performed yesterday? I don't think so.'

'But, Erik,' I said, 'if they are working with Josef – I should leave the competition, go into hiding.'

'If they're working with Josef, they still don't know who you are. To everyone in the world but us, you are Margot Adams. Even if that Palmer Carmichael idiot is Josef's best friend, he has no reason to suspect that you're Josef's missing protégée.'

Hal gaped at him. 'You think they're dumber than they are, Erik.' It was strange seeing them spar like this. The way Hal was looking at Erik – it was as if he was suddenly staring at a stranger.

'They don't know,' Erik insisted. 'And if they are working with Josef, and you manage to infiltrate their ranks, we will have the upper hand. They won't know that we know who they are. And we can destroy them from within.'

I swallowed. 'By "we", you mean me, right?'

He laughed again, though he sounded nervous. 'No, I mean we. I am never going to let you out of my sight – I promise you. I will make sure no one ever hurts you. I give you my word.'

My stomach quivered, and my heart thumped heavily in my chest. I'm so torn. I want to leave the competition, right now. To go far away from anyone who knows Josef.

But I believe Erik. He'd do anything to protect me. He loves me. So I am staying. At least for now.

CHAPTER THIRTEEN

'Vanessa?' Justin called out from backstage. 'Come on. We're up soon.'

In the dressing room, Vanessa hastily pulled on her leotard and pointe shoes, then pinned her hair in a tight chignon. She checked her phone; there were two text messages: one from her mom – *Orchestra row 6 centre. You are amazing! xoMom*, and one from her father, which read: *Good luck, sweetie. I love you*.

Vanessa placed her phone inside her purse, which she left on the chair of her dressing station. As she approached the side of the main stage, the music softened. The theatre was hushed and dim, save for the spotlight hovering over the stage. From the wings, she could just make out the audience – the competition days were open to the public as well as to parents and coaches. The three judges were sitting up front. Different day, same smug attitudes.

In the wings, the rest of the dancers waited in silence, stretching or watching the performances through the backstage curtain. There were fewer of them now, and the backstage area was less chaotic, but it was still brimming with leotards and tutus, girls applying last-minute blush and boys gelling back their hair so it wouldn't fall in their faces.

Onstage, all Vanessa could see were two shadows stretching across the floor. She knew those steps immediately; they were so wistful and tender that they could only belong to one ballet: the bedroom *pas de deux* from *L'histoire de Manon*. Music spilled out from the speakers, lush and intimate.

She could hear the soft scratching of ballet shoes against the wood, the light panting of the ballerina as she tiptoed across the stage towards her lover, his arm running down her leg in a longing embrace, extending it until she was balancing in a perfect arabesque.

Vanessa inched forward to see a pointed foot swathed in satin, an arm so slender it seemed to belong to a child, a chignon tied back with pink ribbon. She recognised the light brown hair, the colour of flat dusty roads and tumbleweeds blowing across the plains: Maisie.

Vanessa had nearly forgotten about her. She hadn't seen her in the dormitory or the cafeteria, and while she knew Maisie had moved into the second round, with everything going on . . . well, Vanessa simply hadn't given her much thought.

Watching her now, however, Vanessa could see what a brilliant talent Maisie actually was, this slight, apparently naive girl who danced with so much power and emotion. There was no longer anything childish and mousy about her. Maisie's legs fluttered gracefully, her pale arms enveloping her dance partner – an American boy with pink skin and a shaved head – as if she were tangling with him between the sheets.

This was one of the things Vanessa loved most about dance – how a dancer could be transformed onstage. All it took was a costume, some make-up, and a bit of talent – a girl could become a woman. For a moment, Vanessa forgot everything that had happened in the dilapidated room in the shadow of the London Eye. This was beauty, she thought. This was why she loved ballet.

A voice spoke softly over her shoulder. 'I could dance that well too, if I'd never gone through puberty.'

Vanessa turned to find Ingrid beside her, her lips painted a glossy red.

'Leave her alone,' Vanessa said.

A cruel sneer spread across Ingrid's face. 'Oh, I didn't know Mother Teresa was a dancer,' she said. 'You think you're so nice and sweet and everyone is going to love you. You sneak out in the middle of the night with your boyfriend, and no one punishes you.'

Vanessa froze. 'How did you know that I snuck out in the night?'

Ingrid snorted. 'I know everything about you.'

Maisie was just coming offstage, beaming from the applause. Without saying anything more, Ingrid sauntered forward, knocking Maisie aside with her shoulder.

'Hey!' Maisie cried, falling to the floor.

'Are you all right?' Vanessa asked, kneeling beside her.

Maisie rubbed her thigh, where the fall had torn a hole through the back of her tights. 'I guess so,' she said, her voice glum.

'I have a spare set,' Vanessa said.

Maisie seemed to cheer up a little. 'You don't need them?'

'No,' Vanessa said, and fished through her dance bag until she found them, still rolled in their package. 'You were exquisite out there,' she added. 'That was just beautiful.'

'Really? You really think so?' Maisie asked. 'Because that's the only thing in the whole world that I want. To be an amazing dancer. Well, and to be in love.'

Vanessa grinned. 'But you already *are* an amazing dancer.'

Maisie looked up at Vanessa, her eyes wide. 'Am I?'

'Of course you are.' On the far side of the room, she spotted Justin stretching. 'I have to warm up now, but I'll see you later, OK?'

'Great!' Maisie said. 'I can't wait to see you perform. I just know you'll be incredible.'

'What was that about?' Justin said when Vanessa joined him. A few paces away, Svetya and Geo were stretching. Geo waved, but Svetya simply looked at her quizzically – surely her roommate had woken up, found Vanessa's bed empty and wondered where she'd gone.

'Maisie's just insecure about her dancing.' Vanessa bent over in a deep stretch until she felt the muscles in the back of her legs burn. 'She's so good; it's actually kind of bizarre.'

'Not Maisie,' Justin said. *Ingrid*. She had the devil's look in her eyes. What did she say to you?'

'Oh, um, just normal stuff,' Vanessa said, lifting herself on to her toes to warm her legs. 'About how I sneak out in the middle of the night, how she knows everything about me, et cetera, et cetera.'

Justin wrapped a bit of tape around his toes, pulling it a little too tightly in frustration. 'She can't just say things like that to you,' he said as he unravelled the tape and started again.

'I'd rather she say them out loud than say nothing,' Vanessa countered. 'At least now I know who to look out for.'

'Oh?' Justin said. 'And what's that? You can't predict what a crazy person is going to do. That's why they're crazy.'

Vanessa didn't like his tone of voice. 'But I *can* watch out for myself. I don't need you to do that.'

'She has a point,' Svetya said to Justin. 'I don't like when people talk behind my back, right? I'd much rather have them tell me what they think to my face.' She stared at Vanessa, like she was waiting for something.

'Thank you?' Vanessa said.

Svetya replied with a soft *hmph*.

Beyond the curtains, Ingrid walked on to the stage, her skin glowing in the spotlight. Her partner, a chiselled boy from the Royal School of Ballet, followed behind her, taking his position just as the first notes of the *pas de deux* from *Swan Lake* floated through the room.

'She's actually not half bad,' Vanessa said, watching.

'Too choppy,' Svetya said, pinning back her hair. 'She's trying too hard to look delicate.'

'I think you're right,' Justin said to Vanessa, and while they turned back to their warm-ups, he whispered, 'Maybe this isn't such a good idea.'

Vanessa tucked a wisp of hair behind her ear. 'Maybe what isn't?'

'Us being here. It isn't safe.' He glanced around backstage. 'Your visions. The Fratellis and their stupid plan. Ingrid.'

Was he actually bringing this up right before they had to perform? 'It hasn't been safe since the day we boarded that plane,' Vanessa said. 'You knew that before we even came here.' She smoothed her chignon, making sure it was in place. 'It's too late for this now, Justin.'

'No, it's not –' he began to say, when, from behind the curtain, the music slowed to a stop and Ingrid and her partner came offstage to loud applause. The judges called out the next pair of names.

'Vanessa Adler and Justin Cooke.'

'Good luck, guys!' Geo said, beaming. 'Rock it!'

'Yeah,' Svetya said drily, staring directly at Vanessa. 'Break a leg.'

The first forceful notes of Tchaikovsky's score sounded, rearranging the air until the entire theatre was drenched in melancholy. Justin let the sombre notes carry him across the stage to Vanessa, his body heavy with guilt, pleading with her to forgive him.

Vanessa channelled all the stress and anger and uncertainty of the past few days until she swooned with sorrow, becoming Tatyana, the spurned lover. That's what dancing was about, right? Turning experience into art? She thought about Margaret – how sad her sister must have been to leave New York, how lost she must have felt.

Dancing as Onegin, Justin complemented her perfectly, their bodies barely touching, as though there was a thin pane of glass between them. She reached out to him, but her hand just missed his, their fingers slipping away from each other, their paths pulling them apart. *Don't go*, his body seemed to plead. *Choose me.*

The music hovered, waiting for her decision. She wanted to throw her arms around him, let him lift her off the stage, the light forming a golden seam around their bodies as they disappeared into the shadows, but she couldn't. She feared she could hurt him.

Then, without warning, the tinny squeal of a violin cut through the room, as if Tchaikovsky's music were somehow distorting itself.

She turned to Justin, wondering if he'd heard it, too, but he carried on with his part as though everything were normal. Vanessa squinted out into the audience, but all she could see were the bright stage lights.

The violin music seeped into Vanessa's body, vibrating through her bones, in counterpoint to Tchaikovsky's score. Concentrate on the steps, she told herself, focusing as her feet followed each other in a swift *chassé*. She felt her fingers, her arms, her neck warming, as if the sun was beating down on her.

The demon was here. She could sense it.

Her limbs began to tingle, as if they had fallen asleep and were struggling to wake up. She could feel the demon coaxing her to hold her position a moment longer, to lift her leg higher.

Do not fear me. As I help you dance, you can help me.

How? she wondered.

I need you so that I can act upon this world. Together, no one will be able to stand against us.

It actually was helping her dance. She almost felt as if it was stretching her, pushing her; her jumps were suddenly higher, her arms reached further. All of the positions felt easy, as if she were weightless.

If I join you, Vanessa wondered, *you'll lead me to my sister?*

She felt its *Yes* thrum through her entire body.

Vanessa spun out of Justin's arms, the routine suddenly second nature. Every move Justin made was flawless, even while he was staring at her. He watched her with a steadfast intensity – he knew something was off, different from usual.

He would stop us, the demon said. *He is jealous. Small-minded. But together, we can have the world.*

The floor seemed to brighten and shift, its wooden planks bending until it looked like the bumpy terrain of a forest. It all suddenly felt *real* to her; she was running through the trees, searching for the man she loved but knew she could never have. She felt herself die inside, her body swooning, her toes fluttering on the wooden floor as she collapsed into Justin's arms. She imagined his hands strong and steady beneath her, his lips inches away from her neck, her collarbone, his body enveloping her in his scent. She didn't want to leave. For that moment, she didn't want anything except him.

But he slipped away, his hands sliding out from under her. Vanessa quivered as she balanced on her own, dripping with sweat. Her entire body ached more than it had since the night she'd performed the *Danse du Feu*. She thought of Josef's body, of his blood soaking the boards beneath him. Hilda's scream before she burned up, consumed by the demon from within. Elly's absolute silence. *I want to find my sister, but I can't be the cause of so much death. So much pain.*

Everything has a price, the demon's voice whispered.

And then she was twirling away in an elegant series of *tours chaînés*, the room around her growing brighter, redder, more beautiful.

The entire auditorium was awash with colour, like an oil painting come to life. For a moment, time seemed to stand still.

Through the colourful blur, all she could make out was Justin, his eyes the only fixed point in the room. He caught her when she landed, his fingers tracing their way down her ribs. She tried to bring his face into focus, but the demon was here, all around her, and she wasn't frightened.

Justin gazed at her, breathless, his fingers spanning the small of her back. His blue eyes were as clear as water. *Stay with me*, they seemed to say. And for a moment she wanted to . . .

Until the demon whispered, *Higher*.

She turned her cheek just before Justin lifted her into the air, his hands gripping her waist, her arms reaching upwards. The Tchaikovsky softened behind the shrill scream of the violin, the sound of the orchestra thinning until nothing was left but the flutes, dying out like whispers.

For a moment, the theatre was silent. Then it erupted in applause.

Vanessa slid one leg behind her and lowered herself into a deep curtsy. But when she looked at Justin, his face was full of rage. She watched him, confused.

He rose from his bow and quickly stalked off the stage. Vanessa forced one last smile at the judges, then quickly bowed her head before dashing off after him.

'Hey, slow down,' she said, but he didn't turn. Instead, he went into the boys' dressing room, slamming the door behind him.

'Justin!' she said, but he didn't answer, so she waited, leaning against the wall, while Svetya and Geo marched onstage to begin their performance.

Vanessa was still there when Justin emerged from the dressing room in jeans and a T-shirt, a towel draped around his neck. 'Wait,' she said. 'Look at me!'

He spun around, his face tight with anger. 'I'm looking.'

'Onstage – what was that about?' she asked. 'We were dancing so well. Why aren't you happy?'

He slung his bag over his shoulder. 'Because of you.'

'Because I danced too well? Because you don't want me to get hurt –'

'No,' he said forcefully, attracting the attention of the other dancers around them. He waited for them to turn away. 'That wasn't *only* you, was it?'

Vanessa averted her eyes. 'I don't know what you're talking about.'

He studied her, as if he could tell from her expression that she was lying. 'Yes, you do.' He took a step closer. 'Do you want to know what I think? I think you're getting help from something else, something that's been in your head before.'

She shrank back against the wall, wishing she could deny it.

'The Fratellis were wrong,' he went on, pointing at her. 'They didn't need to ask you to participate in their plan. You're already doing it. But I can't stand by and watch while you destroy yourself. Once this thing has you, the only way to get rid of it will be to *kill* you. Is that what you want?'

'Of course not,' Vanessa said. 'But –'

'There are no "buts" here, Vanessa,' he said, taking another step forward. 'This is your *life* we're talking about. You said we couldn't be together because you were scared I would get hurt, because the demon was connected to you. But now –' he closed his eyes for a moment –' now I think you're encouraging it.'

Vanessa stared into his pure blue eyes. Was he right?

Onstage, Svetya and Geo were nearing the end of their performance, dancing beautifully.

'So I got a little help,' Vanessa said, turning back to Justin. 'It's not like it hasn't helped me before.'

'This has happened more than once?' Justin said angrily. 'Why do you think it's doing that? Why do you think it wants you to win?'

His words sent a shiver of fear down her spine. 'I don't care why it wants me to win,' Vanessa said. 'I just want to find my sister.'

'I know you do, Vanessa. I get that. But if I had to choose between losing your sister or losing you,' Justin said, 'I'd lose your sister in a heartbeat. Your life is more important to me.'

'I haven't *had* a life since she left!' Vanessa said, her voice shaking. 'The only reason I went to NYBA was because of her. I'll do *anything* to get her back.'

Her admission startled him into silence.

'Why are you so surprised?' she said. 'You know why I came here.'

Justin backed away, his eyes lingering on hers for a moment before he spun around.

Applause suddenly filled the theatre, as Svetya and Geo took a long bow, then marched backstage, Svetya's expression making it clear she was thrilled with how they had performed. She winked at Justin, then strutted towards the benches along the corridor and rolled on a pair of legwarmers. To Vanessa's surprise, Justin followed her.

He looked back at Vanessa and whispered something in Svetya's ear. She giggled and stood. He took her bag and slung it over his shoulder, and together the two of them left the theatre.

Vanessa started after them down the corridor, but was stopped when Enzo intercepted her.

'I have good news for you,' he said.

Good news? Vanessa couldn't imagine anything good coming out of the next few days.

'We're not supposed to know yet, but I overheard one of the judges, and you and Justin have passed,' Enzo continued. His cheeks were red, flushed with excitement.

For a moment, his pride rubbed off on Vanessa; he had an incredible way of making her feel like he was shining a spotlight on her. 'You're both moving on to the final stage of the competition!'

He waited for her to react, but Vanessa didn't know what to do. 'That's great,' she said softly.

Enzo frowned. 'That's it?'

She wanted to be more excited, but she couldn't get the fight with Justin out of her head. 'I'm glad. Really, I am.'

Enzo smiled warmly. 'We're so close, Vanessa!' He couldn't seem to contain his delight. 'I always thought you had a shot at winning the scholarship, but to have all four of you – Svetya and Geo, too – in the final round!'

'Yeah, it's great. I'm going to . . . get my stuff from the dressing room. And I'm sure my mom will want to see me, so . . .' Vanessa backed away.

Enzo gave her a tiny nod, and though she wasn't sure exactly why, Vanessa couldn't wait to get out of his sight.

In the dressing room, Vanessa peeled off her leotard and threw on a pair of jeans and a lavender cotton sweater. The countertops were cluttered with dancers' accoutrements: barrettes and rubber bands and talcum power and Band-Aids and spare tights. Two stations away, Vanessa recognised Pauline's dance bag and wondered if she and Jacques had performed yet. She was about to sling her own bag over her shoulder when she spotted a girl sitting on one of the benches, head in her hands, her shoulders trembling.

'Are you OK?' Vanessa asked.

At first the girl didn't answer. Then she lifted her head, eyes red from crying. She must have danced poorly enough to realise she'd been eliminated.

'Is there anything I can do to help?' Vanessa asked.

The girl shook her head. 'I just love to dance,' she said, and then started to cry again. Her voice was tinged with an accent that Vanessa couldn't quite place, maybe German. 'And now I must go home.'

The girl lowered her head to her hands again. Vanessa sent her a silent hug, then grabbed her jacket and sneaked into the hallway and out the rear exit.

At the door, she looked back. Enzo hadn't noticed her; he was busy watching the final performances, poised as if *he* were the one dancing onstage. His body tensed and swayed ever so slightly with the lilt of the music, elegant even in stasis. And Justin was long gone. His role in this competition was no longer tied to hers.

Vanessa was alone now. And she needed help.

CHAPTER FOURTEEN

Vanessa stared into the fogged windows of Barre None.

The London afternoon was cold and grey, the sun hidden behind a wall of clouds. She was glad she'd brought a pair of gloves with her, and her favourite scarf, red cashmere edged with tiny white flowers.

As she'd walked, Vanessa marvelled at the people filling the city streets, all blissfully unaware of the Royal Court dance competition. She felt a little envious. Was her sister like these people now?

Vanessa adjusted her scarf and gazed inside the restaurant. The chairs were still upside down on the tables, the dining room empty. The sign on the door said CLOSED, but the door was open.

The restaurant felt strange, too quiet, though a heater crackled in the corner. Vanessa glanced up at the dance paraphernalia on the walls, feeling like she was walking through a museum.

'Hello?' she called out.

She heard dishes clanking together; then the kitchen door opened and Coppelia swept out in a long skirt and sweater, her sleeves rolled up as if she'd been cleaning. 'We're not open,' she said.

'I'm not here to eat,' Vanessa said.

'I remember you,' Coppelia said, brushing back a strand of hair. 'You were looking for the girl from the photograph.'

Vanessa clutched her bag. 'Yes. I was wondering if you could tell me more about Margar – I mean, Margot. Anything you can remember would be helpful.'

'I remember her name,' Coppelia said drily, 'because she leased a room from me and skipped out on the final month's rent.'

'She lived here?' Vanessa blurted out, unable to contain her surprise.

Coppelia watched her. 'For a few months, anyway. She and two young men. They were roommates. It's quite a small space to share, but you young people don't need much room, do you?'

Margaret had lived with two roommates? Men? 'Oh,' Vanessa said. 'I guess not. Did she, um . . . leave anything behind?'

Coppelia pursed her lips. 'Indeed. She upped and vanished one day. I think she drove the two boys apart, because they left their things. Quite rude.' She paused. 'It's all still upstairs. I use the room for storage now.'

'May I look?' Vanessa asked. 'Margot was . . . is . . . my sister.' She paused, unsure if she should be telling Coppelia, but . . . why not? 'She ran away a few years ago, and I've been looking for her ever since.'

'Sister?' Coppelia squinted at Vanessa. 'Now you mention it, I do see the resemblance. It's the hair that throws you off at first.'

Vanessa felt a tiny smile form on her lips. 'Everyone used to say that.'

Coppelia ran her fingers through her own grey-white hair and checked her watch. 'I only have half an hour before opening.'

'I promise I'll be fast,' Vanessa said.

Coppelia waved Vanessa further into the restaurant. 'Come on then.'

She led Vanessa into a dim hallway and up four flights of stairs, her skirt sweeping through the dust. At the top was a worn, low wooden door.

'I wish I could tell you more,' Coppelia said, picking through a crowded key ring. 'Like I said . . . the boys split up after she left, and one of them trashed the place. He must have been very upset. He made such a ruckus that I had to call the police.'

She selected an old brass key and unlocked the door. Inside, the attic was hot and stuffy, stinking of woodchips and mothballs. Hazy light spilled through gaps in the window shades and reflected off the dust particles suspended in the air. Boxes littered the room, stacked on top of one another without labels or any recognisable method of organisation.

'Feel free to look around. This is clean compared to what it looked like after that boy went on his rampage – he even broke the window.' She motioned to a small glass window with a large crack running through it. 'I had to change the locks. He came back the next day, pleading with me to let him get his things, but I refused unless he paid for the damage.' Coppelia smirked. 'Served him right.'

'What happened to him?' Vanessa asked. 'The boy . . . What was his name?'

Coppelia sighed. 'I can't remember. Old age is a terrible thing, dear. Anyhow, I cleaned up a bit, and I've been meaning to dispose of all the boxes, but with one thing and another, it hasn't got done.' She cleared her throat. 'I'll be downstairs if you need anything.'

Vanessa blew a wisp of hair from her face. 'Thanks,' she said as Coppelia left.

She went clockwise through the room, opening boxes only to find stacks of plates and napkins, old menus and flyers from beer companies, painted porcelain dolls. Her phone buzzed twice – *Mom* – and Vanessa knew she had only a short time before her mother would really start to worry. Then she noticed a box of more recent vintage in the corner, its lid covered in a thin layer of dust. Inside was a pile of girl's clothes.

She dug deeper and found a pair of ballet shoes, their ribbons tangled together, their soles scuffed. Beneath them was a small change purse. Vanessa opened the clasp and spilled out a handful of coins, a compact mirror and a gym card in the name *Margot Adams*. A tiny photo decorated the front. She raised it to the light and saw her sister's smiling eyes staring back at her.

Margaret's lips were upturned in the beginning of a mischievous smile.

Vanessa smiled back, one step closer to finding her.

Just then, her cellphone vibrated again, interrupting her thoughts. She slipped it out of her pocket. 'Hello?'

'Dear, it's me. Your mother. Where are you?'

'Oh,' Vanessa said, trying to think up something on the fly. 'Um, I just ran out to get some . . . shampoo.'

'Shampoo? Well, all right. Shall I meet you at your room in an hour?'

Vanessa blew a lock of hair from her face. Her mother had a unique talent for inserting herself at the exact wrong time.

'Um, OK. Gotta go! See you soon!' Vanessa shut off her phone and took one more look around the attic room. *Margaret*, she thought, *what happened?*

'Darling, I am simply so proud of you.'

Vanessa stared into her mother's eyes. They were in a pub called the Harwood Arms, on the corner of Waltham Grove and Farm Lane. ('Look!' her mother had said as they entered the restaurant. 'Farm Lane! And in the middle of a city!')

'Here you are, about to enter the final round of the Royal Court ballet competition!' Her mother, who rarely drank anything except wine, had an ale in a pint glass. Vanessa had ordered a soda. 'I texted your father right away,' her mother continued, 'and he is so thrilled for you. He can't wait to join us.'

Vanessa studied her mother, who was dressed exquisitely in a robin's-egg-blue turtleneck and sleek black dress slacks with black pumps.

Vanessa felt slightly guilty not telling her mother that she had found proof that Margaret had come here, to London, and changed her name. It didn't seem fair to worry her though, or to give her false hope before she knew the whole story.

And the truth was, she didn't know much. Margaret had come to London, changed her name and rented a room with two roommates – both guys. She'd entered the Royal Court competition two and a half years ago – and had been a member of the company at some point. But why had she left? And where had she gone? Was she still in London?

'Rebecca and poor Emilie went home this afternoon,' her mother said, chattering on about her friend. 'They didn't want to stick around. A bit of an overreaction, don't you think? I know it's upsetting, but there is so much to do here in London.' Her mother took a sip of her ale. 'I still haven't seen *Billy Elliot*!'

'Maybe you can go with Dad when he gets here,' Vanessa said.

'Good idea! I'll buy three tickets.' Her mother pursed her lips thoughtfully. 'Or should I get four? How is Justin?'

Good question, Vanessa thought.

'Because you two danced so marvellously together, it was almost as if – I don't know – as if you were made for each other.' Her mother took another sip.

Vanessa took a deep breath. 'Things between us are complicated.'

Her mother gave her a sympathetic look. 'Love always is.'

What was that supposed to mean? Vanessa didn't *love* Justin, did she?

Startled, she didn't move away when her mother reached across the table and grabbed her hand. 'Here's the thing about love, dear. It's always difficult.'

'Even between you and Dad?' Vanessa asked.

Her mother chuckled. 'Especially between your father and me. We've been married for nearly twenty years. But I love him, and I treasure our marriage. With you and Justin,' she said, 'you simply have to decide if it's worth the fight.'

On the elegant main stage of a theatre, a lone girl performed beneath a spotlight. The seats before her were empty, the wings of the stage dark and quiet. Her white leotard clung to her, her blonde hair was plastered to her head with sweat.

Invite me in. The hissing voice filled the theatre as Svetya continued dancing, unaware of the evil observing her.

For the first time in her dream, Vanessa answered. *You can get into my head, so why haven't you taken me over?*

I can force *my way in*, said the voice, *but unwilling hosts burn to ash. When I am invited by the right partner, however, we are invincible. And you are the right partner.*

She thought of the man's brittle body collapsing in a heap of ash. Of the others who had perished.

I can't do it, she said.

The air in the theatre grew black and heavy. It seemed to coalesce around Svetya, tightening like an invisible noose.

Leave her alone! Vanessa screamed silently.

The black noose dissipated into shadow. The demon was gone.

And then she saw something else: a pale face watching from stage right. A face she knew well, his eyes lustrous like metal.

Zeppelin Gray.

Vanessa snapped awake in her dorm room and clicked on the lamp on her nightstand.

When she'd returned after dinner, Svetya had been in a deep sleep. A note on her desk read, *Enzo looking for you. – S.* But now her bed was empty.

Vanessa threw off her covers and stood up. She slipped on a pair of black leggings and a matching sweater, twisting her hair into a bun as she quietly snuck down the hallway.

When she reached the theatre's rear entrance, she opened the door gently so it didn't make a sound. Inside, it was dark except for the spotlights shining over the stage, where Vanessa could hear the sound of Svetya rehearsing.

It was strange how the space – which earlier had been full of life – was now empty, as though none of the morning's events had ever happened.

Vanessa crept through the backstage hallway, sticking to the shadows. She could just glimpse Svetya's blonde hair as she lifted herself into a series of *tours chaînés déboulés*, rapid turns that reminded Vanessa of the blur. Svetya's iPod was strapped around her arm, the tinny music from the earbuds insulating her from other sounds.

On the other side of the stage, standing in the shadows, was Zep.

At the sight of him, Vanessa felt her hands tremble with anger. Her feet tightened into third position, her toes curling in her shoes, readying themselves. She closed her eyes and focused, just as Enzo had taught them. Then she arched her arm towards Zep and blurred across the back of the stage, landing silently.

She was behind him now. If Zep had noticed Vanessa or seen her blur, he didn't let on – his eyes were completely focused on Svetya.

He was close enough to touch. Vanessa could just make out his shoulder blades through his thin cotton T-shirt. She could even smell him, the scent unleashing a flood of memories – New York at night, the autumn wind blowing leaves around their feet as they ran, hand in hand, beneath the bright lights of Lincoln Center, the fountain glimmering in the distance; his laughter as they snuck into the basement studio, their bodies damp and trembling when Zep pulled her towards him for a long, salty kiss.

That Zep was gone. Maybe he'd never existed.

And Vanessa had changed. She wasn't the same naive girl who'd fallen for him. She'd never forget the sight of Elly's laptop in his room, the look on his face when he realised she knew he'd been involved in Elly's disappearance.

If he tried to hurt Svetya, Vanessa would do something, only she wasn't sure what. Kick him maybe? Steadying herself with a hand on the wall, she drew her leg back.

At just that moment, Svetya finished her dance. Vanessa held her breath as her roommate padded softly over to her dance bag, threw on a sweatshirt, then sauntered down the centre aisle, disappearing through the far door. Vanessa waited until Svetya's footsteps faded before she snapped her foot against Zep's back.

The impact threw him forward on to his knees.

'What are you doing here?' she said.

He groaned and sat on the floor facing her. 'Vanessa?' he said, his voice strangely warm.

'Yes,' she said. 'Now start talking.'

'I came to protect that girl onstage,' Zep said. 'That was some kick. Ouch.'

'To *protect*?' Vanessa repeated. 'From who?'

'From *what*. The demon was here. But it's gone now.'

'Don't lie to me,' she said. 'You brought that thing with you. I know you did.'

'Are you kidding?' Zep said, sounding perplexed. 'I'm not its master. No one is. That's why it's moving around so aimlessly. It's left a trail of bodies from New York to –'

'Since when do you care about other people?' Vanessa said, trying to control the quaver in her voice. 'Or did you grow a heart after killing Elly?'

She waited for Zep to deny it, but he only slumped back on to the floor.

'I didn't murder Elly,' he said eventually, blinking his long lashes. 'You have to believe me. Josef did.'

'I don't have to believe you,' she said. 'And I never will.'

'I wasn't myself,' Zep insisted. 'I can't even remember what happened.'

'That's all you have to say?' Vanessa said, angry tears blurring her vision. 'That you weren't yourself? That you can't remember? Elly was my friend. She had people who loved her, and now she's gone.'

'I was Josef's puppet,' Zep said. 'After I started working with him and Hilda, my head . . . it wasn't always my own.'

'Oh, please,' Vanessa said.

'Some days I would be myself. Those were the days that I spent with you. I would go to classes and rehearsal, would see you in the hallway and try to ask you out. But then a few days would pass, and I couldn't remember what had happened or what I'd been doing. It was really . . . frightening.' He wrung his hands together. 'When Josef and Hilda died, it was like waking up after a long sleep. I didn't know what I had done, so I ran. I couldn't go home and face my family, so I crashed with a friend. I didn't leave his apartment for two weeks. I was terrified.' He folded his knees to his chest and wrapped his arms around them. 'You were the only part of my life that was real, Vanessa. Being around you – it was the only time I was myself.'

Vanessa laughed. 'After all the lies you told me, do you really expect me to believe that?'

'No,' Zep said, his voice hollow. 'No, I don't expect you to believe anything I say. But that doesn't mean it's not true.'

Part of Vanessa wondered if he was telling the truth, but she quickly silenced it.

'I was going crazy with anger at Josef, and at myself. I couldn't live with what I'd done. The only way I could imagine fixing it was to find you, but you'd gone to London. So I followed you. And from the looks of things, I wasn't the only one.'

She stood up and backed away, reaching for her cellphone. 'You're crazy.'

'Am I, Vanessa?' asked Zep. 'Don't tell me you don't know what it's like to be under the control of someone . . . or *something* else.' He looked over his shoulder at the stage. 'I *saw* you dance yesterday. The demon is here.'

Just the thought of the demon made Vanessa's mouth go dry.

Zep raised his hands. 'I know you have no reason to trust me, but I know more about the demon and the necrodancers than any of your friends or coaches. I was working with them. I was *controlled* by them. I can help you.' His eyes were sad but hopeful. 'It won't make up for what I did, but it'd be a start.'

'You're right,' Vanessa said. 'It won't make up for Elly. Nothing will.' She stood up and backed away, reaching for her cellphone.

Everything in Vanessa's mind told her she should run. Zep was a liar, a murderer . . . and yet Vanessa knew the power Josef had had. Surely what Zep said was possible. It would explain the strange hot-and-cold way he'd acted towards her, one day asking her on a date, the next not seeming to know who she was.

'The demon talks to me,' she said at last. 'It wants me to let it in. It says it can help me.'

'No,' Zep said firmly. 'You *have* to resist it, Vanessa. The more you allow it in, the weaker you'll grow. It will find out what you care about most in the world and will use that to seduce you.'

Vanessa gulped. Was the demon using Margaret as bait? 'Why do you care so much?'

'I did many things I regret,' he said, slowly getting to his feet, his grey eyes barely visible behind his black hair, 'but the one thing I will never regret is getting to know you.'

Just a month before, Vanessa's heart might have swelled at those words, but not now. Not ever.

She couldn't decide which would be worse – to find out that he was lying again, or to discover that he was telling the truth.

Before she could say anything else, Zep stepped backwards and slid his foot across the floor in a slow turn. And without warning, he vanished, the only trace of him the sound of fading footsteps, like a distant patter of rain. So he'd learned the blur step too.

Far away, a door slammed shut.

He was gone now, Vanessa thought, relieved. But was he gone for *good*?

Chapter Fifteen

Surprised to find she could fall asleep again after her encounter with Zep, Vanessa awoke a few hours later to rays of sunlight filtering into the dorm room. For a moment she stared at the white ceiling, willing herself to get up and face the day. The air smelled like hazelnut, and she turned her head towards her desk and saw a mug of coffee, still hot – she could see the steam rising into the air.

Vanessa slipped out of bed and stood up. She picked up the cup of coffee and took a sip. It was good – stronger than what she was used to back in New York. Next to the mug was a brief note: *Get energised. I want to make sure that when I beat you in the next round, you're at your best. –S.*

Sweet, Vanessa thought. Or rather, as sweet as Svetya was ever going to get.

She took another sip and quickly checked her email. She had messages from Steffie, TJ and Blaine, plus one from her dad. But strangest of all was an invitation sent from a blank address.

Full of foreboding, she clicked on it and watched a cream-coloured envelope appear on the screen, its flap sealed shut with red wax. Another click and it unfolded, revealing a slip of paper.

> *Vanessa Adler, you are cordially invited*
> *Time: 8 p.m. on Thursday*
> *Place: The Millennium Bridge over the Thames*
> *There, far from anyone who might overhear us, we'll*
> *lay out our plan.*
>
> *Sincerely,*
> *N&N*

Vanessa couldn't help smiling. Leave it to the Fratellis to make something so serious sound like a party.

To be fair, the twins had been true to their word – they'd promised they'd reach out when they were ready. It would be awkward with Justin, whose name was also on the invitation, but she didn't have much of a choice.

She clicked on her next email, from TJ and Steffie.

> *Vanessa! Hi!*
> *So we did it. We conned our way into Josef's old office! The place was even creepier than before (says me, Steffie), maybe because now we know what he was up to.*

*I know it does not need to be said, but thank sweet
baby Jesus he is gone.*

*Anyway, we found a bunch of stuff about the
Royal Court Company – a binder full of newspapers
and clippings. But none of them mention Margaret.
And, because we're such great friends, we also scanned
in all the Royal Court rosters from the last three
competitions – they're attached here. No mention of
Margaret in any of them, but you can't say we
didn't try.*

*Steffie is staying with me for XXX-Mas in NYC.
Wishing you were here.*

Be careful.

Your besties,
*TJ (& Steffie) . . . (and Blaine, who is still stuck in
Texas and has been super-dramatic about it)*

Silently thanking her friends, Vanessa opened the PDFs and
scrolled down –

She froze, her hand recoiling from the keyboard.

There, on the roster of the Royal Court Company from just
two years ago, was the name *Margot Adams.*

The next email was from Blaine.

Hey Hon,

*I have no info about your sister, only about a hot
new guy I met! He works at Cafe Mojoe! He's amazing!
My lattes never tasted so good!*

*But enough about me. I miss you! Tell me more about
London! Obviously you're whupping the competition.
I only wish I were there to see you in action. I can't wait
for Christmas to come and go, and then to be back at
school, now that all the crazy is gone.*

*Anyhoo, Vanessa for the win! Oh, and give Justin a
big fat kiss for me. Wink wink.*

Kisses,
Blaine

There was only one email left, dated yesterday. She opened it.

Dear Vanessa,

*Congratulations on making it through the second
round! (Though I'm not surprised.) Your mom called to tell
me all about it. I miss you both on this side of the ocean.*

*Take special care of yourself, and know, always, how
proud we are of you. Can't wait to see you for Christmas!
You gals can take me to high tea.*

Love,
Dad

She sat back, feeling a little guilty about not having written
more often.

Dear Dad,

*I still can't believe I made the final twelve. It's so
exciting! Only one more round before we find out who
the two winners are.*

She tapped her fingers against the desk, trying to figure out what to write next, when, out of nowhere, someone slammed her laptop shut.

Vanessa jumped up, surprised.

Svetya stood beside her, a mischievous glint in her eye. 'You stare into a screen too much,' she said. 'It's unhealthy, right?'

'Um, right,' Vanessa said. 'Anyway, thanks for the coffee.'

'And the banana,' Svetya said.

'You left me a banana?'

'Not yet.' Svetya pulled a banana out of her dance bag, which was slung over one shoulder. 'I had to smuggle it out.' When Vanessa didn't move, she said, 'What are you, a gaping monkey? Why aren't you dressed? Practice is in twenty minutes – oh, and take a quick shower. You stink.'

By the time they made it down to the studio, Enzo was already standing in the centre of the room with Geo and Justin.

His face hardened when he saw Vanessa. 'First you disappear from the dressing room, then you don't reappear until the next day's practice,' he said, his eyebrows furrowed. 'You are lucky. Other coaches might not be so forgiving.'

Vanessa dropped her bag by the wall. 'I'm sorry,' she said.

Svetya went to stand beside Justin. He leaned over to whisper something to her, and she threw her head back and laughed. Was he flirting with Svetya just to annoy her . . . or had he really moved on?

'Before we begin,' Enzo said, 'I would like to thank you all for working so diligently. I am the only coach who has four students in the final round of the competition.' He gave them a slight bow, which had the strange effect of making Vanessa feel as though he were the one on display, rather than them. He looked up, his dark eyes softening, as though his words were meant only for Vanessa. Despite herself, she blushed. 'You have made me very, very proud.'

Vanessa clapped, and the others joined in. It was exciting to have got this far – there was no doubt about that.

'Your work is not over, and the most difficult part is yet to come.' Enzo said. 'But before you rehearse for tomorrow's final round, the contemporary solo, I will teach you another step.' He looked around the room. 'Or perhaps *teach* isn't the correct word, as only a few dancers have ever been able to perform it.

'The easiest way to think of it is as a refinement of the blur step,' he went on, tucking his hair behind his ears. 'As you know, in the blur, you're here one moment –' and with a blink he disappeared – 'and in the next, you're over here,' he said from the opposite corner. 'You don't actually become invisible, but you move so quickly that you seem to disappear, and in your own head, it appears that way too.'

'According to dance lore, there is a way to become aware of every moment,' he continued, his words animating him with an infectious excitement. 'To slow time to a crawl. The world around you freezes, and you will be able to move freely between each tick of the second hand.'

'Then show us,' Geo said. 'I would like to know how to do this.' He looked back at Vanessa, Svetya and Justin. 'I mean, wouldn't you guys like to know too?'

'No one that I know personally can do it,' Enzo admitted. 'It means dancing so perfectly that your energy reaches the level of magic. Only the greatest of the Lyric Elite – Balanchine, Nureyev, Martha Graham – could work at that level.'

Beside him, Svetya put a hand on her hip. 'But if you cannot do it, then how are you going to teach it to us?'

'I will show you the steps,' Enzo answered, his feet now in first position, heels pressed tightly together. 'But memorising the steps isn't the same as *performing* them. Still, who knows? Maybe one of you will some day reach this most rarefied level of our common art.' Then, as if in slow motion, he began to walk through a sequence of steps.

It started like a tease, his legs inching forward, then withdrawing, as if he couldn't decide which direction to go in. Even his arms worked in opposition: one moved in, towards his chest, while the other reached out towards the far wall.

As she watched, studying Enzo's every movement, Vanessa began to understand why the dance was so hard to perform. Enzo's motions were unnatural; his body seemed to fight itself, one side trying to move forward while the other pulled back. With every turn he wavered, one leg bending straight through the air, the other lagging behind.

Unlike most ballet, this dance wasn't about passion or love or loss. It was about the oldest and most difficult human flaw: to be at odds with oneself.

Vanessa knew that conflict intimately. Ever since Margaret had disappeared, she'd spent many days arguing with herself: pursue dance or quit it altogether? Go to New York or never leave home? Be with Justin or turn him away?

Enzo raised an eyebrow when he'd finished the demonstration. 'The steps are counterintuitive, but that's the point,' he said, panting slightly. 'But you cannot expect to alter the laws of time and space without altering the laws of your own body. This dance is designed to do just that. It is called "widdershins".'

He relaxed his posture. 'In ballet, you are taught to exert complete control over your body. But you cannot master widdershins by trying to force it. You have to empty your mind.' Enzo clapped his hands. 'Come. Let us begin.'

A murmur rose from the four dancers. They'd barely had time to process what they were supposed to do, let alone memorise the steps.

Enzo strode towards the mirror and, turning his back on it, stood in a stiff first position. 'The easiest way to learn is without looking at yourself in the mirror,' he said. 'Now empty your mind of everything, and when you are ready . . . dance.'

Vanessa pressed her heels together and tried to release all the thoughts that had been distracting her – Margaret, Zep, Justin, Svetya, the Fratelli twins – until her mind was bare, like a deserted dance studio.

As if beginning a normal routine, she lifted a foot and stepped forward. The moment her toe touched the floor, she recoiled. As Enzo had done, she let herself fall into a twirl, one side of her body moving forward while the other tried to wind her back.

She could hear the others gasping and thudding on either side of her, but she willed herself to shut them out, as, slowly, the movements of the dance began to sink in. Instead of trying to control herself, Vanessa let go of her body, closing her eyes. Her arms held at her sides, she rose *en pointe* and slowly extended her right leg into the air.

Then she saw her: *Margaret.*

Her brown hair was pulled into a tight bun, her slender body swathed in a leotard. She wove around the other dancers as if they were props on a stage, her gaze glued to Vanessa.

Was she real? Vanessa reached out to touch her, but the vision only flitted away.

She followed Margaret's lead, listening to her whisper the next step. *Bend left. Arch forward. Now spin, one half-turn. Stop. Left leg up. Higher. Higher.*

A rush of heat filled Vanessa's limbs. Margaret's face rippled like a reflection in a pool. Her hair began to curl and unravel into blackness, her eyes withering in their sockets. Her skin cracked and wrinkled until it was nothing but a swirl of black, two embers burning through it.

You will lose her if you don't let me in.

Vanessa remembered Zep's warning: *It will find out the thing you care about most in the world and will use it to seduce you.* She had to resist. She searched her mind, trying to bring back Margaret, but it was no use. 'Get out!' Vanessa shouted. 'Get out!'

Her voice broke the spell. With one final heave, she thrust the last vestiges of the demon from her head, then staggered and fell to the floor.

When she came to, the room was silent. The others had stopped dancing.

Svetya was gaping at her, and Geo looked worried. Enzo's face had completely drained of colour. Justin was looking away.

'Did I –' she stammered. 'Did it work?'

Enzo's lips parted, though no words escaped, and for a moment he didn't look like a dancer, but like a boy. But he quickly regained his composure. 'No.'

'But she went invisible,' Geo said.

'Only for a moment,' said Enzo. 'It was a good first try, but you have a long way to go.' He crouched down at her side. 'Who were you telling to get out?' When she didn't answer, he helped her to her feet. 'We need to talk, Vanessa.'

He turned to the other dancers. 'Everyone, practice is adjourned. Use the rest of your day to rehearse your contemporary solos for tomorrow.'

Justin caught Vanessa's eye. She could tell he'd guessed what had happened, and he clearly wasn't happy about it. He and Svetya left the room together, their heads down, with Geo following a moment later. She wondered idly which other dancers had made the final round – and realised she'd never found out.

When everyone was gone, Enzo turned to Vanessa. He flipped his ponytail over his shoulder and crossed his arms. 'What happened back there? And no lying this time.'

'It was the demon,' she said. 'It got into my head. It helped me with the steps –'

'Has this happened before?'

'This was the first time,' Vanessa lied.

'I don't believe you,' Enzo said. He studied her. 'This is very complicated.'

'Should we tell the Lyric Elite?' Vanessa asked. 'I mean, the rest of them?'

Enzo studied her curiously. 'No, not until we know what it wants.'

'What do you mean?' Vanessa asked.

'This demon could destroy you in a second if it wanted to,' Enzo said. 'But it hasn't. Which means –' he bit his bottom lip – 'that it wants you for something.'

Vanessa knew what it wanted, and she suspected Enzo did as well. 'What do you suggest I do?'

'Wait,' Enzo said. 'Be careful, as I told you before. Don't leave the lodge without protection. If anything strange happens, call me. And . . .'

'And what?'

Enzo grinned. His teeth were a brilliant white and perfectly straight. Vanessa had always thought of him as her coach, but for a moment she could see how handsome he was, how another girl might fall for him – and fall hard.

'Practise,' he said.

'*Practise?*' Vanessa asked. That was his best advice?

'Your final solo.' He tilted his head, staring at her as if he knew something she didn't. 'This is a competition, after all.'

Beyond the double doors, Justin and Svetya lingered in the corridor.

'Why are we waiting?' Svetya was asking, but fell silent when she saw Vanessa.

'Hey, Vanessa,' Justin said. 'Can we talk?'

Svetya pointed at Vanessa. '*She's* why we're waiting? You pick me only when you can't have *her?*'

Vanessa turned to him, realising that she also wanted to hear his answer.

Justin glanced between the two of them, looking anxious. 'No, that's not what this is about,' he said. 'I like you, Svetya, I do –'

At his admission, Vanessa felt her face grew stony. 'Oh?' she said.

'If you would just let me finish my sentence –' Justin began to say, but Vanessa cut him off.

'What makes you think that I should wait around to hear it?' she said, suddenly furious.

Justin faltered, his eyes growing cold. 'Maybe I don't want you to hear it any more.'

'Then I'll leave you two together,' Vanessa said, and spun around.

Justin called out to her, but Vanessa closed her eyes and blurred. For a moment it almost felt as if her body were being crushed in a vice – then there was a *woosh* of air and she was upstairs, outside the door to her room.

She was getting better at these strange dance moves, she thought, just as her phone buzzed. She slipped it out of her pocket, intending to tell Justin to leave her alone. But a different name flashed across the screen. *Zep*. He'd texted two words: *Meet me*.

And much to her surprise, Vanessa decided she would.

Two And A Half
Years Earlier

From the Diary of Margaret Adler
May 19

I thought we were through talking about the necrodancers. All I wanted to do was to perfect my contemporary solo – from Balanchine's Concerto Barocco *– before tomorrow's competition. Erik guided me as he always has, with a quick eye for where I waver and endless patience. When I fell out of step just before a break, he caught me and stretched me into a low dip, as though we were dancing together in a sloppy dive bar. He smiled as he swept me to my feet, holding me close for an instant.*

'See, I knew there was something off about that step,' I said, and he laughed.

'OK,' he said, trying to regain his gravity. 'Again from the beginning.'

I can't explain how great it makes me feel to make him happy. It happens so infrequently these days, with all the pressure from the competition. I have to savour the small moments. And even at that instant, I could tell he was preoccupied. When we broke for lunch, he said suddenly, 'It's a bit alarming, isn't it? The way these evil dancers have infiltrated the ballet world?'

'I really don't want to talk about it,' I said.

'I understand that, Margaret – really I do. But if these people have wormed their way so deeply into the companies of Europe, then we're going to keep coming across them no matter where we go.'

I stared at the wooden floor in our practice room.

'The only alternative I can see for you is to leave the world of dance entirely.'

At that I looked up. 'No,' I told him.

'Then you have to be prepared.' He ran his fingers through my hair. 'You can never be surprised by the dark dancers ever again. Your life depends on it. It's not going to be like it was with Josef, I promise you.'

'OK,' I murmur.

'After you win the competition –' he continued.

I snorted.

'You are going to win the competition,' he said. 'Trust me. You have a mix of coiled strength and . . . and self-assured grace. There are *famous ballerinas twice your age who haven't half the poise you show onstage. It's amazing really.'*

'Stop,' I said, exasperated.

'After you win, we will work until you've mastered La Danse du Feu,' *he went on.*

'No,' I protested.

'The necrodancers within the Royal Court will not be able to resist trying to recruit you,' he said. 'They'll be like your Josef — looking for that one dancer who can raise a demon for them to control.'

'Please stop,' I said again.

His face softened. 'Of course,' he said, and inched his hand towards mine. Leaning towards me, he ran his fingers down the strap of my leotard, straightening it. His touch distracted me, made me forget where we were or why I was angry. 'I'm sorry,' he whispered. And before I knew what was happening, I was in his arms as he warmed me with a kiss.

'OK,' he whispered, his nose touching mine. 'Let's finish lunch and get back to work.'

Which we did, but I found it hard to focus. I worry that behind his smile, behind the loving looks, Erik is becoming more and more interested in the dark arts, just like the person I fear most.

Josef.

Tonight, after dinner, it came up again.

'We can do this,' Erik said. 'We can defeat the necrodancers at their own game.'

Hal didn't say anything, just blushed fiercely.

'That's easy for you to say, Erik,' I said angrily. 'You're not the one who has to have your soul devoured by a demon if something goes wrong.'

He waved my objection away. 'It doesn't have to be like that. I've read up on ritualistic dance and demon raising, and —'

'WHAT?' I said, and sat down hard on the edge of my bed.

'Calm down,' Erik said, holding up a hand. 'I wanted to know what you'd been mixed up in. Not because I thought we should do what Josef was doing, but because I figured it was better to understand what I was up against.'

'Don't tell me to calm down,' I snapped.

'Josef was on to something,' he said at last. 'And if we want to make sure you are protected against him and his kind, then the thing to do is take control.'

'No,' I said.

At his desk across the room, Hal nodded vigorously. 'Margaret is totally right,' he said. 'We don't want to get mixed up in black magic. Raising a demon is hard, Erik. Dancers typically die while trying to do this. You don't know what you're getting into.'

Erik blinked and said, 'You haven't read what I've read, Hal, so stop butting in on what doesn't concern you.'

Hal snapped his mouth closed.

'There is an ancient guidebook of sorts called the Ars Demonica, which Josef didn't have. If I could get my hands on a copy, then we could iron out the kinks in Josef's methods and not only raise a demon but control it.'

'The kinks?' I repeated. Could Erik hear himself? Just the mention of Josef's name frightened me, even without the thrill in Erik's voice. It was as if he had forgotten what he had been trying to save me from in the first place.

Erik must have sensed my unease for he softened his tone. 'I just think we shouldn't dismiss an idea because it came from Josef. If we work together, Margaret, we can be more powerful than anyone on earth.' He touched my hand, as I tried not to cringe.

Hal eyed Erik suspiciously. 'You,' he said.

'You what?' Erik said.

'You said, "We can be more powerful," but you were talking about Margaret, so you should have said, "You can be more powerful."'

Erik blinked, then said, 'Right, that's what I meant.'

I couldn't listen any more. I grabbed my facecloth and toothbrush and headed for the bathroom. But as I closed the door to our room, I thought that Erik had said exactly what he meant.

The next morning, while Erik showered, Hal said, 'I'm sorry about last night. I don't know what's got into Erik.'

'Thanks,' I said. 'The way he was talking, it's kind of . . . crazy.'

Hal nodded vigorously. 'It's just that he blames them for taking his family away.'

'What do you mean?' I asked. 'They *took his family? Who?*'

'I shouldn't be telling you this.' Hal exhaled sharply. 'Margot Adams was Erik's sister. That's why we were able to put together your new identity so easily. Did you think it was just coincidence that you both have the last name Adams?'

I couldn't think of anything to say. Why had I never put that together? I'd been so terrified of Josef, and so desperate to get away, that I never even bothered to ask Erik about the fake names and papers he provided for me.

'I think Erik really is in love with you, but . . . he's got a personal stake in all this. He was the only one to survive that car wreck. He doesn't talk about it any more, but he is certain that a group of dancers are to blame.'

'The dark dancers?' I asked, leaning on the desk for support.

'Yeah. Those are the ones, from the Royal Court. That's why I think . . . I think you should withdraw from the competition.'

'I can't do that,' I said to him. 'I have to know . . . whether or not I can win this. It means too much to me.'

'I thought you'd say something like that.' Hal shrugged. 'You'll do what you have to do, but if you find yourself getting scared . . . I'm here for you. And not in some I-want-to-be-your-boyfriend kind of way.' He shook his head. 'I'll help you, any way I can.'

'Thanks,' I said, and I hugged him. 'I'm glad you're on my side.'

'Moving in on my girl?' Erik said from the doorway. His hair was damp and standing up on his head; he'd towelled it dry but hadn't combed it yet. He was smiling.

Hal blushed. 'Wishing her luck today, though she's not going to need it.'

'No,' Erik said. 'The one thing she won't ever need is luck.'

I don't need to tell you, diary, that his intense grin was a little scary.

But I can worry about Erik later. First I have a competition to win.

CHAPTER SIXTEEN

It was nearly six when the cab pulled up alongside the thick stone wall. Night had fallen, and a dusting of snow fell from the sky.

'Here you are, love,' the driver said, raising a bushy eyebrow. 'I hope you know what you're doing.'

'Me too,' Vanessa said, handing him the fare.

Vanessa had spent the afternoon practising her contemporary solo, alone in a rehearsal studio. It was hard to concentrate; she kept being distracted by thoughts of Zep, of Justin dancing with Svetya somewhere, her leotard clinging to every curve. Vanessa tried to shake the image from her head, but she kept drifting back to Justin touching, holding, admiring another girl, and there wasn't anything she could do to stop it.

But she had to focus. Margaret – or Margot – had been on the Royal Court roster. Which meant that her sister had probably won the same competition, so Vanessa would have to win as well. Once she had a place in the Royal Court Company, she would be able to find the necrodancers – and she could find out what happened to her sister. Maybe Enzo would finally introduce her to other members of the Lyric Elite, who could help.

After a quick dinner alone in the nearly deserted cafeteria, Vanessa had snuck out of the lodge.

Now, as she watched the black cab drive away up Swain's Lane, she wondered if she'd made a huge mistake. The old wall along the pavement stretched as far as she could see in either direction. Near where she'd been let out stood a Gothic gatehouse, with a windowed spire and an iron gate. A small metal plate read: HIGHGATE CEMETERY.

This couldn't be the right place. Vanessa blew a lock of hair away from her face and looked again at Zep's text. *Swain's Lane and Highgate. 6 p.m. Make sure you're not followed.* The sign on the corner read: SWAIN'S LANE, but he hadn't mentioned that they'd be meeting in a cemetery.

'You've got to be kidding me,' she said to herself, and sent Zep a text. *A cemetery? Srsly?*

She waited, snowflakes catching on her eyelashes. She couldn't see anything through the bars of the gate except a cobbled pathway and the bare branches of trees.

Her phone vibrated. *There's something you have to see here. Meet me in the west wing (left) at the end.*

Vanessa slipped her phone into her coat. She couldn't see any gatekeeper. Other than a black bird perched on top of the spire, there was no sign of life. A heavy chain wound around the bars, but upon closer examination she saw the gate was ajar.

She slipped inside and walked quickly up the path. Along with the occasional lamp post, barren trees lined the way, their trunks as gaunt as skeletons. She saw tombstones along the hills and under the trees, interspersed with creamy statues of angels and saints and lions and other beasts, all covered with a light layer of snow.

Suddenly the path came to a dead end. A circle of pillared mausoleums loomed tall around her, their stony facades cracked and worn with age. One building in particular caught her attention, its columns topped with a frieze of carved dancers and angels.

A twig snapped, and a figure emerged from the shadows.

Zep.

His metallic eyes shone, the wind sweeping his black hair across his face.

Vanessa sighed. 'You could have said something instead of creeping up on me like that –'

'I'm glad you came,' he said. 'I didn't think you'd ever trust me again.'

'I don't, but I came anyway,' Vanessa said. 'What are we doing here?'

He flinched at her words. 'After Josef and Hilda died, I came to London to find the Lyric Elite. Because of what happened in New York, I thought I might know something that could help track down this thing we set loose into the world.'

'So where are they?' Vanessa said, looking around at the empty cemetery.

'If you mean the Lyric Elite, I never managed to talk to them,' Zep said. 'I couldn't find any trace of them.'

'What do you mean, you couldn't find them?' How hard could they be to find, if Vanessa was rehearsing with one of them every day. Or was Zep lying again?

'This is all I found,' he said, spreading his arms. 'Dance families that had been Lyric Elite ages ago. Their legacies go back centuries, but these families have all died out.' He scuffed his toe in the snow, tracing a perfect circle, the graceful motion reminding her that in spite of everything, he was a highly trained dancer, until recently a senior at NYBA. 'All but one.'

He gently smacked his palm against the blackened steel door of the tomb before them. The structure was quite large, Vanessa realised, like a small house. The family name carved into the lintel was so worn and stained with watermarks that it was impossible to read from where she was standing.

'This one?' Vanessa asked.

Zep nodded. 'Come on.' He pushed open the door and disappeared inside.

'Wait,' Vanessa said. She still wasn't sure what she thought of Zep, and now he was leading her into a mausoleum. The perfect place to leave a body – *hers*.

'I won't hurt you,' Zep's voice said from the shadows, 'but you need to see what I found inside.'

'What do you mean?' Vanessa said, her voice unsteady. A dark thought loomed in her mind, one she hadn't allowed herself to consider until now. She suddenly wished she wasn't here. 'Margaret?' Was her sister's body inside?

'Don't worry,' Zep said. 'She's not here. Come in – I'll show you.'

Barely containing her apprehension, she looked up again, and this time could make out the letters engraved above the entrance: *ADAMS*. Just like Margot Adams, the name her sister adopted when she came to London.

Vanessa stepped across the threshold and into the dark interior.

Zep removed a flashlight from his coat and shone it ahead. The mausoleum was actually just the top of a staircase. She followed Zep down the stairs to a stone cavern lined with marble columns. The air was stale and cold. Zep turned left past a chamber flanked by two ancient statues of ballerinas to a room at the end of a dusty pathway.

'I found out your sister was using a stage name: Margot Adams.'

'Yes,' Vanessa said. 'I discovered the same thing.'

'It turns out that Margot Adams was actually a teenager from a dance family who died in a suspicious car crash a few years ago,' Zep continued. 'If she'd lived, she would have been about eighteen, taking her place on the international dance stage. She was in the car with her parents, both of whom also perished. The strange thing was, they never found Margot's body. The fire burned so hot that identifying the remains was near impossible.'

'Gross,' Vanessa said, sticking her hands into her pockets to warm them up. 'What does all of this have to do with my sister?'

Instead of answering, Zep carefully pushed open the door. Inside was a circular chamber holding two stone caskets, each guarded by a statue of a male dancer. Behind each casket was a marble plaque: an urn wall, holding the cremated remains of the dead. A name was etched into one of the plaques, but the second was blank, as if waiting for the name of the only remaining child in the family.

'The thing is . . .' Zep said, 'she died *twice*.'

Vanessa pulled back. 'What?'

'A girl named Margot Adams jumped to her death off Tower Bridge two and a half years ago,' he said softly.

Vanessa searched for words. 'Do you think –'

'It was your sister?' He paused, letting the question linger. 'Yes.'

Vanessa gasped. 'No,' she said. 'Margaret wouldn't kill herself –'

'I'm sorry, Vanessa,' Zep said, 'but it's the truth.'

Vanessa couldn't comprehend his words: she'd heard him, but she couldn't wrap her mind around what it meant. Her sister was dead. She repeated it to herself, trying to grasp how it could be true. Vanessa had been certain that Margaret was alive; she was her sister, made of the same blood, their memories crafted from the same past, their futures woven together, inextricable. Even since her disappearance, she had been a guiding force, leading Vanessa forward. How could she die without Vanessa knowing it? Vanessa steadied herself on the cold stone, feeling as if she was about to collapse. Margaret had taken her own life.

The more she thought about it though, the stranger it sounded. Margaret would never give up; her fragile appearance was deceptive. She would tiptoe on to the stage, her figure so delicate it seemed made of porcelain, and then transform, leaping in a mesmerising trail of light, pulling the spotlight with her. Margaret couldn't be dead. She was out there somewhere, blazing through the night like a falling star.

'Why did you bring me here, Zep?' Vanessa said.

'Almost everyone in this Adams family died, right?' Zep said. 'But before Margaret's suicide, someone signed out the mausoleum key. A young woman. I thought we should find out why.'

The dust and grit on the floor crunched beneath her shoes as she walked forward. MARGOT ADAMS, read the plaque on the wall.

It wasn't until Vanessa touched her hand to its cold surface that she noticed something peculiar. The marble lid of the urn wall was cracked and sitting slightly crooked. Someone had broken into it.

'Zep.' She spun around. 'Did you . . . ? Did you break into someone's –?'

'No,' he said. 'But that's only because someone else did it first. There are no ashes inside. Have a look.'

Zep prised out the lid and set it aside. He shone the beam of the flashlight into the cavity.

Vanessa could see a flash of red and a tangle of browns and blacks. *Clothes*, Vanessa realised, recognising a sleeve, a buckle, a familiar lapel: Margaret's wool coat.

She reached in and pulled out a bundle of Margaret's things. Her red silk dress, her favourite gold earrings and her oldest sweater, the one she'd worn every day at home.

Then she lifted a Ziploc bag tucked beneath the rest. Inside were two passports: an American one in the name of Margaret Adler, and a British one belonging to Margot Adams. Between them was a tattered two-and-a-half-year-old lottery ticket with six numbers. Someone had scribbled *Prince Hal* across the top. 'Why would she save this?' Vanessa asked.

'Maybe it's a winner.' Zep examined it. 'Prince Hal is from *Henry V*, right? Maybe she bought it the night she saw the play. Who knows?'

Also inside the bag were a few pieces of jewellery that Margaret had always cherished: a pair of diamond earrings their parents had given her one Christmas, a bracelet and an opal ring that had belonged to their grandmother.

'Vanessa?' Zep said. 'Are you OK?'

'I just – the demon told me, when it was in my head, that Margaret is alive.'

'Did it?' Zep asked. He looked down at the lottery ticket in his hand. 'There's no trusting a demon, I can tell you that much. It will woo you with whatever it thinks you want to hear.'

'Maybe she became someone else? Or . . .' Vanessa trailed off. *Or was her new life over too?* Margot Adams had died twice, Zep had said. 'If she killed herself, why waste time stashing her new forged documents here?'

'Maybe she didn't want the girl's identity any more,' Zep said.

'Or maybe,' Vanessa said, 'it wasn't just some random girl.'

When they emerged from the mausoleum, the moon was covered by clouds, and all Vanessa could see were the thick white snowflakes floating down from the sky.

'I'm sorry, Vanessa,' Zep said. 'Probably not the final image you want of your sister.'

'It's not,' she whispered. 'I saw her dancing this morning. The demon used an image of her when it got into my head.'

Zep immediately looked concerned. 'What do you mean, *it got into your head*?'

'This morning, in rehearsal. A vision came to me of a girl dancing on an empty stage. At first I thought it was my sister, but really it was the demon, so I pushed it out.'

'Pushed it out?' he repeated. 'That's not what happens with demons. Eventually it gets the better of you.'

'I'm strong,' she said. 'I can fight it.'

'Vanessa,' Zep said, shaking his head, 'you're not strong *enough*. No one is. In your head it probably sounds like a real person – a voice, a personality, whatever. But trust me, it's not.

That's just a mask it wears to win you over. Beneath the mask, it's a malevolent being – something almost unimaginable.'

Vanessa remembered her visions of Justin's and Margaret's faces burning away into a demonic image and, with a coldness in her gut, realised Zep was telling the truth.

'Josef told me this spirit comes from another plane entirely, and I don't even know what that means, but the place it comes from is the same one where we get the idea of Hell and Satan and all that scary business.' Zep grimaced and stared directly at her, moonlight reflecting off his eyes. 'Souls in eternal torment, lakes of fire – real apocalyptic stuff.'

'But it's already *here*,' Vanessa protested. 'What does it need me for? It's already killing people – I've seen it.'

'It doesn't have a living host, one who belongs to this world, so it can't do much. If some idiot tries to summon a demon, it may respond to the call and kill the person,' Zep said, 'but otherwise it's just stuck waiting for you – its chosen host – to come around. Once it possesses you, it will wreak all sorts of havoc. Feed on the souls of innocents the world over, or what-ever it is that it wants.'

'Well, it can wait forever, because that's never going to happen.'

Zep gripped her by the shoulders. 'It's not going to wait nicely forever. It already has access to your memories. Sooner or later it's going to force itself on you.'

'So then, what's the point?' Vanessa said angrily. 'If the demon *can't* be controlled, then I can't do anything about it.'

'It can't be controlled,' Zep said, 'but it *can* be walled out. For a time. And if you trust me, I can teach you how.'

'I don't trust you,' she told Zep. 'And I never will.' She paused, considering her options – which, at the moment, were very few. 'But I'll listen,' she said. 'Tell me what I have to do, according to you.'

For the first time since she'd encountered him in London, Zep smiled. 'First,' he said, seeming glad to be taken seriously, 'you have to find a meditative talisman. Some object that you can throw your energy into. You don't need to have it with you, just in your head.'

'A talisman? Like a magical object?'

'Not magical, just special to you.'

Vanessa's mind drifted to a tangle of memories, all revolving around Margaret. They were small moments, which she'd never appreciated at the time – telling jokes in the back of their parents' car, whispering beneath the covers with a flashlight late at night or laughing while they tried on their mother's lipstick – yet taken together they represented everything that Vanessa held dear. She'd never thought that one day her sister would be gone, that the moments would end. She couldn't let that happen. She *had* to stop the demon and find Margaret.

'I've got something,' she said. Margaret's ballet shoes, the ones that were stolen from Vanessa's suitcase the first day she was in London. 'I think it's powerful enough.'

'You think, or you know?'

Vanessa pursed her lips. 'I know.'

'Great,' Zep said. 'When you feel something trying to enter your mind, the trick isn't to fight, but to focus your entire being on something else – the talisman.'

Vanessa closed her eyes and envisioned her sister's old pointe shoes where they had lain in her suitcase, the well-worn, tangled ribbons, the sweat-darkened insoles, the pale satin smudged from wear. 'OK.'

'Once that object is vivid in your mind, you drop your defences. Your talisman will fill your mind so there is no room for anything else but you and the emotions you feel about that object.'

She saw the shoes in her mind's eye, but the feelings that accompanied it were complicated. They contradicted one another, part sadness, part joy, part anger. 'What kind of emotion?'

'Some big feeling you associate with that talisman,' Zep continued. 'Such powerful emotion that you can barely remember where you were or what was going on.'

Vanessa closed her eyes and tried to forget where she was. Forget that she was standing in a snowy cemetery with Zep, forget what he had just told her. Margaret was as integral to her being as her heart. She couldn't lose something like that without dying herself.

'Now – a memory associated with your talisman. The strongest memory you can think of.'

Sitting on the green couch in her family's living room in Massachusetts, a quilt over her legs, reading. A muffled melody drifted down from upstairs, an aria Margaret had been playing all spring, the soprano's voice pure and perfect. Vanessa had heard it so often

*that she knew it by heart. She rested the book on her legs and lis-
tened, only to be disturbed by a clatter of mail sliding through the
slot in the front door.*

*Her sister burst out of her room and ran downstairs, her pony-
tail bouncing behind her. 'This is it,' she said, kneeling on the floor.
She held up a cream-coloured envelope. 'What do you think it says?'*

*'It says, "We lurve you,"' Vanessa told her sister, laughing. 'Just
open it already.'*

*Margaret tore open the envelope and slid out the letter. She
scanned the page.*

'Well?' Vanessa asked. 'Did you get in?'

*Margaret's hands trembled. 'I got in.' A smile spread across her
face, and she squealed with joy. 'I got in!'*

'Vanessa!'

She opened her eyes to find Zep standing in front of her on
the snow-covered path. He was staring at her, his disappointment obvious.

'What?' Vanessa said. The chill of the night had set in,
and her teeth began to chatter. 'I was doing what you told me
to do.'

'Not good enough,' Zep said, shaking his head. 'Not if I
can simply call your name and bring you out of it. Get *lost*
in the memory. Relive it all over again. That is your only
armour.'

Vanessa stared down at her feet and remembered her last
night in New York, when she'd slipped her feet into her sister's
shoes and seen a flash of Margaret's legs tracing a message in
the ground. *I'm still here.*

Growing up, Margaret had always been the one to help Vanessa get herself out of the messes she'd got herself in. She was ever elegant, the model older sister. Now Margaret was the one in trouble, and she had reached through time and space to ask Vanessa to find her. And Vanessa was determined to answer.

She closed her eyes and focused on that memory of the shoes: the insoles holding the shape of Margaret's feet, the lamb's wool still crushed inside the toe box, the stitching on the ribbons so neat she could envision her sister sitting cross-legged on the floor of her dressing room sewing them on.

Ballet shoes are like puppies, Margaret had told her. *Or boys. Treat them the way you want to be treated. Take good care of them, and they'll take good care of you.*

Vanessa had been only eleven, but she could see that day like it was yesterday: *sitting in her sister's bedroom, watching Margaret break in her new pointe shoes to get ready for NYBA. It was late August, and Margaret was about to leave.*

Margaret came over and gave Vanessa a kiss on the forehead. 'I'll be home for Thanksgiving. It's only three months!' She took out a needle and thread and began to adorn the first shoe. 'These are going to be my favourite shoes, Ness. I can tell.'

'How?' Vanessa asked. 'You've never even danced in them.'

Margaret thought about this. 'True. But sometimes? You just know . . .'

When Vanessa's eyes finally fluttered open, she was standing in the centre of the pathway, Zep beside her.

'Thank God,' Zep said. 'I thought I wasn't going to be able to get you back.'

Vanessa shook her head, realising she was covered in snow. 'Sorry!'

'Don't apologise,' Zep said gently. '*That* memory, whatever it is, is the shield you need to protect yourself. As long as you can tap into that, you'll be safe.'

Vanessa smacked her hands together to warm them. 'Zep, I don't think I can master that before the last part of the competition! It's too soon – tomorrow.'

His eyes were as lustrous as the light-filled clouds covering the moon. 'I know what you're capable of,' he said, his voice soft.

The wind seemed to push him towards her. He leaned in, but Vanessa turned away.

'What's wrong?' he asked.

She averted her eyes, pressing herself against the outer wall of the mausoleum, the marble cold against her back. 'This was a mistake. I shouldn't be alone with you.'

Zep nodded as though he'd been expecting her to say something like that. 'Just promise me that you'll be as careful with other people as you are with me.'

Vanessa's face hardened. 'What do you mean?'

'The Fratellis, Justin, that shady character who's been training you . . . They're no more deserving of your good faith than I am.'

'Why do you say that?' Vanessa said, realising Zep had no idea Enzo was part of the Lyric Elite. 'They're looking out for me, trying to protect me from people like you.'

Zep let out a bitter laugh. '*I'm* the only one looking out for you. The Fratellis are idiots. And that coach of yours . . . I haven't been able to find much information about him. That troubles me. People who leave no trail always have something to hide.'

Of course Enzo had something to hide – he was part of the Lyric Elite. But she wasn't going to tell Zep that. The wind kicked up and made her eyes sting with tears. 'I have to go,' Vanessa said. 'I'm going to be late for curfew.'

She turned and started back down the path to the front gate, waiting for Zep to say something, anything. But all she could hear was the crunch and squeak of her boots in the snow, the wind in the branches of the barren trees around her.

She looked back, but he was gone, the flashlight wedged on the lip of a stone pedestal, its beam illuminating a message scrawled in the snow:

I'm on your side

CHAPTER SEVENTEEN

The wind was bitterly cold.

From this end, the Millennium Bridge was a long, narrow line of lights suspended over the River Thames. Vanessa paid the cab driver, pulled her coat tighter and set off to meet the Fratellis.

With every step she took, Zep's warnings echoed in her mind: why *were* the Fratelli twins going so far out of their way to help? Did they even care about Vanessa's safety, or were they only using her to gain admission to the Lyric Elite?

The bridge was a peculiar place to choose for a meeting – empty save for a few pedestrians, their faces tucked into their coat collars, shielding themselves from the wind.

Soon enough she saw three figures huddled at the centre of the bridge. For a moment she remembered back to when she had thought the twins were scary, when she'd seen them and

Justin together outside Lincoln Center and thought they were stalking her. But the Fratellis had turned out to be far from scary. Her feelings for Justin were more complicated, but she wasn't looking forward to seeing him. Not now.

As soon as Nicholas spotted Vanessa he stopped talking and waved. Beside him, Nicola and Justin turned, their cheeks red from the cold.

'The guest of honour appears!' Nicholas said.

Justin stood against the railing, his arms crossed. 'Where have you been?' he asked.

'I had something to take care of,' Vanessa said.

'Take care of?' Justin repeated. 'What do you mean?'

'I don't see how that's any of your business.' She looked to the side, at the waters of the Thames down below, at the twinkle of lights that was the London skyline. 'Why does it matter to you, anyway? Svetya not keeping you busy enough?'

'Busy? Is that what you think makes a good relationship? Rushing around all the time, never making a commitment?'

Vanessa stepped back, insulted. 'I *have* made a commitment.'

Before she could continue, Nicola said, 'Lovers' quarrel?'

'We'd have to be lovers first,' Vanessa said. 'Which we most definitely are not.'

'Thank goodness for that,' Justin said.

Nicola turned to her brother. 'Let's get this started before my toes freeze off.'

Nicholas lowered the backpack from his shoulder and held it open just wide enough for Vanessa to see the leather-bound *Ars Demonica*.

'While you two were bickering,' Nicholas said, *'we've* been studying the exact ritual required to banish the demon. It's a good thing we got our hands on this book, because it has turned out to be slightly more complicated than we imagined.'

'Complicated *how*?' Justin asked. 'Doesn't sound good.'

'Good is a relative term in this case,' Nicholas said. 'As we said before, usually you have to kill the possessed person to cast a demon back where it came from, but this book reveals a way to trick the demon into hiding itself in an object.'

'Like a lamp?' Vanessa asked, remembering the vision she'd had of the men huddling over an ancient Etruscan lamp in that chilly distant warehouse. Almost reflexively, she turned to Justin. He stood by the railing, his brow furrowed.

'Exactly right!' Nicholas said. 'If we can just get our hands on one.'

'Once it's inside the object,' Nicola continued, 'you destroy the trap, sending the demon back where it came from.' She grinned. 'Easy, eh?'

Justin was speechless. 'We're going to put it into a lamp?' he said. 'That's your big plan?'

For a moment the twins didn't respond. 'No,' Nicola finally said. 'Not just *any* lamp. It has to have certain characteristics. The *Ars Demonica* explains exactly what to look for – silver with a certain percentage of lead, former ritualised use, a particular shape, and so on. Luckily England is a very old place.' She dug around in a pocket for her phone and opened it to a photograph. 'We were able to locate an appropriate lamp in an antiques shop,' she said. 'We'll pick it up tomorrow morning. What are friends for?'

The phone's screen showed a picture of a pot-bellied metal lamp with a round handle and a spout. It looked kind of like the creamer Vanessa's mom brought out for company. It stood on four crooked feet, its spout and lid overlaid with a faded ornate filigree.

'It doesn't look like much, but because it's silver, it takes enchantment easily,' Nicholas said. 'The real challenge will be tricking the demon into entering it. The *Ars Demonica* details a dance ritual involving very precise steps. If we can perform them perfectly, we'll be fine.'

'Are you sure you two are the right ones to do this?' Justin asked. 'I don't remember you being the most amazing dancers.'

'First off, you're wrong,' Nicola said. 'Secondly, we have the book. And thirdly . . . that's why we need you.'

Vanessa stared at Justin, trying to gauge what he was thinking. After a moment he said, 'Even if we do go through with this, the demon wants Vanessa. How are we going to trick him into thinking she is a lamp?'

Nicola said, 'The demon can sense a person, but it can't actually *see* you – not unless it is in someone else's body. That's its weakness.'

Nicholas glanced around to make sure no one was passing by. 'Basically, Vanessa pricks her finger and drops a teeny smidge of her blood inside the lamp. The blood and the enchantment create just enough presence to confuse the demon as to where she is.'

'So let's review,' Nicola said. 'First, Vanessa invites the demon in. It will be unable to resist the invitation.'

That much, Vanessa thought, would certainly be true.

'Second, just when it's about to possess her,' Nicola went on, 'Vanessa blocks it out so that it can no longer sense her.' She gave Vanessa an appraising look. 'Can you do that? Block it out?'

She flashed on her lesson in the cemetery with Zep, thought about how badly she wanted to see Margaret, how she needed to get rid of the demon. 'Yes,' she said. 'I can.'

'Great,' Nicholas said. 'Which brings us to the third bit. The demon can't sense Vanessa, but it *will* sense a touch of her essence inside the lamp, so it will mistake the lamp for her body. It won't know that the lamp is chained with enchantments, ones we will have cast on it using the spells from the *Ars Demonica.*'

'And once it's there, it's trapped,' Nicola said. 'Step four, we destroy the lamp. Done and done.'

The wind filled the silence around them.

'Great,' said Justin sarcastically, 'so all Vanessa has to do is figure out how to block a demon from another dimension from entering her mind and convince it to go into a silver lamp instead.' He let out an angry snort. 'Really great plan.'

While they argued, Vanessa closed her eyes and concentrated on the directions Zep had given her: the talisman, the memory, the blocking of her mind.

'I can block the demon out,' she said again. 'If you two think this plan will work, then I'm all for giving it a go.'

'And if it doesn't work?' Justin said, raising his voice. 'Then the demon will just move right into your head, Vanessa, and we'll have to kill you.'

Nicholas waved his hand in the air. 'That won't happen,' he insisted. 'You've got to trust us.'

Vanessa opened her eyes. 'I do,' she said, just as Justin blurted out, 'I don't.'

'It's my life,' Vanessa said. 'My choice. And I've made it.'

'Good,' Nicola said, before Justin could get another word in. 'Let's leave it at that.'

'Meeting adjourned,' Nicholas said.

'Why did you have us meet you here, anyway?' Justin said. 'Out in the middle of this stupid bridge?'

Nicholas gestured around them. 'We thought it would be more private; we can see anyone coming our way long before they get to us.'

'But also,' Nicola said, pointing to a lit-up building at the other end, 'we're going to an exhibit at the Tate Modern. It's open until ten tonight.'

'We'll call you when we're ready,' Nicholas said, 'but in the meantime, you need to get some sleep. Big competition tomorrow. You don't want to be late.'

Vanessa's stomach sank. The competition. Maybe she could get up early tomorrow morning and squeeze in an extra rehearsal.

All Vanessa remembered about the trip back was that it felt like the longest car ride she'd ever taken. Zep's words were still burned into her mind: Margaret was dead. She had killed herself. And though Vanessa was certain he was wrong, she had no justification for feeling this way.

Meanwhile, Justin quietly seethed on the seat beside her, saying nothing. Vanessa missed Justin, missed having him as a friend, and she ached to tell him everything – especially that she was sorry. She imagined an alternate reality in which Margaret had never disappeared, and Vanessa had met Justin on a brisk autumm day in New York. In that life, they might've bantered and laughed nervously the way people do when they first realise they've met someone special. He'd ask if she'd want to get a cup of coffee, and she'd say yes.

But they weren't living that life. They were living this one.

When the cab finally pulled over beneath the tree-lined drive leading to their dormitory, Vanessa ran inside, blurring down the hallway to get away from Justin.

She paused outside the door to her room, bracing herself to hear a sarcastic comment from Svetya about why Vanessa wasn't rehearsing for tomorrow. But when she entered her room, Svetya wasn't there.

Instead, facing her from her desk chair, was Enzo.

'About time you got back,' he said. 'We need to talk.'

CHAPTER EIGHTEEN

'Sit,' Enzo said.

Vanessa didn't move.

'Vanessa, sit down,' Enzo repeated. He was perched casually on her desk chair, as if it weren't completely bizarre that he'd basically broken into her room.

'What are you doing in here?' she asked. She took off her jacket and sat down on the edge of her bed. 'Where's Svetya?'

'She and Geo are using the rehearsal space downstairs,' Enzo said. 'She let me in after I told her I needed to speak to you.'

Because he was their coach, it was easy to forget that Enzo wasn't all that much older than Vanessa, maybe twenty-one. His long hair was pulled back, as usual, and he was wearing jeans and a black sweater. He seemed to draw the light towards him with an air of authority that was both magnetic and frightening.

'I'm not even going to ask where you were,' Enzo said to her, 'even though you clearly left the lodge against my specific orders.'

'Orders? You don't give me orders. You *suggested* to me –'

'It doesn't matter, Vanessa,' he said, leaning back. 'That's not why I'm here.'

'So why *are* you here?'

Enzo's eyelashes fluttered. 'I haven't been completely honest with you, Vanessa.' He took a deep breath, as though forcing himself to continue. 'I knew your sister.'

'*Knew?*' Vanessa echoed. Another person who thought Margaret was dead? 'What does that mean?'

Enzo looked down at his hands. 'I helped her get away from Josef and create a new identity under the name Margot Adams.'

'You helped her get away from Josef. That's great!' She stood up again, wanting to throw her arms around him and thank him, waiting for him to tell her that Margaret was outside, about to come through the door.

'Please sit down, Vanessa,' Enzo said quietly. Once she was back on the bed he continued, 'The reason I didn't tell you this before now is that I . . . is because she . . .' He paused, and Vanessa got the strong impression that he was on the verge of tears. 'She died. I tried to stop her, but I failed.' He covered his face with his hands for a minute. 'I wasn't able to save her. She's gone, Vanessa.'

'No. She isn't.' Vanessa shook her head. She didn't believe Zep, and now she didn't believe Enzo. Her sister was alive. She had to be.

'There was a girl named Margot,' Vanessa went on, not caring that she was practically shouting. 'She died years ago in a car accident, and that's whose name Margaret took.'

'Who do you think gave Margaret that name?' Enzo said. 'I was Erik Adams. Margot was my sister.' He stood up and took something out of his pocket – a notebook. 'A friend of mine named Hal and I brought Margaret here, to London. We got her involved with the Royal Court, and after she won the competition, she killed herself.' He held out the book. 'This is Margaret's diary. I found it after– afterwards.'

'*No.*' Margaret had left a message for Vanessa, using her pointe shoes, Vanessa thought. She'd probably hidden her belongings in the tomb when she took on a new life. Margaret had to be alive.

'I'm sorry, Vanessa, but it's true.'

'You're wrong,' Vanessa said. 'My sister wouldn't kill herself.'

'It was the dark dancers in the Royal Court,' Enzo said. 'It turned out she hadn't escaped Josef at all. All that time I thought I was helping her, but I just delivered her into their hands. And it was that group who drove her to suicide.'

Vanessa couldn't stop trembling. 'I don't believe you. She's not dead.'

Enzo frowned. 'She threw herself off the pedestrian walkway of Tower Bridge into the Thames late one night. Her body was never recovered, but multiple witnesses saw her jump.'

Vanessa watched as Enzo gently opened the diary and flipped to the final entry. 'Her diary was open on her desk,' he said. 'I found it that night.'

At the sight of her sister's handwriting, Vanessa had to blink away tears so that she could read the entry.

May 21

It is all too much.

The world of dance is forever closed to me. I had hoped that in London I would be able to escape, but they are everywhere, Erik swears, and he says the only way to beat them is to join them. The thing I love most in life, hopelessly perverted? No.

I'm already living one lie. New name, new identity. Unable to be with my family, and now unable even to dance. What kind of life can I have? Maybe I'll be happier in the afterlife.

After all, no one really knows who I am any more.

I am truly sorry, Erik. I did love you.

– M

Vanessa felt sick, dizzy. She shook her head and flipped through the journal. 'Why are there pages missing?'

'Probably she was tidying up, ripping out pages that might upset people.' Without saying anything, Enzo tugged at a thin silver chain around his neck. Vanessa had noticed it before but never thought much of it. Now she realised there was something hanging from it. A ring.

Enzo unclasped the necklace and carefully handed it to Vanessa. The metal chain pooled into her palm, and she immediately recognised the ring – a silver band that had once belonged to their great-grandmother. On the inside of the band were the initials *MA* – their parents had had the ring engraved for Margaret on her thirteenth birthday.

'I'm so sorry, Vanessa,' Enzo said, his voice faltering. 'I'm sure she would want you to have this.'

Vanessa stared at the ring. *No*, she thought. *It can't be true*. Margaret wouldn't have taken her own life, not without reaching out to her for help first. Right?

Her throat felt dry, and her eyes began to water. Was she simply denying the truth? Was Margaret actually gone? Had Zep been right – and now Enzo? Maybe the message she'd gleaned from her pointe shoes hadn't been from Margaret at all; maybe the demon had already begun working on her back at NYBA.

Maybe it was true, and Margaret wasn't out there waiting to be found.

Vanessa's fingers closed over the ring. Her entire body felt numb. 'Why . . . ? Why didn't you tell me this when we first met?'

'I was waiting for the right time,' he said slowly.

'*This* is the right time?' She wiped away tears and tried to steady her breathing. It was nearly 10 p.m. 'With the final day of the competition tomorrow morning? Yes, Enzo – or *Erik*? Or whoever you are? Perfect timing.'

'I loved her too,' Enzo said. 'Not in the same way you did, but I miss her every day. And this is our chance.'

'What do you mean, *"our* chance"?' Vanessa asked, her voice faltering. 'If Margaret is dead, then it's all for nothing. I'm going home tomorrow.'

'*No,*' Enzo said, his eyes suddenly bright. 'That's exactly what you shouldn't do. You can win tomorrow. You can gain a spot in the Royal Court and find out who these dark dancers truly are. And together we can take them down from the inside. Margaret won't have died for nothing,' he said desperately. 'You and I both loved her. Don't you understand?'

Suddenly Vanessa *did* understand. She could almost see Enzo's hand against the small of Margaret's back, his lips pressing against hers under the hazy lights of a dance studio. She didn't know what had happened to her sister, or who to believe, but there was – as hard as it was to admit it – a chance that her sister was truly gone.

Tomorrow Vanessa would dance better than she ever had before. She would channel all her sadness and anger, her confusion and frustration, and perform as if her own life depended on it.

That's what Margaret would have wanted.

'You're right,' she said at last. 'Someone has to stop them. It should be me.'

Enzo reached out and squeezed her shoulder, then stood up. 'Svetya will be back any moment,' he said. 'I think it would be best if you keep what I've told you to yourself.'

Vanessa stared down at her hands, clutching the diary and the ring, then looked up at Enzo, paused in the doorway. 'Dance for Margaret,' he said. And then he was gone.

The girls' floor was empty by the time Vanessa left her room the next morning, since most of the dancers had been eliminated by now. Svetya had given her a curt nod before rushing off. Vanessa understood – her roommate viewed her as competition, always had.

Margaret's gone, Vanessa thought as she headed downstairs. She'd had a restless night's sleep, unable to get Margaret's last diary entry out of her mind: *What kind of life can I have? . . . After all, no one truly knows who I am any more.* Margaret must have felt so alone, so scared – not totally unlike how Vanessa felt now, with the demon out there, hunting her. What kind of life could she have if it was still in this world, if it always wanted her?

The answer was clear: if she wanted to have any sort of future, she needed to get rid of the demon – once and for all. She'd do it for herself, but also for her sister. Enzo was right.

Only five other girls were left: Svetya, Maisie, Ingrid, Pauline and Evelyn. All of them were incredibly talented. Vanessa would have to dance perfectly if she wanted to win – there was no room for error.

As she pushed open the door that led backstage, she looked out and saw that the house was completely full.

'We will now begin our final round, the contemporary solo,' she heard Palmer Carmichael announce to the audience. 'The twelve remaining dancers will each perform a routine set to the music of a contemporary composer of their choice. We will be judging creativity and innovation, as well as technical execution and grace.'

He paused. 'The first dancer to perform will be Justin Cooke.'

Vanessa ran down the corridor, pushing through the dancers warming up in the dressing room.

Svetya was over by the wall in a deep hamstring stretch. 'You are still here?' she said. 'I thought you quit.'

Geo called out from beside her. 'Stop trying to psych her out, Svetya.' He looked at Vanessa and blinked. 'Happy last day! Are you ready?'

Vanessa nodded. 'As ready as I'll ever be.' She rushed up to Geo and gave him a quick hug. 'You'll be fantastic,' she whispered.

'So will you,' he whispered back. He winked at her and continued stretching.

Vanessa pushed forward past Maisie and her eager gaze, past Ingrid and a British teammate who'd been eliminated in the second round.

'Vanessa!' Pauline called out. She was standing still as one of the stage managers zipped up the back of her costume, a gorgeous lavender tutu and a white leotard embedded with crystals.

Vanessa gave Pauline a quick peck on the cheek just as the lights dimmed and the music for Justin's solo began. She found a spot in the wings and looked out on to the stage.

The melancholy notes of a piano filled the performance hall. Justin lowered his head to his chest and waited as the chords repeated. His costume – navy-blue tights and a form-fitting white long-sleeved top – accented his sculpted torso perfectly. With each beat he lifted his head an inch, as if someone were winding him up, controlling him from behind.

Vanessa knew this music from an album her father some-times listened to: Philip Glass's *Façades*. The cry of a clarinet rose over the piano, shrill and haunting, like a voice screaming in the night. Justin's body jolted to life.

The music pushed him across the stage. As the notes of the piano multiplied, like dozens of chanting voices, Justin's pace quickened, the music whipping his body into a state of barely controlled rage.

The music seemed to pulse through Justin. His anger was palpable, his feet thudding loudly against the floor, his fury spilling out of him and permeating every inch of the theatre. Usually so careful, so controlled, Justin was dancing with a fierce strength, a fearlessness that she'd never seen him display before.

Every time he spotted during a *piqué*, his eyes met Vanes-sa's. Every time the clarinet screamed through the speakers, he seemed to extend his arms towards her, as if pointing out her fate for everyone to see.

'Poor girl,' a voice whispered in her ear.

Vanessa didn't need to turn around to know who it was. She recognised the sharp velvety scent of Ingrid's perfume.

'If only you knew what was coming for you,' Ingrid said, her voice deep and syrupy. 'You're going to lose. Or maybe worse . . . Who knows how this dance will end?'

'You're right,' Vanessa said, annoyed. 'No one knows how this will end.' Her fate wasn't already written down some-where – it was under her control. 'Oh, and Ingrid?'

The girl raised an eyebrow. 'Yes?'

'Stop being such a bitch. It's not a good look for you.'

Ingrid's mouth twisted into a scowl. She was about to respond when a bookish-looking girl dressed all in black pushed her way up to Vanessa. 'Vanessa Adler,' she said, 'there you are.'

Vanessa recognised the girl, who was holding a clipboard, as one of the stage managers. 'Yes?'

'You're up in two, after Maisie Teller,' the girl told her.

On the other side of the curtain, Justin's music faded, and thunderous applause filled the theatre. Justin pushed through the curtains, his forehead glistening with sweat. The other dancers surrounded him, Geo slapping him on the back in congratulations.

As Svetya walked onstage, Vanessa slipped on her pointe shoes. She was already wearing her costume, an ivory tutu with a waterfall of coloured rhinestones embedded in the bod-ice. She wrapped the ribbons around her ankles, knotting them in a tight bow. And doing away with convention, she held up a small pocket mirror and unpinned her hair from its chignon, letting it fall loose in red waves.

Svetya stood at centre stage. The bewitching notes of a cello electrified the room. Her eyes snapped open, as if the music had awakened her, and she crept across the stage, her legs long and feline. The sudden bursts of the cello lured her forward, each scratch of the bow sending her into an unexpected spin.

'Shostakovich's First Cello Concerto,' someone said over Vanessa's shoulder. Geo stood behind her, his muscular legs bulging through his nude tights. 'Svetya thinks he is one of the best composers of all time.' He laughed. 'I don't agree. He is good, yes, but a bit too forceful for my taste.'

Vanessa laughed. 'No wonder Svetya likes him so much.'

Geo gave her a vague smile. 'It does capture her spirit, right?'

Justin approached and watched Svetya dance. 'You can take her,' he said to Vanessa.

She was surprised he was even talking to her. 'Thanks,' she mumbled. She couldn't shake the image of Justin dancing onstage, his body swelling with anger as if he were being taken over by a demon. 'You were really amazing.'

'Yes,' Geo agreed. He ran his hands through his orange hair and sighed. 'Stiff competition for me.' He shook his legs out, stretching gently.

There were so many things that Vanessa wanted to tell Justin – about Zep and the cemetery, about Enzo and Margaret, the final diary entry . . . But maybe it was better this way, if he didn't know. He'd only try to stop her from doing what she had to do. How could she explain that rejecting him was a sign of how much she cared for him? Her future had already been decided. Justin's wasn't – and if he faced the demon with her, she might lose him too. That was the problem with loving people: when they were gone, it hurt all the more.

Vanessa tried to go over her own music in her head as Svetya danced. From what she could tell, her roommate was doing a phenomenal job.

The audience erupted in applause, and Vanessa watched Svetya take a low curtsy, knowing her turn was coming soon. She only had to block the demon for a few minutes. It didn't seem so daunting when she thought about it that way. She would dance on her own terms. With no help.

While Vanessa looked on, Maisie took the stage in a pale yellow leotard and skirt reminiscent of the American prairie. Her music matched her dress: the joyful burst of a fiddle, calling out like a rooster at dawn.

Vanessa recognised the piece immediately: Aaron Copland's *Rodeo*. It brightened the room, transforming the stage into a cornfield and the creamy wall beyond into an endless stretch of sky. Maisie soaked up the music, her steps light and capricious, her body brimming with hope. And then the music fell quiet, and Maisie slowed, twirling languidly across the stage like a cloud of dust billowing over an endless parched field.

Vanessa wasn't the only one stunned by Maisie's performance. Ingrid's gaze was fixed on the girl; she even gripped the curtain as Maisie landed her final leap and loud applause filled the theatre. Ingrid pressed herself back into the shadows as Maisie skipped off the stage, a delirious grin on her face.

'Gosh, that was fun!' Maisie said brightly. 'Good luck, Vanessa!'

And then Palmer Carmichael's voice boomed over the theatre: 'Vanessa Adler.'

OK, Vanessa thought. She took a deep breath and stepped on to the stage. *It's now or never.*

TWO AND A HALF
YEARS EARLIER

From the Diary of Margaret Adler
May 20

It's over. And I've won.

I wish I could feel happy about it, but I only feel sick in my heart.

My performance was fine, I'm sure, but I thought it was mechanical. I cannot believe I won, cannot believe that I was truly the best dancer. I am certain that one girl from the Royal Ballet was stronger.

And yet I was the one given the scholarship. Strange.

'It's official now!' Becky Darlington said again and again, smiling so hard I thought her teeth would pop out of her mouth. I wonder if she is one of them. I wonder if all *of them* are *in on it,*

twisted acolytes of some dark, evil religion. And, if Erik is to be believed, killers.

After the winners were declared, they made me and my male counterpart – Brendan Shaughnessy, from Canada – sit for a portrait with the entire company. As soon as it was over, I ran to the bathroom and threw up.

When I came out of the bathroom, all the members of the corps were there. As each one kissed the air around my head and said nice things, all I could think was, Are you one of them?

It was unbearable.

Erik, Hal and I are off to have another stupid celebratory dinner, just the three of us. Maybe afterwards I'll know what to do.

Dinner was strained. Of course Erik went on about my grace and elegance and blah blah – shameless flattery. He still thinks I love him and am going to be his puppet, helping him destroy the evil dancers in the Royal Court.

The night before my final performance, we'd had it out. We were in a practice room going over my routine one last time, just walking through it and talking about possible pitfalls. 'This rest in the music will be the only place you can take a full breath for several measures, Margot. Be sure to use it.'

'My name is Margaret,' I blurted. 'Margot Adams was your *sister.'*

He stared at me silently for a few seconds. 'So Hal told you that.'

I nodded. Erik sat down, his back against the wall. 'They killed my family, Margaret. And they meant to kill me as well.'

'Who?' I asked, even though I knew the answer.

'The necrodancers, as they're sometimes called. My family has been dancing for generations. There was a time when we were like royalty in the dance world. And my mother had all the makings of one of the greats. She joined the Royal Court as a teenager, after winning the competition.

'Over the years, the dark faction tried to recruit her many times. She wouldn't join them, and at last she promised to expose them, so they arranged an accident. Everyone was in the car but me. In one night I lost my mother, father, brother and sister.'

'That's horrible. I'm sorry,' I said, but he shook his head. 'How do you know the dark dancers were behind it?'

'The accident was suspicious,' Erik said. 'The fire that destroyed the car burned hotter than a mere gasoline fire – three thousand degrees at one point. They were incinerated, Margaret. There wasn't anything left to identify.

'Afterwards, when I was dumb with grief and staying with relatives – I was only ten, mind you – someone broke into my family's house and ransacked it. The police said it was simple theft, and it's true, valuables were stolen. But thieves would not have taken all the paper records to do with the Royal Court. No, whoever robbed my family's house was after very specific things.'

The room seemed to close in around me, the walls shrinking, as I understood what Erik's plan had been all along. 'You always knew there were necrodancers in the Royal Court. So I'm . . . bait.'

'No, no – I mean, yes, you're an especially enticing prospect for them, but that wouldn't matter if you weren't the exquisite dancer that you are. When you win – and you will win – you'll be right in their midst. You can find out who they are, and the two of us can make them pay for what they've done.'

I searched his words for some hint of the boy I had fallen in love with, but the Erik standing in front of me now was a stranger. Had it all been a lie?

'I don't want to be your tool of revenge,' I said. 'I want to dance. That's all I've ever wanted to do. I don't want to be Josef's doll, and I don't want to be part of your vengeance. I'm sorry, but I can't do this.'

'You have to, Margaret. If you love me, you won't say no to me.'

I backed away, horrified, not just at Erik, but at myself. Who was this person? Every touch, every kiss – it had all been part of Erik's plan. I had let myself fall in love with a façade. The boy that I loved had never been real.

'I'm sorry if I deceived you,' Erik said, standing up. 'I just didn't know how to tell you. Get some rest tonight. I know you're going to win.' He smiled. 'I'm counting on you. And I love you.'

I should have walked out, diary. I should have run away or called for help or done anything but go out on to that stage and dance.

But where would I go? Except for Erik and Hal, I don't know anyone in England. I don't even have my own identity. At least for today, I am Margot Adams.

Even if I didn't do everything Erik wanted me to, I reckoned I could at least try to win for that dead girl whose name I was using. That would have to be motivation enough.

I'd figure out what to do afterwards.

But now it is *afterwards. I won, and at dinner I sat and let Erik praise me – and let him think, after all, that I would be his puppet. It's midnight, and Hal and Erik are asleep across our attic room. I wish I could call Vanessa. She would listen to me and remind me that no matter how hopeless things may seem, there is more to life than just ballet.*

I think I know what to do, but I'm going to need help.

CHAPTER NINETEEN

The stage was illuminated by a single spotlight.

The theatre was silent, the audience nothing more than a sea of black. The three judges scrutinised her from the front row. Becky Darlington crossed her legs and jotted something down on a notepad.

Vanessa took her place in first position. She hadn't had another chance last night to rehearse her solo, but it didn't matter; she knew the moves by heart.

Vanessa dropped her arms to her sides as the buttery trill of a clarinet drifted over the speakers, enveloping the theatre in the first notes of Gershwin's *Rhapsody in Blue*, warm and lazy like a Sunday morning.

The spotlight spilled down like sun filtering through a window. Vanessa lifted herself on to her toes, stretching her arms wide, her body arching back in a deep yawn.

She twirled across the stage, her steps quick and delicate, the piano fluttering like the patter of footsteps. She skidded to a stop, the horns pushing her back, forcing her in the opposite direction. So far, so good.

And then a hiss of dry heat blew over the stage. It was here. She could feel the demon close by, its warmth seeping into her skin, making her head throb. It was more overpowering than she remembered.

She strained her mind, trying to focus, to find a memory of her sister, but she couldn't. The force within her pushed back, twisting, reaching deeper inside her. She wasn't strong enough.

Do not fight me, Vanessa, she heard it say. *Embrace me. Together we can win.*

Vanessa took a breath, steadying herself. The raspy heat coiled through her, making her sweat. The piano on the sound-track seemed louder than normal, filling her ears and making it impossible to concentrate. She willed her limbs still, then bent forward in a deep bow and saw the pink satin tops of her ballet slippers, exactly like her sister's.

Margaret.

She thought about everything her sister had been through – all because of necrodancers and demons. She felt rage boil up inside her.

Slowly Vanessa raised her head, moving into a deep *port de bras*. *Think of Margaret's shoes and nothing else*, she told herself. She dragged her feet across the floor, tracing her sister's name as they wove in and out of each other. The abridged version of *Rhapsody* that she was dancing to seemed to burst out of the speakers, the orchestra bathing her in a cacophony of sounds. Her body felt as if it was being gripped in a vice, but she fought – fought as hard as she could as the music played and she whirled across the stage.

Margaret's shoes, that memory – they were her talisman. That's what Zep had taught her. She jumped into the air, her feet switching position in a *changement* as the tempo of the accompaniment changed. Vanessa struggled to recapture the memory she'd recalled in the cemetery last night, when Margaret had got her new ballet shoes for NYBA: *These are going to be my favourite shoes, Ness . . .*

Images of her sister flashed before her: Margaret's smile. Her hair. The smell of her perfume and the sheen of her lip-gloss. They came and went in seconds; trying to hold on to them felt like grasping for water.

Let me in, Vanessa, the demon said, its voice harsher, almost desperate. *Now.*

Vanessa shook her head, lifting her arms and rushing across the stage in quick steps. *Focus*, she thought. *Margaret's shoes.*

The *couru* section of her solo was here; swiftly she brought her back leg forward and poured herself into a *pas de basque*, then twirled into a *sauté* mid-air. All she could see was Margaret's ballet slippers; it was almost as if her sister was right there with her. She focused on images of the ribbons, the fresh satin, the square toe box. She felt the demon's heat begin to dissipate, and she was able to unclench her jaw and let her limbs relax. Zep had been right – picturing the shoes filled her mind's eye completely. There was no room for the demon.

She felt its grasp waver. *Vanessssssa, my love . . .*

The air around her cooled just enough for her to take a sharp, deep breath. The loneliness of the years since Margaret's disappearance seeped into her, and the warped notes crackled and faded until the only sound that filled her was the nostalgic lilt of Gershwin's piano.

The music swelled, the orchestra crescendoing and then a quick diminuendo, leaving only the sounds of a piano, softer and softer until there was only a trickle of sound, and then: silence.

Vanessa opened her eyes.

The room was quiet, the faces of the judges and the people in the audience motionless, as if caught in time; the only sound was her breathing. In the wings, Justin stood frozen, as if something had surprised him. Between them, dust glimmered in the beam of the spotlight, suspended in the air like specks of gold.

And then – a crashing of sound as the room exploded with applause. She planted her feet in third position and raised her arms.

Vanessa's temples were damp with sweat. She had blocked out the demon and finished the dance without his help. She gazed out into the audience, the dazzle of lights and camera flashes making the entire theatre glitter. And sliding one foot behind her, she lowered herself into a deep curtsy, her eyes lingering on her sister's shoes.

'For you, Margaret,' she whispered, lifting her head and listening to the applause.

The clock ticked above the open doors of the dressing rooms.

Vanessa sat cross-legged on the floor, her hair still loose around her face. Justin sat on the bench a few feet away, taking nervous swigs from his water bottle. She couldn't tell if he'd watched her performance or not.

The rest of the dancers were scattered on either side, Geo leaning against the wall next to two boys from the Paris Opera Ballet Academy, his head bowed in his hands. He had performed a quiet but elegant dance to Rachmaninoff's *Danse Orientale*. An olive-skinned boy paced in front of him, muttering to himself in Italian, while a Chilean boy shushed him. Pauline had performed beautifully, almost ethereally, to a solo from Prokofiev's *Romeo and Juliet*.

Ingrid whispered to a teammate, glancing at Vanessa every so often with daggers in her eyes. Nearby, Maisie sat quietly on the floor, bandaging a blister on her heel. The clock kept ticking like a communal pulse.

Through the curtains, Vanessa could hear the loud chatter of the audience, could swear she could even make out her mother's voice. Standing, she made her way to the girls' dressing room, but when she entered, she realised she wasn't alone.

Svetya stood by the mirror, blotting her lipstick with a tissue. 'What are you looking at?'

'Nothing,' Vanessa said, startled. 'I just . . . nothing.'

'You know,' Svetya said, 'whoever wins – and it will be me, most likely, but anyway – it's been nice getting to know you.'

Vanessa was completely taken aback. Svetya liked her? 'Um, you too.'

Just then, one of the stage managers poked her head inside. 'Dancers, they're ready for you.'

Vanessa and Svetya joined the other ten dancers on the stage.

The audience grew quiet, the last stragglers scampering down the aisles to find their seats. The three judges sat in the front row, Palmer Carmichael gesturing while he whispered to the others, as if they were still arguing about the rankings.

Becky Darlington stood up, holding a clipboard. Carmichael rubbed his hand over the smooth crown of his head, then stood with her. Finally Apollinaria Marie joined them, her long legs unfolding like a gazelle's.

'We would like to thank you all for your beautiful performances,' Palmer Carmichael said, his eyes travelling over the dancers. 'If we could take each and every one of you, we would. Since that is not possible, we would like to announce the winners, starting with third place.' He turned to his left. 'Becky, if you will.'

A hush fell over the theatre.

Becky gripped her clipboard. 'In third place for the women . . .' she looked up at the crowd, 'Svetlana Chernovski.'

Svetya's face went blank when she heard her name.

'Svetlana?' Becky said, smiling. 'Congratulations.'

Reluctantly Svetya inched forward, glaring into the photographers' flashes.

'And in third place for the men, Geoffrey Scott Alexander.'

Geo shot Vanessa a miserable look, then stepped forward beside Svetya, forcing a smile.

'In second place for the women,' Becky continued, 'Vanessa Adler.'

Vanessa felt her heart plummet as she came forward, forcing herself to smile. She'd failed. She hadn't won a spot in the Royal Court. She wasn't going to be able to avenge Margaret.

'And in second place for the men, Jacques Lecole.'

Pauline's partner from the Paris Opera Ballet Academy stepped forward proudly, flashing a million-dollar grin at the cameras.

'And finally, our first place winners and Royal Court scholarship recipients . . .' Becky said, her voice tinged with excitement.

Behind Vanessa, the other girls held their breath. Vanessa closed her eyes.

'In first place for the girls, I would like to introduce . . . Pauline Maillard.'

Vanessa felt herself clapping instinctively, but all she could think of was that she had let her sister down. She'd never find the people who drove Margaret to her death. And she had let herself down. She felt tears on her face and knew people would think she was crying about coming in second, but she didn't care.

'And in first place for the men, I would like to introduce . . . Justin Cooke.'

Vanessa was so stunned she could barely believe she had heard correctly. *Justin* had won?

Becky cleared her throat. 'Could you both step forward, please?'

Justin stepped out of line, then reached for Pauline's hand, pulling her towards the front of the stage. For an instant he smiled at Vanessa – wistfully, she thought. She had spent so long thinking about what she would do once she won, that she had never once considered the possibility that Justin might win instead.

'I would like to formally welcome you both to the Royal Court Company,' Palmer Carmichael said. 'I am sure you will both be invaluable assets to our company and to the art of ballet.'

Palmer turned to the audience. 'I would also like to thank all of the dancers who participated in the earlier rounds. There will be a ceremony tomorrow evening, and all of our competitors are invited. I hope you, your coaches and your families will join us.' He clasped his hands together. 'But tonight, you are free to celebrate. You're all winners to us.'

Apollinaria bowed her head. 'We all know that dance is an ongoing competition. I look forward to seeing each of you on the stage in future.'

Justin led Pauline into a low bow, camera flashes flickering as the audience erupted in applause. Behind them, the other winners followed suit. Vanessa scanned the theatre for Enzo, but there was no sign of him.

As they filed off the stage, Svetya turned to Vanessa and said, 'I did not see that coming at all. And I have twenty-twenty vision.'

Vanessa was about to respond when Ingrid pushed past, knocking Vanessa's shoulder as she stormed into the dressing room. She turned back, glaring at Vanessa with an expression so cold it was frightening. She hadn't even placed.

'Vanessa!' Maisie said. She pushed through the other dancers and ran towards her, a wad of tissues in one hand, a bouquet of flowers in the other. 'I just wanted to congratulate you.' Her eyes were red and swollen from crying. 'You almost won the whole thing.'

'Thanks, Maisie,' Vanessa told her. Nobody liked sore losers. 'I thought you were amazing. You should be so proud.'

'Really?' Maisie said. 'Thanks. That means a lot coming from you.'

Maisie gazed down at the flowers in her arms. Their pale yellow matched the colour of her hair. 'I bought these to motivate myself, but I guess they should go to you.' With a nervous laugh, she held them out to Vanessa.

'No,' Vanessa said. 'You don't have to do that.'

'I want to,' Maisie insisted, and thrust the bouquet into her arms. 'Take them. I can't bear the sight of them any more.'

Maisie backed into the crowd, covering her face as she slipped through the door to the dressing room. Vanessa gazed down at the flowers, then followed her inside. She could hear her sobbing from the bathroom stall, her voice echoing off the stone walls. Vanessa sighed and left the bouquet by Maisie's locker, then changed out of her costume.

Backstage was bustling with parents and dancers and coaches when she emerged. 'Darling!' called her mother, who was standing on tiptoe and waving. She scooped Vanessa into a hug. 'You were wonderful!'

Vanessa wrapped her arms around her mother. 'But I lost,' she said. *I lost Margaret.*

'You were robbed,' her mother said, stepping back. 'But it's not all about winning, dear. It's about doing the best you can do. And really, you were marvellous.' She lowered her voice and whispered into Vanessa's ear. 'Besides, I hear that Pauline's father donates *beaucoup* to the Royal Court.'

Vanessa had to laugh. Leave it to her mother to comfort her while spreading gossip at the same time.

'And Justin, winning the whole thing!' Her mother pulled back and smiled. 'You must be very proud of him.' She paused, peering into the crowd. 'Where *is* he?'

Vanessa turned around: a flurry of people surrounded Justin and Pauline, including several reporters. She *was* genuinely proud of him, even though she was disappointed she hadn't won herself. He caught her gaze and excused himself.

'Vanessa,' he said. 'Hey.'

'Congratulations,' she told him. 'You were wonderful.'

He blushed. 'Thanks. So were you.'

'You watched?' she asked.

'Are you kidding? I wouldn't miss your dancing for the world.'

Vanessa felt herself blush. 'Where's Enzo?' she said, scanning the area. 'It's weird that he's not here to congratulate you. I'm sure he's thrilled you won.'

'Maybe,' Justin said.

'Of course he is! You're a Royal Court scholarship recipient.' She forced a smile.

'I know you're disappointed,' Justin said softly. 'But, please, Vanessa – don't do anything rash.'

'Rash? What do you mean?'

He looked around and lowered his voice. 'Don't go through with the Fratellis' plan. Your performance was . . . mesmerising, but how much of that was you? And how much was *it*?'

'It was all me,' Vanessa said. 'I said I would shut it out, and I did. Zep was right.'

Justin's face darkened. 'What do you mean, *Zep* was right?'

'Justin, there you are.' Palmer Carmichael placed a hand on Justin's shoulder, interrupting their conversation. 'There's a reporter from *The Times* who wants a picture of you and Pauline.' He noticed Vanessa and nodded. 'Congratulations, Ms Adler. You danced beautifully. You made our final decision a very difficult one.'

'Thank you,' Vanessa said.

'Vanessa,' Justin started to say, 'please –'

But Carmichael whisked him away before he could finish. Which was fine by her.

'Mom,' Vanessa said, walking back over to her mother, who was on the phone, 'I'm going to find Enzo and thank him for all his help.'

'All right, dear,' her mother said, covering the mouthpiece with her hand. 'I'll call you in a little while, and we can go out for dinner. Our last girls' night before your father arrives in the morning.'

'Absolutely,' Vanessa said, kissing her mother's cheek. 'Sounds great.'

She turned on her heels, leaving the backstage area. Only instead of going to her dormitory, she headed straight for the coaches' residence.

CHAPTER TWENTY

The lawn behind the White Lodge was bustling with people. Vanessa kept her head down and walked quickly. Under different circumstances, she might have been proud of her runner-up status. She was only fifteen, and she'd nearly won one of the most competitive ballet competitions in Europe, if not the world.

But none of that mattered. She'd lost everything: the scholarship, a spot in the Royal Court and the possibility of finding the people who'd driven Margaret into taking her own life. She'd even lost Justin, she thought. He'd be here for the next two years, while she'd be back in New York. She tried to convince herself that it was for the best – after all, they hadn't exactly been getting along these past few days – but the thought only made her feel lonely.

Behind the White Lodge was another, smaller, more modern building – the faculty residence. In a moment she was in the foyer, reading the room assignment directory.

She climbed the stairs to the second floor. It was no surprise to find that the coaches' dorm was nicer than the students', the walls filled with framed black-and-white pictures of various ballets the Royal Court had staged over the years.

Vanessa walked down the quiet hallway, her footsteps muffled by the plush beige runner, until she reached room 202 at the end of the hall.

She knocked gently. 'Enzo?'

No answer. Vanessa knocked again. 'Enzo? Hello?' She rapped on the door again, harder this time, then tried the doorknob.

It turned easily and the door swung open.

'Enzo?' She had no idea what she was expecting his room to look like, but it was surprisingly bare. A bed with a white duvet, still rumpled from the previous night; a small suitcase in the corner; and in the open closet, a few clothes on wire hangers. Piled in a corner on the floor were a bunch of dirty leotards, T-shirts and tights. The air smelled stale.

Vanessa pushed the door open a bit wider, then stepped inside. Next to the bed was a wooden desk. Vanessa walked towards it; she knew she shouldn't be snooping, but . . . what the heck.

Inside the desk were a few pens, some writing paper and a photograph of her sister.

Margaret's face smiled back at her – her sister looked carefree, happy, resting her head on Enzo's shoulder. Another boy was with them in the picture, with dirty-blond hair and wide, eager eyes. *That must be Hal*, she thought. Below the picture were a few folded papers. Vanessa picked them up and recognised the handwriting immediately: the missing pages from Margaret's journal. Clearly Enzo had torn them out.

Enzo had lied. What had Margaret written that he didn't want her to see? Vanessa pocketed the papers and the photo. She had to get out of here.

She took one more quick look around the room, and her eye caught something pink in the mound of dirty laundry, under one of Enzo's T-shirts. Using her little finger, she moved aside the shirt. What she saw took her breath away.

A pointe shoe.

And not just *any* pointe shoe – Margaret's. She'd know it anywhere. She pushed the T-shirt away completely and saw the other shoe. When they'd gone missing from her room the day she arrived in London, Vanessa had accused Svetya of stealing them. Only the culprit hadn't been Svetya at all.

It had been Enzo.

Or Erik. Who was he, really? Could she trust anything he'd told her?

Vanessa picked up the shoes and slipped them into her dance bag. She was just about to leave when Enzo burst into the room.

'Vanessa,' he said, staring at her strangely. He looked stylish in a simple black suit, white dress shirt and a thin red tie. 'What are you doing here?'

'Oh, um . . . I came looking for you.'

'I'd imagine that's why you're in my room.' He stepped inside, leaving the door open behind him. 'What's going on?'

Vanessa tucked her hands behind her back so Enzo couldn't tell they were shaking. Would he know she'd gone through his things?

'I wanted to say that I'm sorry.'

'Sorry?' Enzo scrunched up his forehead. 'For what?'

'For not winning,' Vanessa said. 'I was dancing for Margaret, like you said I should. And I tried my hardest, really I did –' she thought back to the competition, how much she had wanted to win – 'but I failed. I disappointed us both. I'm sorry.'

Enzo placed a hand on her shoulder. 'There is nothing to apologise for, Vanessa. You danced incredibly well.'

She frowned. 'At least you have Justin.'

'Hmm?' Enzo said. 'What do you mean?'

'He can go undercover for you and the Lyric Elite,' Vanessa said. 'In the Royal Court.'

Enzo nodded. 'Yes. He can – if he wants to. But he hasn't been touched by the dark arts personally, like we have.' He sat down at the desk. 'Vanessa, you may not have won a spot in the Royal Court, but there is still a way you can avenge your sister's death.'

'There is?' Vanessa asked.

'Your connection to the demon is strong,' Enzo said. 'Stronger than anything I've ever seen or even read about. If you call it to you and offer yourself as a host . . .' He looked at her, his eyes wild, unfocused. 'I know it sounds crazy, but if you were its willing consort – or partner, let's say – you would have an otherworldly power at your disposal.' His voice trembled, his hands curling at his sides. He leaned closer. 'You could wreak havoc – stop the evil dancers once and for all.'

Vanessa stepped back. 'I'm not sure I want to do that.'

'Not yet you're not,' Enzo said with a small smile. 'But you'll come around – I just know it. You'll see that this is the best way. You've been given an opportunity no one else has ever had. Aren't you upset about what happened to Margaret?'

'Of course I am.' She had to get out of there. 'I'll have to think about it and get back to you.' Vanessa tried not to let her voice quiver and betray her.

Without speaking, Enzo reached into her dance bag and pulled out one of Margaret's shoes. 'Ah,' he said, 'so I see you found Margaret's pointe shoes.' He sighed. 'Aren't you going to ask why I took them from you?'

Vanessa shook her head. 'Um, no! I mean, I'm sure you had a reason.' She turned and headed for the door. 'I really have to go now, so –'

Suddenly there was a rustle in the air and Enzo was on the other side of her, blocking the door. 'It's just that I miss her so much. When I saw her shoes in your bag, they reminded me of her, and I just – well, I took them without thinking. I'm sorry.'

Vanessa had never thought of Enzo as being particularly large before, but he was quick on his feet and all muscle. There was nothing she could do to him. And if she screamed, no one would hear her.

'Vanessa,' he said, reaching out for her, 'I –'

She didn't stay to hear him finish his sentence. She side-stepped and then leaped into a twirl – blurring through the door and into the hallway. She slammed into the far wall, and turned just long enough to see Enzo, his face a mask of rage.

And then she ran.

Vanessa had never run this fast or for this long in her life.

Adrenalin pumped through her as she sprinted down the long driveway of the White Lodge and across the park to the city streets. She ran without looking, without thinking, until her breath came in painful gasps and she reached a famil-iar building.

Barre None.

She stopped, heaving in gulps of air. A warm glow shone through the frosted windows of the restaurant.

Inside, the dining room was quietly busy, with a few fami-lies and couples cosied up in the corners, sipping drinks and talking softly. The smell of mulled cider warmed the air.

Vanessa's phone buzzed as she spotted Coppelia. The older woman was near the front, sharing a joke with one of the waiters.

See you at the hotel at 8.30, her mom had texted. *So proud.*

When Coppelia saw Vanessa walking towards her, she beamed. 'If it isn't the princess!' Her long hair was in a single braid over one shoulder, and the bangles on her arms clinked together. 'Congratulations, dear. You placed very well in the competition.'

'How did you know?' Vanessa asked.

Coppelia motioned to one of the televisions on the wall. 'It was on the news!'

Vanessa blushed. 'Thanks,' she said. 'But it's not really that exciting. There's not much to tell.'

Coppelia put her hands on her hips. '*Not that exciting?* But OK, no big deal. I get it.'

'It's just . . . I have something more urgent on my mind.' She leaned forward as a waitress walked by. 'Could we find a more private place to talk?'

'Only if I can join you.'

Vanessa swung around to see Justin standing behind her. He'd changed out of his dance clothes and was wearing an emerald-green sweater and tight blue jeans. The sight of him startled her, and for reasons she couldn't explain she suddenly wanted nothing more than to wrap her arms around him. 'Justin, what are you doing here?'

He shrugged. 'I saw you run off – *everyone* did, Vanessa. So I went after you. I'd done enough interviews. They can talk to Pauline for a while.'

'If it isn't King Justin,' Coppelia said with a grin. She swung her braid over her other shoulder and pushed a stack of menus under the bar. 'How about I make you a deal – we can talk privately, if you both promise you'll give me photos with your autographs for my dancer wall.'

Justin chuckled. 'Sounds like a deal.'

Coppelia waved to a booth in the back of the restaurant. A pair of old ballet shoes hung on the light over the table, ribbons dangling.

Vanessa slid over the cracked leather seats next to Justin and gazed up at the pictures that adorned the walls.

'I wonder how many of these dancers were part of the Lyric Elite,' Justin murmured.

'The Lyric Elite?' Coppelia laughed. 'Oh, you kids. The Lyric Elite hasn't existed for decades. It was already ancient history when I was a dancer, and that was . . . Well, let's just say that was a very long time ago.'

Vanessa remembered how Zep had told her in the cemetery about his search for the Lyric Elite, and how he hadn't been able to find or contact any of its dancers. Then she thought of how the Fratellis had been unable to get the Lyric Elite to stop Josef.

'But that makes no sense. We've –' Vanessa cut herself off.

Justin gave her a worried look. 'We've been working with a man named Enzo, who told us he was from the Lyric Elite.'

Coppelia leaned closer, the light illuminating her face. 'Why *wouldn't* he say that?' she said. 'People always try to dress up the bad things they do in a uniform and say it's *for the greater good*. But trust me, the Lyric Elite died with the last of Diaghilev's Ballet Russes.'

She pointed to a daguerreotype hanging high on the wall. A male dancer stood in the centre, wearing an ornate beaded costume, his impish eyes peering out as if he were in on some secret. Vanessa recognised him as Vaslav Nijinsky, one of the most famous dancers of the Ballet Russes, a travelling dance company that had broken off from the Imperial Russian Ballet.

'That was the company that enlisted Stravinsky, wasn't it?' Justin said.

'That's right,' Coppelia said. 'Diaghilev commissioned him to write *The Firebird*.'

'*The Firebird*?' Vanessa blurted out. That was the dance Josef had cast her in to call forth the demon – the same dance he had cast Margaret in three years earlier, not long before she disappeared.

Justin leaned forward. 'So what happened with the Lyric Elite? They were still around during the Ballet Russes. Why not after?'

'Diaghilev inducted many of his young prodigies: Nijinsky, Fokine, Balanchine.' Coppelia fingered her bracelets. 'But then Diaghilev died, and without a strong leader, the Lyric Elite fell apart.'

'And this happened a long time ago?' Justin asked.

'Ancient history!' Coppelia drummed her fingers on the table. 'Dancers shouldn't mess about with dark arts. The magic we do touches our audiences' hearts – isn't that enough?'

Vanessa felt her stomach lurch. If Coppelia was telling the truth, then Enzo had been lying to them from the first moment he'd shown up at NYBA. He wasn't part of the Lyric Elite at all. Somehow he must have got wind of the Fratelli twins' calls for help about Josef. But if that was the case, who was he *really*?

He had known about Margaret all along and had never said a word. Every day that Vanessa had shown up for rehearsal, every time he corrected one of her steps or criticised her form, he had been holding this secret from her.

She thought back to Margaret's diary, Enzo looming over its pages like a dark shadow, and shuddered as she reached into her dance bag and pulled out the diary pages along with the picture of Enzo, Margaret and Hal.

'What's that?' Justin asked.

'A picture of Enzo and my sister and a friend of theirs,' she said. Before he could ask how she got it, she added, 'It's complicated.'

One of the waiters called Coppelia to the bar. She stood up, her skirt swishing about her ankles. 'I can talk more after we close.'

'Right,' Justin said. 'Thanks for your time.'

'Thank *you*,' Coppelia said. 'And remember . . .' She pointed to the wall, reminding them that they owed her their own photographs.

After Coppelia walked away, Vanessa told Justin everything she'd kept to herself over the past few days – about Zep and the empty space in the Adams tomb; how Erik's family had died; Margaret's journal and the missing pages, and how Margaret had ended her life by leaping from the Tower Bridge; how she and Enzo – *Erik* – had been in love.

The rush of words left her breathless, and though Vanessa still felt drained of the hope that dance could somehow bring her sister back, she felt lucky to have Justin by her side.

'I'm so sorry, Vanessa,' Justin said. 'For everything. Poor Margaret.' He unfolded the pages from the diary. 'Have you read these yet?'

Vanessa shook her head.

'Then I guess we should do that. There has to be some reason Enzo or Erik or whatever his name is hid them from you.'

Vanessa took a sip of water and said, 'He wants me to let the demon possess me. To invite it in. He says that's the only way we can have vengeance on the dark faction in the Royal Court.'

'No way are we letting that happen,' Justin said. 'I bet that's been his game plan all along. Clearly he has a history with the darker elements of dance, or he wouldn't know all of those magical steps. Somehow, when the Fratellis reached out for help, Enzo got wind of it and pretended to be a member of the Lyric Elite just to get us to London.' He narrowed his eyes. 'Or really, to get *you* to London. After what happened, he realised you would make the perfect host . . .' Justin shook his head in disbelief. 'He's as bad as Josef.'

Vanessa looked at the photograph. 'He's set on vengeance for Margaret,' she told him, 'or for his family. Maybe both.'

Justin nodded. 'The question is, what are we going to do about it? How are we going to stop him?'

'*We?*' Vanessa asked. 'This is my battle, Justin, not yours. You don't have to –'

'Don't be silly.' He rested his hand on her shoulder. 'I'm with you, Vanessa. Until the end. Whether you want me there or not.'

'Thanks, but –' Her phone vibrated. She saw an earlier text from her mom, something about meeting for dinner at her hotel, and then Nicola Fratelli's name scrolled across the screen.

It's time.

CHAPTER TWENTY-ONE

Battersea Power Station stood dark beside the Thames, its four massive white smokestacks dwarfing everything in their midst. There was a high chain-link fence around the former power plant, with curls of razor wire along the top edge.

In the parking lot were trailers and construction machinery, and the shadows of enormous cranes loomed alongside the building. Justin stopped at a key box on a pedestrian gate just off the road. He checked a text from the Fratellis, entered a code to open the locked gate, then closed it behind them.

In front of the building was an enormous lawn. 'I thought this place was abandoned,' Vanessa whispered. 'This looks like a park.' It worried her that things were already not going as planned.

'Used to be abandoned,' Justin said. 'Maybe the park is part of the redevelopment that's going on.'

They crossed quickly, the lawn soft under their feet, and soon reached the shadows along the wall.

'Nicola said we'd find an open stairwell door on the south-west corner,' Vanessa said, shivering, though Justin had given her his coat. 'Is this the south-west corner?'

'I don't know north from south here,' Justin said. 'I guess we just check all the corners and hope we're lucky.'

The first corner they checked was all locked up, but at the second corner a door was propped open with a brick. 'Subtle,' Justin said.

Inside, the air smelled of cement dust, and it was pitch black. 'Do we climb the stairs in the darkness?' Vanessa asked.

'Probably for the best,' Justin said. 'Nicholas said security is lax here, but there's no need to advertise our presence.' His hand found hers and grasped it tightly. 'We'll go up together.'

It was a long climb. 'Largest brick structure in Europe,' Justin wheezed on one of the landings while they rested.

'Feels like it,' Vanessa replied.

Finally they reached another propped-open door that spilled out on to a long, narrow rooftop. To one side was the grassy area they'd crossed, the silvery band of the Thames visible in the distance. On the other side was a central courtyard filled with machinery and other signs of construction. 'This place really is enormous,' Vanessa said.

They trudged forward, Vanessa hunching down into Justin's jacket. A thin panel of glass ran down the middle of the roof in a geometric skylight. The cold air stung Vanessa's cheeks as she followed the panel to the centre, where she could see a flickering light.

'That must be them,' Justin said.

Two figures huddled around the light as Vanessa and Justin approached. Vanessa recognised Nicola's hair dangling around the hood of her coat as she held open the yellowed parchment pages of the *Ars Demonica*.

Nicholas stood a few feet away from her, pushing a broom over the roof. He barely looked up when they approached.

'What are you doing?' Vanessa asked.

Nicholas gestured at a pattern of intersecting lines drawn into the snow on the surface of the roof. 'It needs to be perfectly clean,' he said.

'A pentagram,' Justin said, standing back.

Vanessa turned around. She was standing in the centre of a giant five-pointed star inscribed in a circle. Five other pentagrams had been drawn, all meeting at one central point. A large candle stood on the ledge behind Nicola.

In the middle stood the pot-bellied silver lamp, the one the twins had found in the antiques shop. Glimmers of light chased around its edges, as though it were catching the beam of a non-existent flashlight.

Nicholas followed Vanessa's gaze and said, 'We've already worked the preliminary enchantments on it.'

'Justin – here.' Nicola tossed him a ratty-looking black peacoat. 'I brought an extra just in case, and you look like you need it.'

Justin gave her a nod. 'Thanks.'

'There's something we should tell you,' Vanessa said, not sure how to begin.

'The Lyric Elite doesn't exist,' Justin said.

Nicholas stopped sweeping. Nicola narrowed her eyes, the candle flickering behind her. They didn't say a word while Justin told them what Coppelia had said about the Lyric Elite.

'No wonder Enzo wouldn't let us join,' Nicola said finally. 'And that explains why they only answered us in New York once the demon had actually been summoned.'

Nicholas still looked confused. He frowned, trying to piece together what she was saying. 'But there are still necrodancers in the Royal Court, right?'

'Right,' Vanessa said. 'And that's Enzo's excuse – he wants the demon for himself, so he can use it to sniff out the evil dancers and destroy them.'

Nicola whistled. 'Who's left that we can trust?'

They exchanged glances. 'Right,' Nicholas said. 'Only us.'

'Is a roof really the best place to do this?' Vanessa asked. 'I can't remember when I've ever been this cold.'

'Yes.' Nicholas finished sweeping the sixth pentagram. He nodded at the silver lamp. 'We don't want anyone else to get hurt if something goes wrong, so we wanted a place that was very isolated. Which is why we're on the roof of a decommissioned power plant.'

'You two have been hard at work,' Justin said, examining the pentagrams.

'No kidding,' said Nicola. 'You can't just paint a pentagram, at least not for these purposes. You have to dance its shape first, barefoot.'

Vanessa wrapped her coat tightly around her. 'You danced barefoot in this cold?'

'That's nothing, Vanessa,' Nicholas added. 'Not compared to what you're going to have to do.'

Nicola rolled her eyes. 'Don't frighten her,' she said. She opened the book again and picked up the candle. 'Here's how it's going to work. Vanessa, you'll stand in the centre of the pentagrams by the lamp. Nicholas and I will dance a simple containment spell around you. When it's time – you'll know when – you have to cut your hand and let it drip inside the mouth of the lamp. Once the spell is completed, the demon will be called to mingle with the blood of the host. Then you, Vanessa, just have to invite it in.'

'And this part is key,' Nicholas said sternly. 'You have to say the formal, binding invitation. Without saying the exact words, the demon won't be *bound* to enter you – or the lamp. Do you understand?'

Vanessa swallowed. 'Yes.'

'Good,' Nicholas said, and nodded to his sister, who picked up the *Ars Demonica* and read from it, translating from the Latin.

'I declare myself your willing partner. The one who gives herself to your will and desires. I am nothing and you are everything. I demand that you join me.'

'We wrote the Latin out phonetically for you to read,' Nicholas said, handing Vanessa a slip of paper. 'Once you chant the invite,' Nicholas said, looking at Justin, 'we have to act super-fast and fling Vanessa out of the circle into safety. And the demon, already drawn in, will sense her blood and inhabit the next best thing.' He motioned to the lamp, which was resting in the centre of the pentagrams.

'Then we just have to destroy the lamp,' Nicola said, closing the book.

'That sounds way too simple,' Justin said.

'Does it?' Nicola said, her voice uncharacteristically grave. 'It's actually quite dangerous. Lots could go wrong.'

'Once you speak the invite, the demon is going to make a beeline for you,' Nicholas said to Vanessa. 'Remember what happened to Hilda?'

Vanessa shivered, picturing the way Hilda's skin had blistered and cracked until she'd been destroyed in a brilliant burst of light.

'That's why we have to act fast,' his sister continued. 'Once you're out of the circle, you should be safe, because the demon will be trapped within the pentagrams.'

'And if we don't get her out in time?' Justin said. His voice wavered at the end of the sentence, betraying his anxiety.

The Fratellis exchanged an uneasy look. 'That's not an option,' Nicola said.

Vanessa spoke up before Justin could reply. 'I want to start. Let's get this over with.'

'OK,' Nicola said, nodding at her brother, who pulled a small penknife from his jacket and handed it to Vanessa. 'Let's do this.'

A silence fell over them, the moment suddenly real. Vanessa walked back into the centre of the pentagrams. With each step she felt as if the air were tightening around her. Moonlight glinted off the engravings on the lamp, highlighting the fine filigree.

Nicola opened the book and began to read instructions to the others, but all Vanessa could think about was the offer the demon had made her days before. *When I am invited by the right partner, however, we are invincible.*

What would happen if she actually let it in – would it destroy her? Or was she strong enough to control it?

'Vanessa.' Justin was at the outside ring of the pentagrams, 'I'll be here,' he whispered. 'Until the end.'

Nicola threw her arms wide. Nicholas did the same. And on the beat of three, they began to dance.

Vanessa held the knife, waiting. To her surprise, the Fratellis were good dancers, their legs moving swiftly around the circle, their weight shifting, giving them momentum. There was no music; they seemed to be driven by the sounds of the night: the creaking of the building beneath them, the roar of the wind. Justin stood back, watching the twins with an unreadable expression on his face.

The lamp seemed to quiver, the brass developing a slight sheen, as if it were drinking up the dim light from the stars above. It glowed bright, brighter, the engravings on the lid and handles suddenly ablaze.

It was time.

Vanessa gripped the knife more tightly and pricked the tip of her ring finger. A sharp sting, and a crimson bubble of blood welled up.

With her other hand, she reached out and touched the lid. Pain shot through her fingertips as the metal scorched her fingers, so hot that she almost couldn't bear it. But she had no choice. Clenching her teeth, Vanessa lifted the lid, then held her cut finger over the top until a few small drops of blood pooled inside.

With a gasp, she lowered the lid on to the lamp and stumbled back into position. At the same time, the dance around her began to change, growing quicker, as Nicola's and Nicholas's feet retraced the pentagrams until each line glowed with an eerie yellow light.

Vanessa felt the ground beneath her shift, a strange heat grazing her arms in a tender caress, sending a prickle of goosebumps up her skin. All the while she concentrated on an image of her sister *en pointe*, seeing the faded pink ballet shoes, the satin stitching, the talisman she had practised with Zep that had worked so effectively in the competition.

Beside her, the lamp hissed and spat. Vanessa could feel the demon, his breath turning the night hot and foul, his presence constricting the air around her. Then a voice crackled in her head.

Here you are. At last we will be one.

Vanessa felt her legs begin to buckle. In the distance she heard Nicholas's voice.

'It's here!' he shouted, the words swallowed immediately by the rush of wind.

Vanessa closed her eyes, remembering what Zep had taught her to do: she thought of the box of Margaret's old things that had been shipped home after she disappeared, of her ballet shoes inside. Then she pictured Margaret standing in front of her with the shoes on her feet, alive and well. Waiting for her.

With renewed strength, Vanessa opened her eyes. She read the phonetically spelled words of Latin from the scrap of paper, squinting at it in the darkness. As she spoke a ripple of heat passed through her body. She could feel it seep into her pores, rushing through her veins, making the bones in her neck crack.

The shield in her mind began to quiver, as if something were banging against its walls. She read the final syllables from the paper, and was nearly blown off her feet by the demon's answer. She felt it in every corner of her being.

You have called and I have answered. You are mine.

Heat wrapped itself around her. Her fingers trembled as warmth radiated through her, bringing her blood to the surface.

She felt herself weaken.

Then a hand grasped her wrist, cold and pale, jerking her from the pentagram's cage of light, back out on to the icy roof.

The cold was a shock. She turned, feeling Justin's arms holding her close, his hand still clasping her wrist. 'Vanessa?'

'Yes,' she said.

Justin's eyes welled, and then she realised he was looking past her.

She spun and watched as something swirled within the grid of light, where the silver lamp stood, waiting. They all fell back as the air within the pentagram twisted and erupted into flames. The fire in the air curled into a thin braid and poured itself into the lamp's narrow spout.

The rooftop was suddenly dark and silent, and Vanessa blinked as her eyes adjusted. 'Is that it?' she asked. 'Did we do it?'

The lamp rattled in the centre of the pentagram, the sides bulging as if something inside were trying to force its way out.

Justin backed away, pulling Vanessa with him. But the Fratelli twins looked on with wonder.

'We pulled it off,' Nicholas said in awe, and turned to his sister. 'It worked!' They slapped palms and stepped away, breaking their circle of protection.

'Now all we have to do is destroy the lamp,' Nicola said. 'Then the demon will be cast back to its dimension.'

A loud crack silenced them all.

They turned to the lamp just in time to see its metal split at the seams. Vanessa looked at the twins. 'Guys, is this supposed to happen?'

Slowly, something began to rise out of the lamp.

They watched in horror as a shape stretched and warped against the sky. It grew brighter with each passing second, sending off flicks of golden light like embers from a campfire.

Nicholas gasped. 'What the . . . ?'

And then it began to change. Within moments it had formed a hulking silhouette, a dark outline with flecks of golden light: a head, broad shoulders, arms and legs. There were no eyes, just a whistling black hole where a mouth should have been. And then it began to speak.

I am Werzelya, the demon said. *And it is time for us to dance.*

'Oh crap,' Nicola whispered.

CHAPTER TWENTY-TWO

The demon's figure grew, eclipsing the stars in the sky. Its outline crackled as it moved leisurely towards them. Eyes began to form in its head, dozens of eyes that burned a terrible orange. As they expanded and contracted, Vanessa could almost see herself in their reflection.

Justin thrust himself in front of her. 'Stay behind me!' he said. The Fratellis scrambled to their feet and closed in on either side of Vanessa, shielding her.

'You skipped part of the invitation!' Nicholas said, looking back at Vanessa.

'I did?' she cried.

'The nothing and everything bit. I'd hoped it wouldn't matter. I'm sorry.' He took a deep breath and turned to face the demon. 'Let's get this over with.'

Summoning her courage, Vanessa pushed past Justin and the Fratellis. 'I'm the one it wants,' she said. 'I'm the only one who can stop it.'

The black swirl of the demon's lips parted, and it laughed at her.

'No!' Justin grabbed her arm. 'I won't let it take you!'

Vanessa called forth her sister's pointe shoes, but the mental image blew away in tatters. The demon's wrath was too strong. As it pulsed through her, Vanessa felt her limbs begin to shake, her neck arch back, her lips crack and sizzle.

Justin grasped her hand. 'Stay with me,' he pleaded.

Frantically Vanessa called to mind the people she loved – her mother, who was likely back at the hotel, waiting for her in the restaurant; her father, who would be arriving tomorrow morning for Christmas; her friends, TJ, Blaine and Steffie, and Elly too. Justin. Even Svetya and Geo, Pauline and Maisie. Margaret. But their faces boiled away into a hot black nothingness that seared the air in her lungs and filled Vanessa with fire.

Then a new, familiar voice sounded across the roof.

'I welcome you, Werzelya.' The words were followed by a string of hurried Latin.

Zeppelin Gray stood halfway to the stairwell, by the roof edge. How long had he been there?

Distracted, the demon had to obey the invitation. Suddenly able to breathe again, Vanessa gasped and fell to her knees. Why was Zep doing this? And how had he found them?

'No!' Vanessa cried, struggling to her feet. If Zep finished the incantation, the demon would destroy him.

But before she could move, Justin tightened his grip on her hand. 'Let him do it,' he said.

'No!' Vanessa called out again, but by then it was too late. Zep had finished speaking the Latin, and she felt the demon's hold on her loosen completely and disappear.

Zep hopped up on the raised edge of the roof, drew his hands close over his heart and looked at the gold-flecked form of the demon. 'Come and get me,' he said.

The demon's outline trembled, its form disintegrating until it was nothing but a snarl of particles, a terrible black wind. It raged over the rooftop in a shrill whistle, straight towards Zep. Vanessa watched, and for a moment she saw the Zep she'd first fallen in love with. The handsome boy who'd smiled at her as he walked up the stairs of the ballet theatre in Lincoln Center. The boy who had swept her away to the quiet streets of the West Village, where they'd sat, their knees touching as they laughed over their pizza. The boy who had taken her hand and run with her through the brisk autumn night into the studio, where they had danced in the darkness, their bodies tangling together as he bent over her in a soft kiss. The boy who'd helped her remember why she loved ballet.

There was a split second when Vanessa thought she saw Zep smile at her – and then his expression froze as the dark cloud enveloped him, seeping in through his skin, his lips, grasping at his throat.

A flash of red lit up the sky, and for a moment everything was silent.

All Vanessa could hear was the sound of her own breathing; all she could feel was the staccato beat of her heart.

'I found her,' Zep said as his body began to crackle with light. He curled his fingers into fists and raised his arms. Then he turned to Vanessa, his expression soft. 'This is my proof!' he called.

Vanessa knew then that the Zep she'd loved was real. He had been there all along. This was his way of atoning for his role in Josef's evil scheme, his final sacrifice. His gaze never left hers as he took one step backwards and tumbled off the rooftop.

With Justin and the twins beside her, Vanessa rushed to the roof's edge and looked down to where Zep lay, his body bent awkwardly on the pavement.

Vanessa turned away and sat down, her eyes closed, stunned.

'Is it truly gone?' Nicholas asked.

'Only one person can tell us the answer to that.' Justin put his hand on Vanessa's shoulder.

She felt for some hint of that other presence in her head, but there was nothing. 'As far as I can tell, it's gone,' she said softly. 'Zep killed himself and took it with him.'

'He did it to save *you*,' Justin said.

Zep, Vanessa thought. There had still been good inside him. Though he had done terrible things, she knew now that he had been telling the truth. He'd merely been a pawn, swept up in Josef's sinister plan.

'There was nothing you could have done,' Justin said firmly. 'He helped bring the demon into the world in the first place. This was his choice.'

Nicola stuffed her hands into her pockets and said, 'Who was the *her* he mentioned?'

Vanessa was about to answer when they all heard a quiet pattering of footsteps. Someone else was here.

Nicholas snapped his flashlight beam around to the other side of the roof, and they saw a pair of eyes staring calmly at them.

Enzo.

He stepped forward, his long hair tied back, his face stony in the light from the torch. 'The demon – have you already summoned it?' He stared directly at Vanessa. 'We can still avenge your sister, Vanessa. There is still time –'

'The demon is gone!' Vanessa called out, her eyes trained on Enzo. 'Sent back.'

Enzo blinked rapidly. 'I don't believe you,' he said, 'I am sure that it –'

'Believe it,' Vanessa said. 'We took care of it.'

'Only the Lyric Elite can make sure it is gone,' Enzo said.

'You're not the Lyric Elite,' Justin said. 'There is no Lyric Elite. Not any more.'

Enzo scanned the roof, his gaze resting on the twisted metal shards of the lamp in the centre of the pentagrams. 'You are liars,' Enzo said, contempt in his voice. 'There is no way you could have –'

'Zep invited it in,' Justin said, interrupting. 'And then he killed himself. Sorry you weren't able to make use of the demon – we know that was your plan, what you've wanted all along.'

Enzo's expression passed so quickly from disbelief to anger to something far more malevolent that Vanessa could barely keep up.

'I did it for your sister!' Enzo shouted. 'Everything I've done has been for her. Everything!'

Vanessa let out a desperate laugh. 'How can you say that, when you were the one who betrayed her?' She thought back to Margaret's journal entries. 'She trusted you. You were supposed to keep her safe. But instead – instead . . .' Her voice tailed off as she remembered her sister's final diary entry. It wasn't the dark faction at the Royal Court that had frightened Margaret so badly – it was Enzo. 'All you cared about was using her to get your revenge. And now she's gone. And it's all because of you.'

Enzo shook his head. 'That's not true –'

'*You* were the one who brought her to the competition,' Vanessa said, 'who pressured her to win, to face the demon. She thought you were taking her *away* from danger, but instead you pushed her towards it, because you were too afraid to face the demon yourself. And now you want me to finish the job.'

Enzo took a deep breath. 'I was never afraid. I was unable. I don't have the talent that your sister possessed, that you possess. We can still call the demon back,' he said, sounding strained. 'You mastered *La Danse du Feu* once. You can do it again.'

'You're a coward,' Vanessa said, moving her feet into fifth position. 'You brought us here to London and told us you would help us. Instead you've been using us.'

Enzo reached into his coat and pulled out a gun, its barrel shiny in the moonlight. He trained it on Vanessa. 'As fast as you are, you can't dance past a bullet.' He cocked the hammer and tightened his finger on the trigger. 'You forget that I trained you. I can anticipate your every move.'

Vanessa gazed down the muzzle and said, 'Not this one.'

As she arched her body, her arms stretched into a *port de bras*, Justin shot her a bewildered look – guessing, maybe, what she was about to attempt. She had never danced widdershins successfully – she hadn't even tried it since that first time in the studio. She called to mind the unnatural steps, the way her entire body had to fight itself. How she had been guided by Margaret and the demon.

But now they were both gone. There was only Vanessa. She gazed at her feet, allowing herself to imagine her sister's shoes one last time. She could almost make out the shape of the letter M accidentally drawn into the snow by footprints, but the wind quickly blew it away. She gazed up at Justin, the gentle angles of his face reminding her of New York, of home. Maybe she wasn't alone.

She took in the stars that blinked above them like thousands of tiny stage lights, then lifted herself on to one toe in her sneakers, and stepped forward.

The moment her toe hit the ground, she flinched back, one leg thrusting her into a spin while the other made her body teeter in disagreement. The wind guided her as she spun into a dazzling pirouette, only to be thrust out of it, folding herself into the dark as if she were nothing more than a shadow.

The night around them blurred, the stars melting together in brilliant streaks of light. Justin's body grew quiet, his face frozen, the Fratellis suspended mid-step beside him.

Enzo didn't move at all, just held the gun steady.

Even the air itself stood still, and as she moved forward, Vanessa's hair bumped over frozen eddies of wind and bounced loose about her face.

All around her, the world was silent. But her senses were filled by the rushing of her own heart, the pulsing of her blood. Emotion flooded her.

She missed her sister. Margaret was three years gone, and yet the sadness only grew with each passing day. It was always there in the background, dulling every single experience. Worse, she felt guilty – guilty about being here when Margaret was not, about not living life to the fullest, stuck in the shadow of someone who wasn't even there. And hot on the heels of the sadness and guilt came a new feeling: rage. Vanessa had done this to herself, but someone else had done this to Margaret. Her sister had been ripped away from her, and Vanessa ached as if the wound was real, physical. A prickle of wind grazed her arm, the phantom of her sister dancing beside her. Vanessa turned, expecting to feel her presence, to speak to her, but there was only emptiness.

So this was widdershins.

A few feet away, Enzo stood like a statue.

With one final step, Vanessa reached out and calmly took the gun from his hands.

Then she turned and flung it off the roof. For a moment it hung in the air, a glimmering line of moonlight along its barrel.

Then Vanessa pressed her heels together and stopped dancing. She dropped her arms to her sides, and let a breath of air escape in a delicate cloud.

Time rushed to catch up.

The gun spun out into the night and disappeared.

A shout burst forth from Justin's throat, warning her to move aside.

The Fratellis turned their bodies as shields for a bullet that would never be fired.

And Enzo clenched his hand, his finger pulling at nothing but air.

He gazed down at his empty hand. 'What?' Realising what had happened, he backed away from Vanessa, his eyes darting from her to Justin to the Fratellis.

'I threw your gun off the roof.' She wasn't scared of him any more, just emotionally drained. 'I would leave now if I were you.'

'Before we rip you to pieces,' Nicola said with a hearty growl.

For the first time since Vanessa had met him, Enzo looked frightened. With a quick flick of the leg, he spun backwards towards the door to the roof, blurring into invisibility, the staccato patter of his footsteps the last trace of his presence.

No one moved for a moment.

'I'm sure he'll turn up again sooner or later,' Justin said.

'He'd better not,' Nicola said.

'Don't worry,' Nicholas said. 'If he does, we can take him.'

Vanessa drifted towards the edge of the roof. She should have felt relieved, but instead she was numb, empty. This must be the price of dancing widdershins. She wanted to go somewhere and have a good, ugly cry.

With the twins out of earshot, Justin whispered, 'Are you OK?'

'No.' Her chest felt heavy, her thoughts so bleak they frightened her. 'Zep swore that everything back in New York was because of Josef, that he was being controlled by him and Hilda. I didn't believe him. I told him to prove it to me . . . and so he did, and now, he's . . . he's . . .'

A tear trickled down her cheek. Justin wiped it away, his touch sending a prickle of warmth through her. 'If Zep hadn't done what he did, we'd all be dead,' he said. 'And you would be possessed by a demon. He did a good thing.' Justin paused. 'Is there more to it than that? Were you still in love with him?'

Zep had been Vanessa's first boyfriend, responsible for some of her best memories, yet he had betrayed her. 'No,' she said. 'I'm not in love with him. Maybe I never was.'

She slipped her fingers into Justin's hand and squeezed.

'The demon is gone now,' Justin said.

She nodded. 'We're safe,' she said softly, brushing strands of Justin's sandy hair back from his eyes.

'That,' he said, 'but also . . . ? You're not going to hurt me.'

'Hurt you?' Vanessa said. 'Why would I –'

Justin leaned forward and pressed his lips to hers in a soft, familiar kiss, his fingers running up her neck like frost blooming on a windowpane. She had been waiting for this, wanting this, for so long – ever since they came to London. Her body sighed as his hands tangled in her hair, pulling her up on her toes in the kind of dance that she could lose herself in. Her body melted into his, her arms pulling him closer, tracing her fingers up his chest. She wanted to keep this moment, this kiss, forever.

But she knew she couldn't.

She pulled away and stared into Justin's brilliant blue eyes. 'We can't be together, Justin.'

He blinked, looking nervous. 'What? Why not?'

'Because,' Vanessa said, 'you just won the largest scholarship a high-school dancer can win. You're going to be in London for two years, and I'll be in New York.'

'I don't have to accept,' he said to her. 'Not if you don't want me to – I'll come back with you.'

She shook her head. 'I couldn't let you do that.'

Justin clenched his hands into fists. 'You're not being fair,' he said. 'We can be good together, Vanessa.'

'I know,' she said. She knew in her heart that she cared deeply for Justin, maybe even loved him.

'All this time,' she said, 'I've been convinced that Margaret was just waiting somewhere for me to come and find her. But she's gone, Justin. Forever. I need to tell my parents and we need to do whatever families do. Grieve. Heal, I guess.' She wiped at her eyes. 'I – I'm sorry.'

But if she was honest with herself, she wasn't apologising to Justin, she was apologising to her sister. She had always assumed that when she went home, it would be with Margaret by her side, and now that she was standing alone, she didn't know how she was going to live with herself. If she had only made it to London sooner, if she had danced better, maybe she could have caught her in time . . . And now Vanessa had to move on without her. She would grow older, would change and get married and have children, while her sister would stay the same age, her memory frozen in time. The thought was unbearable.

Justin ran his fingers through her hair, tucking a wayward strand behind her left ear. He leaned forward and gave her a gentle kiss on the lips. 'I'll be waiting for you. Whenever you're ready.'

They turned towards the Fratelli twins, who'd been standing at the edge of the roof, watching. Nicholas pointed at flashes of red and blue approaching down Battersea Park Road. 'Not to be a nuisance,' he said, 'but the police are coming. There *is* a night guard at this place. We should scoot.'

Vanessa looked down. 'I feel bad about leaving Zep. His body, I mean.'

'Yeah, me too,' Justin said. 'But I'd feel worse if we stayed and got arrested.' He took her hand. 'Come on. Zep wouldn't want us to get into trouble.'

Together the four of them ran towards the stairwell, as behind them, the wind and snow blew away all traces of the pentagrams.

CHAPTER
TWENTY-THREE

They slipped out of Battersea and were already a block away hailing a cab before the first police cars arrived.

'Shotgun,' Nicola said, pushing Vanessa inside and shutting the door behind her. The back seat of the black cab was roomy – there were two jump seats as well as a bench seat, plenty of space for the four of them.

'What does *shotgun* even mean in this situation?' Nicholas protested, but Nicola moved past him, pulled down the seat behind the driver, and planted herself.

In her pocket, Vanessa's phone buzzed. There was only one person who'd be texting her right now. 'Oh no,' she said. '*Mom. I totally forgot. Justin, what time is it?*'

'Almost nine.'

'We were supposed to meet her at the restaurant in her hotel at eight thirty,' Vanessa said. She leaned forward and told the driver where they needed to go, then glanced down at her phone. There was a text message, but it wasn't from her mother.

Where are you? it read. *Tired of waiting for you at the dorm. S*

Svetya? Confused, Vanessa texted back *Waiting why?*

Svetya replied quickly. *Your mom said she was buying us all dinner. Geo too.*

Her mother had invited Svetya and Geo? *We'll meet you at the hotel*, she responded. *We had something we had to do first.*

She thought that would be the end of the conversation, but her phone vibrated with another text. *2 people came here looking for you. We will bring them.*

Who? Vanessa replied. *What 2 people?*

But Svetya was apparently done conversing. No reply came through.

'What's going on?' Justin asked.

Vanessa showed him her phone. 'Svetya has apparently decided to make my mother's dinner invitation into a party.'

'We'll deal with it when we get there,' he said, grabbing her hand.

'Deal with what?' Nicola asked. 'We'd like to come to dinner too.'

Nicholas nodded. 'We love parties. Also? We're completely starving.'

Justin paid the driver as the four of them piled out on to the street in front of the Trafalgar Hotel. Another cab pulled up behind them, and Vanessa watched as Svetya and Geo climbed out.

'Why didn't you text me back?' Vanessa said. 'Who's with you?'

Svetya simply looked at the cab. After a moment, two other people emerged: a young man with a mass of blond hair and freckles, his neck wrapped in a white woollen scarf. He wore a green peacoat and a pair of slim-fitting jeans. And a girl.

She had flowing black hair and piercing blue eyes, and there was something immediately familiar about her. With a start, Vanessa realised that she'd seen this girl nearly every day of her life – until three years ago. The hair colour and the clothes were new, but Vanessa would recognise that face and those eyes anywhere – even in her dreams.

'Vanessa,' Justin said, confused, 'who's that?'

For a moment Vanessa was so full of emotion that she couldn't say anything more. The girl stopped in front of her, opening her arms for a hug.

'Margaret,' Vanessa cried. 'It's Margaret. My sister.'

And then she understood what Zep had said on the roof, that final *I found her*, though she didn't have time to ask, because she was throwing herself into her sister's arms, her eyes blinded by tears, and she was saying her name over and over again. 'Margaret!'

'I don't understand how you're here,' Vanessa said, a few minutes and several bone-crushing hugs later.

'It's a very long story,' Margaret said. 'Too long to tell on a cold street. This is Hal, by the way.'

Vanessa nodded at Hal, who nodded back at her, and hugged her sister again. 'Let's go inside, and you can tell it to me and Mom together.'

The eight of them moved up the steps towards the hotel entrance. Svetya, Geo and the Fratellis swept in through the doors, but Vanessa stopped short.

'What's wrong, Ness?' Margaret asked. And the easy familiarity of her sister's voice and that nickname made Vanessa's eyes sting with tears.

She glanced back at Justin and said, 'I'll be with you in just a moment.'

'Take your time,' Margaret said. 'I've waited this long to see you, another minute or two won't kill me. I'll be in the lobby.'

Vanessa watched her sister disappear inside, then turned to Justin, whose hands were buried in the pockets of the jacket the Fratellis had lent him. His jacket – the one Vanessa was wearing right now – smelled citrusy, like his shampoo. Vanessa breathed in the night air and looked around at the couples walking to and from the theatres and restaurants around Trafalgar Square. Everyone was happy, in love, full of life.

So why did she feel so sad?

'Justin,' Vanessa said, 'if anyone deserves this scholarship, it's you. I don't want you to give that up because of me.'

He smiled. 'I don't plan to give it up. There are still dark dancers in the Royal Court. And even if there isn't a Lyric Elite, that doesn't mean I can't stop them from whatever nasty business they're doing,' he said. 'Corny, but true.'

'I can't wait to see you on a ballet stage one day so I can tell everyone, "I knew him back when he was my dance partner,"' she said, smiling sadly.

Justin let out a small laugh. 'What about you? I'm sure you'll grace a thousand different stages all over the world.'

'Maybe,' Vanessa said. 'Though, to be honest? I think I've had enough dancing for a while.'

Justin leaned forward, wrapping his arms around her waist. 'You just found your sister. This is a big deal. Maybe the biggest deal.' He paused. 'But does this change anything between us?'

She thought for a moment. The demon was gone. Her sister was back. And Justin loved her. He might not be coming back with her to NYBA, but that didn't mean they couldn't be together. Or at least try.

There were a million things she could say to him, but instead of all that she simply tipped her head upwards and pressed her lips to his.

Then she pulled back. 'I'll see you in London for spring break.'

A wide grin took over Justin's face. 'Sounds like a plan,' he said. 'A perfect plan.'

Inside the hotel, Margaret was waiting, watching through one of the front windows. 'Are you OK?' she asked.

The Fratellis, Svetya, Geo and Hal were seated in the lobby. Vanessa looked at them. 'You go ahead,' Svetya said. 'Let us know when we can join you.'

Vanessa nodded and took her sister's hand. She led her through the hotel lobby, towards the bustling restaurant. 'Let's go give Mom a heart attack.'

'Good luck!' Nicola called after them. Nicholas just gave her two thumbs-up.

Margaret laughed as she followed Vanessa into a modern-looking dining room with bright white tables and low mood-lighting. Most of the tables were full.

'Adler,' Vanessa said to the hostess, who muttered, 'Only a little bit late,' and then led them towards the back of the restaurant.

In the distance Vanessa could see her mother sitting by herself at a large table, sipping a half-empty glass of white wine. Her brown hair was swept up, away from her face, and she was wearing a chic grey dress with a low neckline.

When she saw Vanessa, her mother stood up from her chair, her face pinched together into a swirl of angry lines. 'Vanessa! Where on *earth* have you been?'

'Mom –'

'Don't *Mom* me. I've been waiting for you. I texted you –' She pivoted and looked at Margaret, her wine glass in her hand. 'And who's this? Another friend?'

'*Mom*,' Vanessa said.

Vanessa watched as her mother studied her older daughter, waiting for her to see past the clothing and the dyed hair and the years of being apart.

She waited.

And then it happened.

All the muscles in her mother's face relaxed. The sadness that had covered her like a dark cloud for years lifted, and Vanessa saw the mother she used to know – the beautiful woman who was devoted to her husband and daughters, the former ballerina who loved her life and her girls and had never suffered the loss of a child.

The wine glass fell to the floor with a crack.

'It can't be,' her mother whispered.

But it was, and finally, as she watched her mother rush to Margaret and take her in her arms, both of them weeping with joy, Vanessa felt whole.

TWO AND A HALF
YEARS EARLIER

From the Diary of Margaret Adler
January 1

A new year, a new diary.

*When I went into hiding, I had to give up a lot. The big things
I regretted every day: my dancing, my name, my parents, my sister.
But there were smaller things I lost too, things that sound silly: my
walk to class across the NYBA campus, the Lincoln Center fountain glittering in the distance. My birthday cards from friends and
family. And my diary.*

*Hal insisted I leave it behind. 'If you take it with you,' he said
to me that night after I won the Royal Court competition, 'Erik
will never believe you're gone.'*

'But he'll know what I was thinking!' I protested.

Hal only nodded. 'Right. He'll see how you were thinking, and he'll believe that you fell into a pit of despair that no one could rescue you from. That's why you have to write one last entry, one that will convince him never to look for you.'

And that was when I did something I'd never done before: I lied to you, my diary. I wrote how my despair (all too real) had overcome me, so I had nothing to live for. And then I left the diary on my desk, sure I'd never see it again. I didn't mind leaving behind the things I'd acquired since arriving in London. The clothes, the IDs – they all belonged to some fake person, to Margot Adams.

None of it was mine.

But leaving the diary was different.

But then Vanessa returned it, and now I can be sure that what I write will be read by you alone, Diary, and no one else.

Hal was as good as his word: he called on a bunch of his hacker friends to 'witness' a girl plunging to her death from Tower Bridge. He told them she had to change her identity for political reasons, that her life depended on it, and he wouldn't ask people to lie for him otherwise. And, because Hal is the most decent person I have ever met outside my family, dozens came forward and swore they saw me jump.

I didn't even have to be at the 'suicide' site in the end. Hal told his people the time, the site, the distance from either end of the bridge and even the exact phase of the moon. And then seventeen 'witnesses' came forth for the police.

There were so many of them and of so many ages (the youngest was twelve, the oldest in his sixties), and from so many walks of life, the police accepted their accounts without question. The river was searched, and though no body was recovered, the witnesses were too reliable to be doubted.

And so Margot Adams died for the second and last time. And I was free of Erik.

Hal's friends also found me a place to live, though at first I was handed from person to person like a relay baton. Five apartments later, I ended up on Streatham Place in Brixton, a lively area of London with a multicultural community, a neighbourhood I'm told used to be dodgier than it is now. All I know is that the people on the streets are warm and polite, that the best jerk chicken in all of London can be found a block away and that no one there thinks about demons or dance or any such things.

When I arrived, Harriet gave me a new passport and a work visa – in the name of Glynnis MacMurray. 'Don't blame me for the name,' she said. 'It was Hal's doing.' Harriet worked for a small music label, programming their mixing boards and helping produce records, and soon enough I did too. 'You'll be our web designer,' she told me when I moved in. 'Though first you'll only be an intern.'

'I don't know how to be a web designer,' I told her.

'Don't be daft,' she said. 'That's why you'll start as an intern. Trust me, it's easy.'

At first Hal kept his distance. He was still in touch with Erik, and he didn't want to risk the truth coming out. But he kept checking up on me, and he was sweet and kind and thoughtful, and he cared about me. Not because I was a dancer or talented. Just *because of me. He took care of disposing of the evidence of my old lives, and I never found out exactly how. Only later did I learn that he'd left them behind in Margot Adams's empty grave – along with a losing lottery ticket that had his phone number coded in the numbers.*

When I asked him why, he said that on the off-chance someone came to London snooping around, he needed to know about it so he could protect me.

Little did I suspect that someone would be my sister – or rather, a friend of hers named Zeppelin Gray, who figured out the code, called Hal and explained who he was. He told me that my sister was here in London, competing in the very same competition that I had won. The rest, as they say, is history.

Erik, or Enzo, as he calls himself now, is still out there. And still, throughout the world, there exist dark dancers who try to use the art of dance for evil purposes . . . But I know that Josef is dead and no longer hunting me – or my sister – and for the first time in years I feel safe. Anything else, I can worry about tomorrow. Or the tomorrow after that. I don't know what the future will bring, but I will figure it out. But not this moment, because now, back in my childhood home, Vanessa is calling me downstairs to dinner, and I know better than to keep my parents waiting.

I am no longer Margaret Adler the ballerina. Instead, I am Margaret Adler the friend, the daughter and – especially – the sister.

READ ON FOR A TASTE OF
DANCE OF SHADOWS,
THE CAPTIVATING
PREQUEL TO
DANCE OF FIRE

PROLOGUE

In the harsh glare of the lights, Chloë's shadow stretched across the stage. Her toes pointed and taut, her arms fluttering like wings, she arched her neck and watched as her own silhouette seemed to move without her . . .

A drop of sweat slid down her chest and seeped into the thin fabric of her leotard. There was no music. The room beyond was dark and empty, yet she could feel her master's eyes on her. She tried not to tremble as she lifted her chin to meet his gaze. Slowly, she extended a long, slender leg into the air.

He rapped his staff on the floor. "Again."

Chloë wiped her temples. The floor was speckled with sweat and blood from hours of practice, but still she took her position. On the choreographer's count, the thirteen ballerinas around her began to flit in and out in cascades of white, their shoes pattering softly against the wood.

"One and two and three and four!"

And before she knew it, her feet were moving soundlessly across the stage. She dipped her head back, fanning her arms toward the light.

"Now rise!" he yelled as she thrust herself toward the circle of dancers, keeping in step. "Transcend your body! Your bones are hollow! Your feet are mere feathers!"

Chloë twirled, her back flexed into a crescent as the dancers flew past, their faces vacant, their feet moving so quickly they seemed to blur.

"Yes!" cried the choreographer, his smile wide and triumphant. "Yes!"

Chloë was dizzy and exhausted, her leotard damp with sweat, but she didn't care. The routine was finally coming together. Her legs wove around each other with effortless grace, and her body followed, smooth and slippery, like a strip of satin gliding over the stage.

Letting herself go, she cocked her head back in a flush of rapture. Her chest heaved, and hot, thick air filled her lungs.

The other dancers reached for her, their faces a pale swirl. Chloë bowed out of their reach, dipping low and letting her fingertips graze the wooden floor. It felt strangely hot. The thin smell of smoke coiled around her, tickling her nose, and the choreographer's voice grew distant and watery. The overhead lights seemed to flicker, casting eerie shadows against the walls.

A wave of heat rippled through her body. It was strange, unidentifiable—a hot presence spilling into her veins, making her head throb.

A string of whispers began to unravel in her mind, the voices too soft to understand. She jerked her head, trying to shake them off, but they melded into one another, foreign and indecipherable, growing louder, shriller.

Her eyes burned. The room swam with red. The ribbons of her pointe shoes tightened around her ankles. Without warning, her legs bent backward, as if boneless. Her arms cracked and swung over her head. Against her will, her chin jerked upward to face the overhead lights.

Mine, a voice said inside her head.

Chloë teetered, her legs trembling as she fought to maintain her balance. Using all her strength, she forced her lips to move. "No!" she screamed convulsively, and fell out of position.

The dancers stopped midstep, their faces empty and distorted. From somewhere in the darkness, the choreographer's voice cut through the room. "That, my dear, was a fatal misstep."

"What?" Chloë whispered. "How can—" But her words were consumed by a stifling breath of heat. It enveloped her, licking at her legs, and she twisted in pain as the presence took hold, her blood boiling as it pulsed through her fingers, her arms, her chest, until she was filled with an unbearable, burning ecstasy.

The colors around her sharpened until they were so bright they burned her eyes. Something screeched in her ears—a shrill, deafening cry that she suddenly recognized as her own voice.

She blazed into a brilliant, coruscating light, her body dissolving into ash.

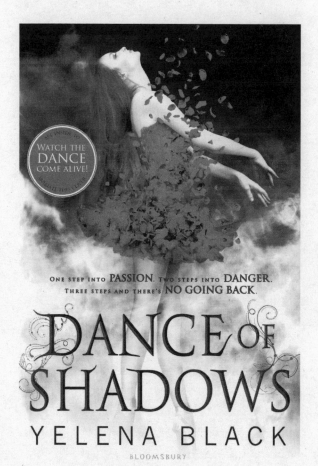

WATCH THE
DANCE
COME ALIVE!

ONE STEP INTO **PASSION**. TWO STEPS INTO **DANGER**.
THREE STEPS AND THERE'S **NO GOING BACK**.

DANCE OF
SHADOWS
YELENA BLACK

BLOOMSBURY

OUT NOW